THE HORSES RETURN

The Horses Know Book 3

LYNN MANN

Coxstone Press

ISBN 978-1-9161721-2-8
Published by Coxstone Press 2019

In memory of Pie,
who started it all.

Prologue

*T*he Drifters are in constant pain and their suffering only increases with time. I feel their distress as if it were my own and I want to go to them, but my parents stop me. They tell me that the Drifters' decision to be outcasts should be respected. They are wrong. The Drifters live as they do because they see no other way. They need help, I know it and so does Aunt Amarilla, despite her refusal to admit it. I see her smile to herself whenever I bring up the subject and am shouted down, and sometimes, when she knows I'm about to explode, she'll give me a wink that nobody else sees. She guards her thoughts completely, as very few can. She won't tell me what she knows and she won't tell me why she keeps her silence. I'm beyond being frustrated. People avoid me. I disturb their peace with the dark cloud that hangs over me as I thrash around inside myself, trying to see a cure for the Drifters' predicament. I've been told over and over that when I can stop my personality overpowering my Awareness, I will understand. Apparently, it's my strength of will that gets in my way. Yet my will doesn't prevent the Drifters' anguish from seeping almost constantly into my mind. Their need for help is urgent, now, and I won't be told otherwise. I am right. I am determined. I am Will.

ONE

Amarilla

I love to sit and watch Infinity while she grazes. The rhythmic sound of her munching distracts my mind from all of the thoughts battling for attention within it, and the sight of her reflecting the sun's rays with a dazzling brilliance calms my soul.

It's been a long twenty-two years since Will, my nephew, was born. He's struggled through lessons and experiences that have been both lengthy and difficult, and knowing that they have been necessary in order for him to be who he needs to be hasn't made it any easier for me to just sit back and watch.

Will was named after the character trait that he has demonstrated in abundance from the moment he was born. As a child, his wilfulness was cute, especially when Candour, Bond-Partner to Will's father, Jack, was still around to tame it; whenever Jack was seen riding his grey stallion around the village with a tiny, laughing, blond-haired Will sitting in front of him, everyone would smile and wave, knowing that another of Will's tantrums was in the process of being diverted. By the age of four, Will was often seen riding Candour by himself. The child who could leave a path of destruction in his wake similar to that of a tornado when on his own two feet, would be mellow and smiling as he sat astride Candour with a poise akin to any of the Horse-Bonded. It came as a surprise to nobody when Will achieved perfect balance aged only five. With all blocks to Awareness out of his way, he should have been as Aware as any of the Kindred youngsters, yet unless mounted upon Candour, who would ease him past his will to his Awareness, he couldn't access it at all. He still can't. His personality is all of him and there is no room for anything else.

We have all tried to help him to be more centred – to find a better balance between his personality and his Awareness – as Candour used to be able to help him to do, although admittedly in Justin's and my cases, we haven't tried very hard; I have seen aspects of the future and the part that my nephew will play, and since I hide little from the man I have loved for more than twenty years, Justin knows what I do. We both bury deep within our minds what we know, so that nobody, whether an interested party probing for information, or merely an innocent mind trying out the extent of its Awareness, can find it. And we wait.

Will is right; the Drifters do need help. Yet his parents are right to insist that he doesn't try to inflict it upon them. When there are opposing views and both of them are right, it is a case of waiting while the lesson that Infinity has instilled in me over and over becomes apparent to all involved: everything happens as it should.

Over the years, I've given Will the tiniest indications possible that I support his views regarding the Drifters. Being the sensitive lad that he is, he hasn't missed a single one. I am Aware of the lift it gives him every time he realises that I agree with him; even a will as strong as his needs a little boost every now and then, when his love and respect for his parents, combined with the duration of his disagreement with them, threatens to wear him down. I've spotted Justin putting a hand to Will's shoulder in solidarity for the briefest moments, too, when he's sure my sister won't spot him.

The waiting has taken its toll. Justin has suffered the agony of staying behind with me when Gas, his Bond-Partner of twenty-six years, left this physical existence of ours, years ago. I told him I would be fine if he wanted to move on with his horse; I still have Infinity and we can both be with Justin and Gas in the oneness whenever we want to – we all spend enough time there together anyway – but he was resolute. As long as I am here, he will stay with me. He doesn't say what he really means, but of course he doesn't need to. I know he has stayed to make sure that when it is Infinity's time to leave, I'll have the strength to stay here too, at least until I have given my nephew the help that only I can give him.

The time is approaching when we will find out whether Justin's sacrifice was warranted. Infinity, my beautiful, blue-eyed mare, whose soul is woven so tightly, so intimately with my own, is twenty-eight years old and her body is failing.

'But that's okay, Aunt Am, you can just heal her,' Vinca, Will's youngest sister, told me when I explained Infinity's situation to her.

'Not this time I'm afraid, sweetie,' I replied.

'But you can heal everything, you're nearly as good as my mum,' my twelve-year-old niece persisted.

I swallowed the lump in my throat that formed whenever I thought of what was to come. 'Vinca, quieten your mind and pay attention to your Awareness of Infinity. What do you feel from her?'

There was a pause and then Vinca said, 'She feels the same as she always does... only further away.'

'That's because she's preparing to leave. We need to respect her decision. Any attempt to heal her would be for our benefit rather than hers and it would greatly upset the process she has begun.'

'Is… is she going to die soon?'

'She's going to leave her body soon, yes, but no one ever dies, Vinca, it just seems that way to us. You'll be able to reach Infinity after she moves on, almost as easily as you did just now.'

'Then why are you upset?' Vinca took my hand and squeezed it as she looked up at me with my sister's blue eyes.

I smiled a sad smile, and drew her into a hug. 'Nothing gets past you, does it. I'm sad because knowing what I know doesn't stop me from being human. Infinity and I have been here together for a very long time and although we'll always be together in the way it really matters, I'm scared of being here, in my body, when she isn't in hers.'

Vinca pulled back from me enough to look up into my face. A lone tear trickled down her face. Then, her eyes widened as we both felt the mental equivalent of a snort from Infinity. I felt my mare focus her thoughts at Vinca, so that my niece could hear them in her head as easily as I could. *It is as I have always observed. Give a human the opportunity for excess emotion and she will take it.*

I managed to grin but Vinca ran up to Infinity and hugged her as she grazed. 'Don't go for a while, Infinity. Auntie Am isn't ready yet and neither am I.'

I bit my lip in an attempt to stop my own tears from forming.

Vinca came back and stood in front of me. 'I know Will's your favourite, Auntie Am, but he's always so angry. He won't be able to help you when Infinity goes, but I will. I'll try to be Aware of Infinity when she isn't here anymore, and then when you're busy,

I'll talk to her so you'll know she has company. And whenever you need a hug, I'll come running.'

I managed a grin. 'I'd love that, Vinca. But just so you know, I don't have a favourite among you and your brother and sisters, I love all six of you very dearly. Will just needs a bit more help than the rest of you, and so I check in with him more often. That's what you pick up from me.'

'As well as the fact that he's like you? You changed things and he's going to do it too?'

This time, Infinity's thoughts were for me alone and came as the faintest whisper on my mind. *She knows not exactly what it is that she feels yet she feels it as keenly as do we. The time is very close when you and I will need to do what we have waited so long to do. I will hasten my body's decline.*

Grief threatened to swamp me for the loss that would now approach even more swiftly. *You're still absolutely sure that you need to leave your body, Fin?*

A wave of Infinity's love wrapped itself around me. *We have discussed this many times. I will be able to influence what is to come far more powerfully when I no longer have a physical body to maintain.*

Panic warred with the knowledge that Infinity was right. It still does. She and I have indeed discussed everything that will come to pass and we both know that it will all happen as it should. Yet my human personality still struggles to conceive of being here without Infinity's physical presence, and it grieves for the era that is coming to an end – for Infinity is the last of her kind. There will never again be a need for horses to bond with humans, now that we have achieved Awareness and the horses all have perfect balance.

All of the other horses who were bonded lived out their lives with their Bond-Partners and then departed at their chosen time.

Some of the Horse-Bonded chose to pass on with their horses, but most are still here, spread out amongst the villages, helping people adjust to the changes initiated by Infinity, me and our friends more than twenty years ago; some individuals, such as my sister, immediately embraced the feeling of being at one with All That Is, and then accepted as much help as was offered by the Horse-Bonded and Kindred alike in order to identify and get past any blocks they had to even greater Awareness. But the vast majority of people have been far more cautious. They have taken much longer to accept that the only things stopping them from reaching out and knowing everything and everyone as intimately as they know themselves, are the personality traits and negative experiences – their blocks – that they allow to cloud their ability. They have needed help to find the courage to identify and address their blocks, bit by bit, and then have needed further assistance to adjust to the resulting increase in their Awareness.

And then there are the Drifters. When the Kindred first moved into our villages and began to help people to be Aware, there were some humans who would accept their assistance to a certain extent – just enough to be Aware that we are all one – but then slammed down barriers to greater Awareness. While these villagers were happy to sense their connection to the rest of existence, they were terrified that having a higher level of Awareness of their oneness with All That Is would result in them losing all sense of themselves as individuals. Continued exposure to the Kindred, with their ability to broadcast aspects of themselves to all, wore away at the barriers to Awareness that these people had erected within their minds, so they drifted away from our villages to live in small villages of their own, with other equally fearful people. They have existed ever since as forlorn, dejected outcasts who can sense what is possible but cannot bring themselves to overcome their fear and embrace it.

The pattern for Awareness has grown ever stronger within the human collective consciousness over the years, and the Drifters have felt its pull. In their desperation to protect themselves, they have added more and more fear to their barriers, resulting in ever-increasing misery. Despite the isolation and internal conflict from which the Drifters suffer, however, they have found a way to negotiate life. Many have married, although they now raise their children to be as fearful of embracing the truth as they are.

Infinity and the other bonded horses could have helped the Drifters at any time, but since it was the Horse-Bonded who brought Awareness to our communities, the Drifters have avoided us and our horses as much as they have avoided the Kindred. I know whose help it is that the Drifters need. I just have to find the strength to play my part so that when the time is right, I can make sure that help reaches them.

TWO

Will

---

*E*veryone is hurrying out of my way as I walk to Aunt Am and Uncle Justin's house. I suppose I'm not really walking, though. I'm stomping. I sigh. If only that were the only reason they're moving out of my way. I know they feel my anger as "a hundred knives being hurled simultaneously in their direction," as Levitsson put it yesterday, during one of his many unsuccessful attempts to help me access my Awareness. I think he was trying to be poetic. He's tried everything else to get me to have the faintest interest in softening my personality so that I can "stop messing around and be Aware," but I don't understand how anyone can think that is even remotely important when there are people suffering.

I bang furiously on the solid oak door with my fist. Uncle Justin flings it open and beckons me inside. 'It seems that time has proven Amarilla correct when she insisted on such a sturdy door with you in mind,' he says.

I take a deep breath. 'Today is the day that you are going to give me the answers to my questions. The answers that you and

Aunt Am have always refused to give me. And don't tell me that you don't know what I'm talking about, because I know you know.'

Uncle Justin smiles and I feel my face go hot. He holds up his hands. 'Keep your temper, I can't help smiling when you remind me so much of your aunt.'

I love him, but I want to punch him. 'DON'T CHANGE THE SUBJECT. EITHER YOU TELL ME WHAT I NEED TO KNOW, OR I'M LEAVING ROCKWOOD TO GO AND FIND THE ANSWERS FOR MYSELF. I CAN'T STAND THIS ANY MORE.'

Uncle Justin nods and puts a hand to my shoulder. 'We knew this day was close. You're feeling what's happening with the Drifter children?'

I nod, my anger evaporating. Those poor kids. Their whole lives, they've felt the human collective consciousness pulling at them to bypass the barriers that their parents have drummed into them to keep them from their Awareness. And now that they're old enough to challenge their parents as to why they aren't allowed to do what feels natural, their parents just respond by putting even more fear into them to strengthen the barriers they never asked for, and don't want. The parents think they're protecting their kids, but they're not. The kids are angry, frightened and confused and they're starting to rebel.

'Enough is enough, the Drifters might have chosen to live like they do, but their kids didn't. They need our help, and they need it now,' I say.

I'm surprised when Uncle Justin nods. 'Yes, they do. And the situation is giving their parents even more agony to bear, which means that, finally, they'll be open to having some help, too.'

My heart lifts. 'So, at last, you'll help me to help them?'

'It's not really my help you need, Will.'

'Then Aunt Am? Where is she?'

'She's out in the paddock. Infinity is dying.'

'She's... she's what? Why didn't you say before? Don't you need to be with them both?'

'For now, no. This is something Fin and Am need to do on their own. Once Fin's left her body, then yes, your aunt will need me.' Uncle Justin's eyes widen slightly. 'And that time is now. Come on, Will, we'll go to her together.' He gestures for me to follow him down the stone-walled hallway to the back door.

'I should just leave, Uncle Jus.'

He stops and turns to face me. His hair may be greying but his dark brown eyes are as intense as ever as they bore into mine. 'What has Amarilla told you over and over, almost from the moment you were born? In fact, weren't they your first words? When your parents were expecting you to say their names, what did you, in fact say?'

'I said, "thin shud," as I'm obviously never going to be allowed to forget. I know, everything happens as it should.'

'Then you're here at Infinity's passing because you should be. Now let's go and remind Amarilla that we love her. For the time being, that's going to be all we can do.'

We make our way to Infinity's paddock. When I catch sight of Aunt Am kneeling by Infinity's head, stroking her cheek and sobbing, I stop walking and let Uncle Justin go on ahead of me. As I replay the memories I have of Aunt Am and her Bond-Partner in my mind, the enormity of her loss washes over me and I experience one of my rare breaks from anger and frustration. I sense my Awareness available to me and I plunge into it, while I can. I feel the grief that swamps my aunt as she relives the last moments of Infinity's life.

My aunt had prepared herself well, anchoring herself in her centre, where her personality – which understood Infinity's reasons for leaving, but wanted her to stay – was in perfect balance with her Awareness that it was time to let Infinity go. From there, she managed to hold on to the knowledge that everything happens as it should, giving her the strength to not follow Infinity as she left her body.

This wasn't like all the times Aunt Am and Infinity have left their bodies before to be together in the oneness – to "fly the oneness" as my aunt calls it. Then, there has always been a sort of cord tying them to their physical bodies, that they have followed when they needed to come back. No, when Infinity left this time, she absorbed the cord behind her, slowly but surely. She will not be returning to her body, ever again.

Aunt Am sent her love to Infinity all the while that her Bond-Partner was leaving her body. It was only after Infinity took her last breath, that my aunt broke down.

As I watch Aunt Am cry so hard that she heaves, I'm Aware that she is more than she was before. Her bond with Infinity is as strong as it ever was, and there's something even more than that. It feels as if some of Infinity's soul has infused Aunt Amarilla's body, so that both souls are occupying the same physical space. How on earth? And why?

Because of me. I feel what should have been obvious to me a long time ago; they have stayed in Rockwood all this time for me. And now Infinity has left – well, sort of – for me.

I feel Infinity's approval of my being Aware. She nudges my mind to remember all of the times I've managed to use my Awareness for any length of time before. Candour. When I achieved perfect balance whilst riding him, it was easy, like it was whenever I rode him after that, before he passed on. When I was with him, being Aware felt like the natural way to be. All of a sudden, I see how to help the Drifters. I need horses. Wild ones. Lots of them.

My excitement breaks through Aunt Am's grief and as she picks up on the cause of it, I feel her add her approval to Infinity's. I walk slowly up to where she still kneels by her horse's body. As she wipes her eyes and turns to look up at me, I take a step back. From behind Aunt Am's blue eyes, a second, paler blue pair of eyes stares out at me.

THREE

Amarilla

Will's blond eyebrows almost touch his hairline as he looks down at me. I realise that I can feel what he is seeing – that which Infinity assured me I would feel.

'Infinity is here with me,' I say to myself as much as to him. 'That's lucky for you, I'd have no idea what to do with you on my own.' I manage a weak smile, which he returns uncertainly.

I feel Infinity's presence more strongly than ever as she sits within me. And she is more intense, more powerful, somehow. My brain can't seem to catch up with what my mind knows, though. All it can process is that I am still here in my physical body, whilst Infinity's lies empty in front of me. My heart feels as if it is being crushed from all sides as another wave of grief washes over me and sweeps me away, preventing me from feeling anything other than the shock and sorrow of loss. I put my hands to my face and rock backwards and forwards on my knees, keening.

Will drops to his knees beside me and puts a hand on my arm, squeezing it as if he can wring the pain out of me. Justin wraps his arms around my shoulders and gently pulls me to him, holding my head to his chest. 'Feel everything you need to feel, love,' he says. 'The sooner you feel it, the sooner you can let it go.'

Memories flood my mind. I remember the first time I saw Infinity, the first time I saw her beautiful blue eyes and heard her words in my head: *You are here.* I want to scream, 'I'M STILL HERE, BUT YOU AREN'T. YOU'VE LEFT ME HERE WITHOUT YOU.' I remember the first time I woke up curled against her, comforted first by her warmth and then by the knowledge that I'd found the horse I had dreamt of finding for so long. I remember our early discussions, when I constantly felt stupid. I remember riding Infinity for the first time, and all of the times after that. I remember the times I felt scared, overwhelmed, frustrated or sad, and then, with Infinity's help or even just her presence, found a way to feel the opposite. I remember feeling complete. And now I feel nothing but all-consuming, heart-wrenching sadness.

It is dark when I finally stop crying. Neither Will nor Justin have left my side. They have endured feeling everything that I've felt as they've hugged me, held my hands and supplied me with endless handkerchiefs.

I feel Justin's arm tighten around my shoulders as he draws me to my feet. 'Come on, Am, it's time to go inside,' he tells me and I find that I don't have the strength to argue.

I allow myself to be guided to the back door, where my sister is waiting. She takes me into her arms. 'I'm so sorry she's gone, Am,' Katonia whispers into my ear.

'She hasn't really though, has she,' I murmur.

'And when you really know that, instead of trying to convince yourself through all the pain you're feeling at the moment, you'll be fine,' my sister says.

She leads me to a chair at the kitchen table, where a sandwich awaits. My throat is so tight, I can't imagine how I can possibly eat it. 'Thank you, but I'm not hungry. The night's coming on, Kat, you should be at home with Jack and the children.'

My sister turns me to face her. 'They know where I am if they need me. I'm your big sister and when you're hurt, I take care of you, just like always. If you won't eat, then you need to sleep, come on.' She steers me towards the stairs and guides me up them in front of her. Bed sounds like a good idea. I know where I will go once I'm asleep.

As soon as sleep allows me to break from my humanity, Infinity welcomes me back to the truth of who we are. We soar through the oneness, blissful in our shared knowledge that whatever happens in the dream, we are never truly apart, and ecstatic that the time has come for which we have waited so long. The Drifters are the wedge, Will is the mallet and the horses are the hand that will guide the mallet to hit the wedge at just the right spot in order to split the log apart, releasing humanity from the last of what prevents it from achieving its full potential. Infinity and I have seen what will be and finally, finally, the time has come...

I wake up feeling excited and happy. Then my world crashes down around me as I realise that I have to face the first full day for more than twenty years that I haven't been able to see Infinity. Instantly, I am overwhelmed by grief. I try to remember the time I have just spent flying the oneness with her, but my brain refuses to let me think past its anguish at the prospect of life, here, without my Bond-Partner. I already feel as tired as I was when I went to sleep.

The door opens and Justin comes in with a mug of greenmint tea. He puts it down on the bedside table carved by him with Infinity's likeness, and sits on the side of the bed. 'How was it? Gas and I stayed away to leave the two of you to yourselves,' he says and I remember Infinity and I having done the same for him the first night after Gas passed on.

'It was as it always is when we're in the oneness. Nothing has changed there, at least,' I tell him, my lower lip and chin trembling, 'but I can't seem to bring that happiness back here. Infinity told me we would be the same together here as we are in the oneness, but I can't even feel her at the moment, I just feel empty and s… sad.'

Justin takes my hand. 'It doesn't matter how prepared you are, losing a Bond-Partner is a massive shock to the system. But the shock will wear off and then the grief will start to lessen, and then you'll be able to feel Infinity and the extent of what you can both do now. It's actually very exciting.'

I nod miserably. 'I felt that last night, I know I did, I just… can't…'

Justin draws me into a hug. 'You can't feel it through the fog you're in at the moment, I know, love. Come with me.' He takes my hand, waits for me to get out of bed and then leads me to the oak-framed mirror that hangs on the stone wall of our bedroom. 'All you have to do, any time you can't feel Fin and you're panicking that you've lost her, is to look into your own eyes.'

I gasp and take a step backwards, putting a trembling hand over my mouth as I see Infinity's pale blue eyes looking out at me from behind my own. Her gaze bores straight into me, as calm and assured as ever. All is well. And we have a purpose. Tears fill my eyes and stream down my cheeks. I take a deep breath, then another, and another, until my tears stop.

Justin hands me a handkerchief. 'She's always with you, Am. Now shall I let Katonia up with your breakfast before she wears a trench in the kitchen floor with her pacing, or will you come downstairs?'

'I'll get dressed and come down. Did you... did you bury Infinity?'

'Will and I buried her between us. When he's not raging, it turns out that he's every bit as strong an Earth-Singer as your brothers. He's struggling this morning, though,' Justin says.

'Struggling? How?' It feels strange not having easy access to my Awareness.

'It's such a habit for him to feel angry and frustrated that he can't help himself, despite having been Aware of you and Infinity yesterday and knowing that everything you went through was in order to help him. He's been desperate to be Aware again this morning, but he can't calm himself enough, so he's more frustrated than ever.'

'That means Kat will know why Infinity left too. Will doesn't have enough control over his mind to be able to hide anything from her. Her pacing won't just be from concern for me,' I say wearily, realising that despite how I'm feeling, I'll need to tell my sister everything.

I get a faint sense of events moving forward at speed and recognise the imprint of Infinity's energy on my thoughts. I smile a heartfelt smile as I realise that she is still the same Infinity, pushing onwards with little time for the excess emotion in which I am currently indulging. I set about pulling clothes out of my wardrobe.

'You're feeling Infinity's influence,' chuckles Justin.

A dull, empty feeling creeps back into my stomach. 'I felt it briefly. It's gone now, but I know things need to be moving on apace.'

Justin takes both of my hands. 'Absolutely, but at the same time... be kind to yourself, Am, okay?'

I nod. He hugs me and waits while I dress. Then he goes down the stairs in front of me and I see him raise a hand to keep Will and Katonia where they are while he leads me past them.

Katonia nods. 'Breakfast will be ready for you whenever you want it, Am,' she says and nudges Will, who is scowling. He manages a stiff nod in my direction.

'Thanks,' I say, unable to bear the sympathy I see in my sister's eyes. I'm almost relieved that I can't feel it. Grief is giving me a glimpse into what it's like to be Will, living amongst those who know my thoughts, whilst I am deaf to theirs. I feel a surge of determination to get on and help him with that now that the time is right, but then as I catch my first glimpse of Infinity's grave, I am swamped yet again by acute, heart-wrenching sorrow.

I don't know how long I spend sitting on the pile of earth that covers Infinity's body, while Justin sits a short distance away on his own horse's grave. Slowly, I find myself beginning to come to terms with my new situation. Something moves within my mind and I feel restless.

'Infinity isn't going to let up, is she?' Justin grins at me from his own place of contemplation.

I get to my feet. 'Nope, and she's right. She didn't leave her body so that I could waste time moping around, she left it so that she could put a load of energy into a situation that needs it. I need to do my part too, as we agreed.'

'And the being kind to yourself bit?'

'When I need a hug, you'll be the first to know,' I say and we both smile, knowing that he always is.

One of the many advantages of my sister being Aware is that it's impossible to go hungry when she's in the vicinity. Almost the second I sit down at the kitchen table, a plate of scrambled eggs on toast is placed in front of me.

'You're feeling a little bit better,' she tells me.

I nod while stuffing a forkful of egg into my mouth. 'I have to get on, which means…'

'…that you need to tell me what this is all about,' Katonia finishes for me.

Will nods. 'And me. I know you and Infinity have stayed around all this time for me, but you've done nothing to help me. You've sat back and let the Drifters suffer and you've let me argue their case without once backing me up. I've been right all this time that they need help, and except for doing all your little smiles and winks, you've done nothing to support me, NOTHING!'

'WILL!' Katonia stands up and puts her hands on her hips. 'You have no right to speak to your aunt like that, especially now.'

'Better out than in, Kat, it's fine,' I say. 'Will, I'm sorry. I'm sorry you've had such a difficult time growing up and that it didn't get any easier once you reached manhood, but I can't apologise for how I've behaved because, in the words of a very dear old friend who once did the same for me, "sometimes it's a case of knowing when to keep to one side and allow another to tread the path they were meant to, even if it means watching them struggle".'

'WHAT'S THAT SUPPOSED TO MEAN?' Will rages. His blue eyes, every bit as piercing as his father's, bore into me with fury. He runs a hand through his short, blond hair, ruffling it as he always does when he's agitated, and raises his broad shoulders in defiance.

Justin lifts a hand in Katonia's direction to stop her from intervening. She sighs and shakes her head, but stays quiet.

'It means that I've known what the future holds for you since you were born. And it isn't just the Drifters who need your help, actually, it's all of us.'

Will looks at me in disbelief. 'All of you? What do you mean? And why didn't you tell me this before?'

'It's best if you just focus on helping the Drifters until the meaning of everything else becomes clear on its own. As to why I didn't tell you before, it was because I had to wait until the right time.'

'WHAT?'

'Let me finish.' I wait until his shoulders relax back down before continuing. 'If I'd given you any more encouragement than I did that you were on the right track, you would have acted too soon and your attempts to help would have just made things worse. The time had to be right for both the Drifters and for you – and now it is. There's a huge amount you'll need to learn, and determination alone won't be enough to ensure you learn it. You're going to need to add maturity and a willingness to listen, to the strength you've always had. Even then, you're going to find it tough.'

Will frowns as he stares at me.

'It may not feel like it, Will,' I say, 'but Infinity, Justin and I have helped you as much as we possibly could. Now that the time is right, we can help you much more. Infinity has left her body in order to do her part, as you already know.'

'Am, can I ask why she had to leave in order to help?' Katonia asks gently. 'And what is it that has happened between you and Infinity? I mean, I felt her leave her body, but then I felt part of her settle within you and I can see her looking out of your eyes. When the other bonded horses passed on, they all – sorry Justin – they all actually passed on, but Infinity's still here with you, and I can feel her focus on Will. I haven't delved any deeper because it didn't feel right when you haven't chosen to tell me what's happening, but since it involves Will…'

I nod. 'I'll explain as best I can. Infinity allowed her body to fail so that she could be free of it. Now that she doesn't have a body to uphold, she'll be able to use the full force of her energy to influence the events to come – to make sure that what needs to happen, will happen. Some of what she'll need to do, she'll do through me and some of what I'll need to do, I'll do through her. That's why part of her is within me. There'll be times when she'll speak with my voice and times when I'll speak with hers. There'll be no need for communication between the two of us, though, apparently, which I'm already finding very difficult.'

My sister puts a hand to her mouth. 'But why? Justin, you can still communicate with Gas even though he's passed on, can't you?'

Justin nods and looks to me.

I take a deep breath but I can't keep the shake from my voice. 'Infinity told me that once she was out of her body and with me in mine, there would be no reason to indulge the illusion that we're separate in any way. She assured me that once my grief has passed, I'll be able to accept our shared existence and we'll know ourselves as one in the same way we do when we fly the oneness together. There'll be no need to communicate our thoughts, because we'll have thought them together.'

'But you have a whole lot of grief to get through before that can happen, and in the meantime, you can hardly feel her there at all. Oh, Am, I'm so sorry.' Kat reaches for my hand and squeezes it.

I bite my lip hard and shake my head. 'Don't be. When I was with Infinity in the oneness last night, I was happy. She's told me that there will come a time when I'll be like that here, too, and I trust her. In the meantime, we need to focus on the fact that the time has finally come for Infinity and me to help Will learn what he needs to, in order to help the Drifters.'

Will opens his mouth and then closes it. Finally, he looks at his mother and glares. 'You see, Mum, I was right. All this time, I was right. The Drifters need my help.'

'Your parents were right too though, Will,' Justin says. 'It wasn't up to you to go steaming in and demand that the Drifters accept it from you. Even now, when they'll be more open to help because they risk losing their children, their fear will prevent them from trusting you.'

Will slams his fists down on the table, making us all jump. 'WELL THEN WHAT AM I SUPPOSED TO DO? HOW DO I HELP THEM?'

I have a blinding headache and feel more tired than I can ever remember feeling before, but I think of the determination I felt from Infinity to push onwards. 'You need to remember what Infinity helped you to see yesterday,' I tell him. 'You're so busy focusing on everything you have to be angry about that you've forgotten you already know the answer to your question.'

Will glares at me. I stare back and hope he'll be able to resist arguing. Katonia's eyes flicker between the two of us anxiously.

'Deep breaths, mate,' says Justin. 'If you want your aunt's help, you're going to need to get used to taking them.' He winks at me and I smile feebly in response.

Will breathes in and out slowly, as my sister has taught him to do when trying to release his anger. Then he closes his eyes. They flick open again. 'The horses. It's the wild horses' help that the Drifters will accept. I need to go and find some wild horses and take them to the Drifter colonies.' His eyes widen. 'Flaming lanterns, that's better, how did I do that?'

With grief still blocking me from my Awareness, I have no idea what he is talking about.

Katonia smiles in amazement at her son. 'You don't feel the Drifters' suffering anymore. Something has changed. Oh, Will, thank goodness, after all this time, you deserve a break from it.'

Justin nods and grins. 'Nice one, Will, now you've

remembered your agreement with the Drifters, your soul doesn't need to keep their predicament at the forefront of your mind.'

Understanding dawns on my sister's face, but Will looks confused. 'My agreement? What are you talking about?'

'Your soul made an agreement with those of the Drifters before any of you were born,' replies Justin. 'You're a sensitive lad, Will, and your soul has had little trouble filtering the Drifter's emotions through to you, despite your lack of Awareness.'

'Is this like the agreement you told me about between your soul and Dad's?' Will asks Katonia.

Katonia smiles. 'I think it's exactly like that, son. It all makes sense now. I remember how it feels when your soul is prodding you to take notice of something – it's like having an itch that you can't scratch and you feel so restless all the time.' She sighs and looks up toward the ceiling, and then looks back at her son. 'Will, I'm sorry. I thought it was you being... well, you, all this time, refusing to let go of the argument and constantly obsessing over it. I didn't delve deeper, because you're always like this about everything, but this time, it's been your soul at the root of it all. I've let you down.'

'Thin shud, I suppose.' Will gives his mother a rare smile and a wink.

We all laugh but I stop suddenly and put my hands over my stomach; laughing feels at odds with the sadness that is lodged there.

Justin reaches for my hand and squeezes it. 'Another cup of tea, love?' he asks.

I nod gratefully.

Will is watching his fingers as he taps the table. 'So, I need to go and find some wild horses,' he nods to himself. 'I've no idea where they are or how long it will take me to get them to come with me once I've found them, so I'll need to pack for a long journey. There's no time to waste.' He leaps to his feet with such force that his chair topples over backwards and crashes to the stone floor.

I need to stop him from rushing off, but I can't seem to find the energy. Will is striding for the front door and Katonia is rushing after him, telling him to wait. I think of the times I used to sit astride Infinity, knowing that there was nothing we couldn't do. I feel a glimmer of strength.

'STOP,' I shout, and they both stop in their tracks and turn around. 'Will, please come and sit back down.'

'No, sorry, Aunt Am, I have a huge amount to do, the sooner I leave, the sooner I'll find the horses and the sooner I can get help to the Drifters.' Will turns back towards the front door.

'WILL, COME BACK AND SIT DOWN!'

Will stops and turns to face me and I see the colour rising from his neck up to his face. Katonia puts a hand on his arm in an effort to calm him, but he shakes it off.

'I'm only going to say this once, Will,' I say. 'Infinity left her body while I stayed here so that we could b…both h…help you. If you refuse our help, then it will have been for nothing.' Tears stream down my face and I don't have the strength to stop them.

A mug of steaming tea appears in front of me and I stare at it miserably as Justin's hands squeeze my shoulders.

I hear a chair scrape the floor as it is pulled up to the table and then Will's hand takes mine. 'Okay, I'm listening.'

FOUR

Will

I hate being told what to do, but I know Aunt Am is telling the truth. Infinity left her body while Aunt Am stayed behind, so that they could help me. I should listen to what she has to say.

'I'll help you to find the horses you need to find,' she tells me, 'but first you must join forces with someone else. You'll never get near the horses without him. He's been living in the woods over towards Goldenglade, and judging by his condition when I checked in with him a few days ago, he needs you as much as you need him. Pack a sack for three to four days travel, and when you get back here with him, we'll be ready to leave to find the horses.'

I frown. 'Goldenglade? The Drifter village? Who is this person? How will I find him?'

'He finds you, as best as I can tell. You'll know him when you see him.'

'He finds me? Oh, don't tell me, this is something else you've seen in my future? Right, Aunt Am, this is the time to tell me everything you've seen, come on, no more secrets now that we all know the score.'

'First of all, you can stop calling me Aunt Am now, Am will do. Second of all, now is absolutely not the time to tell you any more of your future than I already have. All it will do is distract you. You'll learn more about the dangers of that once you can see the future for yourself. And thirdly, if you want to find...'

'Once I can see the future for myself? What are you talking about? I can't use my Awareness in the most basic of ways, so how am I going to be able to see the future as you do? Not even Uncle Jus or any of the other Horse-Bonded have ever managed it.'

Aunt Am – no, Am, as I need to think of her now – ignores me. 'As I was saying, thirdly, if you want to find your new friend in any fit state to be able to help you, you are going to need to leave as soon as you have packed your back-sack. He can't wait, Will.'

'But...'

'Use the time on your own to let what I've told you settle in your mind. It's the first step.' Her voice is sounding stronger now.

I look into Am's eyes and see what I saw yesterday. Another pair of blue eyes looks out at me from behind hers. While Amarilla's eyes look tired and sad, the other pair have a calm, steady focus. I find myself becoming focused too, and for once, strangely, my urge to do something isn't being fuelled by anger or frustration. Infinity could never affect me this way while she was here. I begin to have a glimmer of what she might be able to do now that she isn't.

'Okay, I'll leave within the hour. So, I just head for Goldenglade, and at some point, I'll come across this person?' I say.

My mother gasps and looks from me to Am in disbelief.

Am nods. 'We'll be ready and waiting for you when you get back. See you, Will.'

'I'm going to stay here for a little bit and have a chat with your aunt, then I'll come home and see you off, okay?' my mother says.

I nod, wave to them all, and leave, wondering how this all came about. It feels completely unnatural to be doing something I hadn't intended to do. I won't be making a habit of it.

All of my family are waiting by the front door as I come down the stairs, dragging my back-sack behind me.

'Flaming lanterns, Will, I thought Am said you'd be gone for a few days, not several months,' says my father. 'You've got your bow and arrows, though? Good. I don't think you'll encounter any wild cats between here and Goldenglade but the dogs are getting braver all the time.'

'Jack!' my mother says under her breath. It's too late. Vinca and Tully, the two youngest of my five sisters, both look as if they're going to cry.

I grin. 'I'll be fine, I'm a good shot when the situation calls for it.'

'Good job too, you've no chance of being able to outrun anything with that lot on your back,' Mabel, the eldest of my sisters, tells me.

'He wouldn't be able to outrun a dog even without his back-sack,' says Ivy, 'he can't even outrun you, Vinca.'

That makes all of my sisters laugh, and I wink at Ivy gratefully. I know I'm not an easy person to be around, but I love my sisters and I hate seeing any of them upset.

They are all blond-haired and blue-eyed like me, but that is where the similarities end. My sisters are all lively and happy-go-lucky, and I know they lift my parents as much as I bring them down. Hopefully they won't have to for much longer. They line up from youngest to eldest, so I hug Vinca, Tully, Mija, Ivy and Mabel in turn and then find myself pulled into a bone-crushing hug by my father.

'It'll be alright now, son,' he whispers into my ear. 'You've had a rough time getting to this point, but you've got here. Candour always told me that you are the future. Now take care of yourself and we'll see you in a few days.'

I nod and pretend not to notice him wiping a tear from his eye as he lets go of me. Before I can say anything, my mother hugs me. 'I know it isn't easy for you to be doing this when you want to be off searching for horses, but you're right to trust your aunt. Keep trusting her, okay?'

'Yes, Mum, ouch! You're squashing my bow and arrows into my back.'

My mother lets me go. 'Off you go then, before your grandmother finds out you're going off adventuring on your own. It's a good job Mother Elder isn't with us any longer, or she'd have been clucking after you too. Take care and promise me you'll eat properly? I've packed all your meals ready, so there's no excuse not to. Will, did you hear me?' she yells after me as I walk away, waving and laughing.

Vinca calls after me, 'Will, I'm just off to tell Gran you've gone without saying goodbye to her.'

'No, you aren't, and, Ivy, neither are you,' my mother tells them.

'I only wanted to see him run.' Vinca's voice fades away as I turn the corner onto the main street through Rockwood. I smile at everyone I pass and their faces show their surprise.

Once I've left the stone cottages and cobblestones of Rockwood behind me, I walk as fast as I can through meadows dotted with summer flowers. The sun is hot on the top of my head and the breeze carries the smell of honeysuckle. I actually feel happy! It's a foreign feeling, but I suddenly remember that I used to feel this way sometimes, when Candour was still alive. After all this time, I'm finally doing something that feels worthwhile. I wonder who this mystery person is that I need to find. If I can stop my mind racing, maybe I'll be able to access my Awareness and find out. I can't do it. Aaagh! It's usually because I'm too angry, too frustrated, too determined to have my own way, too this, too that, according to Levitsson, whenever he has tried to help me. Now what is it that keeps me from my Awareness? Am I too happy?

My mind races on and I wonder what's happened to this mystery person and why he needs me. Maybe he's injured? Maybe he was attacked by a wild cat? I'm told that there was a time when the only danger of attack came from the Kindred. The Kindred! I can't imagine how anyone was ever frightened of them. Or how they ever lived apart from us – I mean, they're family. Apparently, they used to live in the woods and the younglings used to roam far and wide during some sort of survival challenge. They were amazing hunters and their presence deterred wild cats and dogs from inhabiting our part of the country. Since the Kindred have settled in our villages and taken up our farming way of life, the wild predators have gradually spread into the areas the Kindred left behind. They don't bother me. As I reminded my family, I'm a good shot and I can climb trees if need be.

I power on through my first day of freedom, almost running in my hurry to find who I need to find. I curse the long grass that slows me down in the meadows and pastureland, and slash irritably at the low branches and dense undergrowth that snag my clothes and back-sack as I pass through woodland. Why do the

Drifters have to live somewhere so isolated? It's not as if any of us have ever been allowed to come and bother them.

I eat lunch while on the move, and then cover a good distance before stopping just as the light begins to fade. I get a decent fire going to deter wild animals, eat another of my food rations and then try to decide whether to sleep against a tree trunk, or climb it and settle in the branches for the night. I grin as I realise that Am has seen my future and that means I'm in it. I'll be safe tonight, wherever I sleep. But wait, will I be safe regardless, or am I only in the future she has seen because I take precautions? My mind goes around in circles until it is spinning. I won't be able to sleep now. I'll carry on travelling through the night. The longer I spend walking, the sooner I'll find this mystery man, anyway.

Something is poking me in the face. I open my eyes and see the fallen branch I have been using as a pillow. I remember walking for as long as I could into the night, before collapsing to the ground in exhaustion. I must have fallen asleep straight away, because my back-sack is still on my back. I shake my head and rub my hair to get rid of insects and dirt. I grin to myself as I imagine what my mother would say if she could see me. I stand up, brush myself down and find another food packet in my back-sack. I'll eat while I'm walking.

By mid-afternoon, the trees are thinning out and eventually, through them, I can see scrubland. I'm at the edge of the woods and that means Goldenglade must be just over those hills. I'm tempted to carry on and find the village. Surely someone among the Drifters will give me a bed for the night if I promise not to question their beliefs? But Am said that the person I'm looking for has been living in the woods and that he'll find me. I'd better stay here.

I collect some wood and light a fire, despite the warmth of the day. Hopefully, it will serve as a beacon, making me easier to find, and if I'm still alone by nightfall, a healthy blaze should keep animals away.

Once I have a decent pile of firewood gathered and the fire is burning hot enough to keep itself going, I'm restless. I see a game trail running through the undergrowth off to one side, and follow it until the trees grow more densely and the undergrowth peters out. I jog through the spaces between trees, circling back to my camp. Pleased with my circuit, I decide to carry on jogging laps around it. I can't just sit and wait.

When I've worn myself out, I flop down a short distance away from my fire, sweating. I look around slowly as I eat from another food parcel. The birds are chattering and calling, a squirrel is sitting on a low branch nearby, nibbling on something and I can see some rabbits hopping about between the trees in the distance. Nobody is coming. I'm where I'm supposed to be, so where is he? How long is he going to keep me waiting? We have to get back to Rockwood within the next few days – Am will be waiting for us to go and find the horses. I hope he isn't injured, that will just slow everything down. Where is he? WHERE IS HE?

By the time darkness falls, I'm steaming mad. I break twigs into little pieces and hurl them as hard as I can into the fire so that sparks fly up. Wait until he gets here, whoever he is, I'll tell him what for.

All of a sudden, I notice two small, green lights over to my right, low down in the undergrowth. They blink off and then on again. My heart thumps as I realise that they are the eyes of an animal. I slowly reach for my bow and arrows. Stupidly, I'm sitting out of reach of them. I close the fingers of my other hand around a large stick from my wood pile just as a whine reaches my ears.

I don't need to be able to use my Awareness to know that whatever the animal is, it's in distress. I let go of the branch and get to my feet very slowly. The eyes continue to blink every now and then, but they don't move as I edge closer, cursing the firelight for making me blind to most of what is beyond its reach.

When I'm a couple of arm lengths away from the eyes, there is a rustle and they disappear. I stand up, squinting into the darkness and see them blinking at me from further away. Another whine reaches my ears and pierces my heart. Whoever it is that is supposed to be finding me will just have to wait. This animal needs to be either helped, or put out of its misery. I walk slowly to where it waits for me, only for it to move away again, staying out of my reach. I follow it until I'm far enough away from my fire for my night vision to kick in, and I see that the animal is now slinking a short distance in front of me, turning every now and then to check that I'm still following. It looks like a very small wild dog.

I hear whimpering in the distance and stop in my tracks. How many dogs are there? What if I'm walking into a pack of them? The dog lowers itself to the ground and crawls back towards me, whining. I have to help it. I lower myself into a crouch and hold out my hand, but the animal turns back away from me and continues on the way it was going. I follow. There is a huge tree lying across my path and the animal turns to slink along the length of it, towards the whimpering. As I reach the base of the tree, its enormous roots poking horizontally into the air, I make out a dark hollow that appears to have been dug out beneath it, too dark for me to see inside. Cowering at the entrance to the den is the dog I have been following.

I crouch down to make myself smaller, and edge sideways towards the dog, trying not to frighten it. It crawls towards me on its belly until its nose almost touches my outstretched hand. It sniffs me slowly and carefully, then a warm tongue licks my finger. Instantly, my mind stops leaping around. Awareness floods me. I know that this young, brave puppy hasn't seen his mother in days. He and his litter mates are starving. As the strongest, he has managed to hunt and kill a few mice but his search for his mother has left him nearly as exhausted as his brother and three sisters who have remained in the den. He sensed me nearby and was drawn to an energy so similar to his own.

Like resonates with like... Am's thought flits lightly through my mind and I know that she's smiling.

I tune into the puppies and find their mother's energy. She left her body when it was attacked and killed by a wild cat. If I don't take all of these puppies, they will die, except maybe for this strong, determined boy. Maverick. That's who he is. He gets braver and sniffs my hand and then my arm. I can just make out his tail switching from side to side in the darkness. When I move my hand to his chest and gently rub it, he stiffens. I send him everything that is warm in my heart. He relaxes and within minutes, he is a warm, wriggly mass of fur, snuggling into me and licking my chin. I stroke him all over and am horrified to feel his bones protruding all over his body.

'It's okay, I'm here now,' I tell him and then instantly know that if he could talk, it would be him saying that to me.

FIVE

Amarilla

---

*H*e's found him, then,' Katonia says, letting herself in through my front door.

'Yep. Help yourself to toast.' I wave my own slice at a huge pile on a plate.

'Feeling hungry this morning then, Sis?' Katonia grins as she sits down at the table opposite me.

'No more than usual, Justin made this lot before he went out to work on the litters. He told me to tell you that he's not offended that you feel the need to check up on me every morning, and you can help yourself to as much toast as you need while bending my ear about Will.'

'I'm not checking up on you, I'm checking in with you and… why am I even rising to the bait? As for my son, how amazing is it that all the dog has to do is touch him, for Will to relax enough to access his Awareness? I wish we'd known about this, we could have tried to find him a puppy before now.' My sister looks at me pointedly.

'I know you think I could have made something like this

happen before, but it wasn't me who made it happen this time. We lost the right to ask anything from the dogs when our ancestors cast them all out into the wild to fend for themselves. The wild dogs are just that until they choose not to be, and it took this particular situation with this one particular man for one particular dog to make that choice.'

Katonia holds her hands up. 'Okay, okay, it's just lovely being able to share thoughts with my son now that he can be Aware for long enough at a time, and I just wish it could have happened before he was twenty-two years old. Will he always need to be in physical contact with the dog in order to be calm enough to use his Awareness?'

'For now, yes. He'll feel less agitated just by the dog – Maverick, isn't it? – by Maverick being near him, but the effect will always be greatest when they're in physical contact. Maverick's energy grounds him, calming his personality so that his Awareness can get a look in and he's in a position to learn.'

'From the horses?' Katonia says.

'Yes, he has a lot to learn from them before they'll help him with the Drifters. It's pretty exciting, I'm beginning to remember that.' My words forge a path through my grief to my Awareness, as is beginning to happen from time to time.

'Well, as his mother, I...' Katonia jumps as someone thumps on the front door. A smile lights up her face. I, too, am Aware who is standing on my doorstep and my heart leaps.

I take a deep breath and fling the door open with an attempt at a smile. Rowena charges across the threshold and throws her arms around me. It isn't long before Marvel's arms enclose us both. None of us need to say anything; Marvel and Rowena both know what it's like to remain behind while a Bond-Partner passes on. They hold me tightly as, together in our Awareness, we remember. We remember helping one another to experiment with our horses as we tried to ride them better. We remember galloping Broad, Oak and Infinity along the river bank at The Gathering, yelling with joy. We remember riding towards Rockwood, laughing and joking, at the beginning of our mission to find the Kindred. We remember our horses showing the wild horses what it was to be in perfect balance. We remember galloping as one over the wet plains towards Shady Mountain. We remember our horses racing one another through the trees while the Kindred swung in the branches above us on our journey home to Rockwood. And we remember what it was to feel the strength and power of our beautiful Bond-Partners as we sat astride them, at one with them, each other and all else. Grief takes me over again and my Awareness fades.

'A group hug without me?' Justin's voice breaks the silence. 'Katonia, how could you allow this to happen?'

Marvel's arms disappear from around me and there is much back slapping as he greets his friend. Rowena stays where she is. The close presence of the person who was involved with Infinity and me from the very beginning of our relationship, who was there with us through all of the difficult times and who shared our triumphs, gives me enormous comfort. Rowena knows it and doesn't move.

'We knew she was going, so we were already on our way here. We got here as soon as we could,' she whispers.

When I finally step back from her, I notice how much of her black hair is now grey.

'Well, you're no spring chicken yourself,' she grins. 'As I keep telling Marvel, if you're going to have thoughts about the degradation of my physical appearance, do us both a favour and guard them carefully.' Her dark eyes look deeply into my own. 'We weren't a hundred percent sure you'd stay here without her, you know, but you aren't, are you? Here without her? I can see her looking out of your eyes every bit as easily as I can feel her imprint on you. None of the rest of us were affected like this when our horses left.' Rowena's eyes widen. 'But Infinity isn't done, is she? She didn't pass on because it was her time, she went because you both still have things to do here and she can influence things more powerfully now that she's free of her body... Will! How have I not known about this before? Aaah, I see, because it wouldn't have been right for everyone to know what he didn't. Oh, Am, this is so exciting!!'

'Judging by the way Am's mouth has opened and closed several times, Ro's having one of those conversations where no one else needs to join in,' Marvel calls out from where he is now sitting at the kitchen table with Justin and Katonia. 'Come and sit with us, Am, we're polite enough to allow you to answer out loud, instead of digging around in your mind for what we want to know.'

'Polite? This is coming from the same man who belches so loudly that our neighbours can hear it through the wall?'

'Fabulous ale I managed to brew this time, Jus, I've brought some for you to taste for yourself,' Marvel says.

'The light help us all,' Rowena groans and we all laugh.

Katonia stands up and beckons Rowena to take her chair. 'You've been walking since dawn, come and sit down. There's plenty of toast here and I can scramble some eggs? Unless you'd rather have porridge? And I'll make a pot of greenmint tea. You sit, too, Am, you four have lots to catch up on.' My sister kisses the air in my direction on her way out to see how many eggs the chickens have laid.

'So, what's all this about Will?' Marvel says.

'Thanks for your manners, mate,' says Justin with a wink at Rowena, 'but it'll be a whole lot quicker if you catch up the same way Rowena did. Prepare your mind and I'll get you up to speed. Ready?'

Marvel nods and then only seconds later, whistles as he processes all of the information Justin has transferred to him. He slaps his hand on the table. 'Now it all makes sense. We knew you weren't telling us the whole truth when we kept asking you to travel the villages with us and you kept saying that your family needed you. You guarded your thoughts so well that we realised there must be more to it. So, Will is the one to watch, is he? And he's teamed up with a dog – interesting. The dog will keep him on a level. I see that the lad's realised the same thing.'

'Huh?' says Rowena.

'Has he?' says Justin.

Marvel shrugs. 'Check it out for yourself.'

'I can't, Marvel, not at the moment,' I say.

Marvel looks at me with love and understanding in his hazel eyes. 'It takes a while, doesn't it? I'll tell you what the rest of us can feel. Will's emptied his back-sack and is using it to carry Maverick's four litter mates towards Goldenglade. He's been hunting and all five puppies have full bellies, the four in the back-sack are asleep and one of them's snoring. Maverick's full of energy, though, and is trotting along at Will's side. He won't be parted from him, now. Will's amazed at the effect Maverick has on him and is planning to persuade the Drifters to raise his dog's litter mates, not only ensuring the puppies' survival, but hopefully providing advance help to the Drifters before he can return with horses.'

I smile at the news. Will hasn't stopped to question his actions, which is normal. He has, however, forgotten that he is meant to be on his way home to us, to begin his search for wild horses. It is no small thing for Will to be diverted from a course of action on which he's already decided; Maverick may be small in stature at present, but the impact of his presence on Will is already huge.

'It'll be more than a couple of days before he's back,' says Justin.

'Great, it will give me and Marvel time to rest before we all go off horse-hunting,' says Rowena.

'We?' Justin's eyes narrow as he grins.

'Well, obviously. I can't let Am go adventuring without me, she just gets into trouble as we all know, and before you say it, Jus, she needs a firmer hand than you'll provide. The only reason I agreed to settle in Coolridge was because I knew I could always get here in time to prevent anything going on without me – that and the fact that Adam wanted me to have his cottage, saving this lazy arse from having to build us one…'

'Oi!' says Marvel. 'I simply suggested we stay there for a while to recoup our energy after all of the work we did getting the Horse-Bonded organised and settled where they were needed when Fitt, Sonja and Aleks were on their rampage spreading Awareness everywhere…'

'Lazy, just like I said,' says Rowena.

'And yet here I am, instantly willing to come with you while you pretend to protect a friend who doesn't need protecting, just so you can be one of the first to know what is going on,' retorts Marvel. 'I wonder what excuse the others will use.'

'Others?' I say weakly.

'Well you can't think they'll accept being left behind if you take off when they've just got here,' Rowena grins.

Someone bangs on the front door and Justin leaps to open it. 'Well, look who it is.' He hugs Vickery and is just closing the door when Holly bursts in, looking apologetic.

'I arrived at Mum's just after Infinity… well, you know, left, and I knew you wouldn't want visitors for a while, so I've stayed away, but I saw Vic arrive and I knew that Rowena and Marvel were here, so I thought it would be okay if I joined you?'

I rush to hug her and Vickery just as Katonia arrives with an apronful of eggs. My sister smiles delightedly at our friends and then looks down forlornly at the eggs she has gathered.

Rowena hugs the new arrivals, then takes the eggs from my sister and puts them in a basket on the kitchen worktop, telling her, 'Come on, Kat, I'll help you fetch some more.'

It's been a long time since so many of the group who went to bring the Kindred home, were together at once. We spend the day reminiscing and from time to time, my grief lessens and Awareness seeps through. We are overjoyed when the remainder of our group – Fitt, Sonja and Aleks – join us in our thoughts. There is a sense of wistfulness from them as we fill them in on our plans, as well as of amusement at the speed at which Justin and I have been forced to accept that our plans are now those of six people.

At various times, our reminiscing causes Justin and my friends to reach for their departed Bond-Partners, drawing them closer and including them as they always were when we were together before. The only person who can't do that is me. It is impossible to draw Infinity to me when she has never left, and in the fleeting moments that I can feel that, warmth floods through the being that we now share. Infinity was right; when I manage to sidestep my grief, it is just like when we are in the oneness together – we are one in thought and intention. And that makes it even harder when grief kicks back in and blocks me from being able to feel her again. But I am human and I learnt long ago that denying my humanity is no better than ignoring my Awareness. I just need time to work through the shock and sadness of losing Infinity's physical presence – time that I don't really have if I am to help Will.

As the day wears on, though, the easy company of my friends and the comfort of sharing our memories help me to stumble further along the pathway through the grief that pushes in on me from either side, blinding me and clouding my mind.

'Thank you,' I say suddenly.

Everyone stops talking and looks at me. They know why I am thanking them and Justin squeezes my hand as warm smiles spread around the room.

Hopefully, when Will returns, I shall be ready for him.

SIX

Will

_____

*M*averick is trotting along at my side as if it's normal for us to travel together like this. I spend so much time looking down at him, I nearly fall over Goldenglade. It looks just like any other village, with its stone cottages and cobbled streets, but I don't need to touch Maverick and be Aware, to know that Goldenglade is very different. It reeks of pain, sadness and fear. I am finally looking at one of the sources of the emotions that have bombarded me my whole life. Not for much longer though, I'll make sure of it.

Maverick is finally looking tired, so I pick him up and carry him. He snuggles into my arms and quickly falls asleep. It is as if the world comes into focus. All of the thoughts that are always darting around in my head slow down, and Awareness of All That Is seeps through them to me. I stare at this tiny being who has decided I am his. How can he have turned my world around in a matter of hours?

He is pure, unconditional love.

The saying "jumping out of my skin" is not so much a

metaphor as an actual phenomenon, I realise, as Am's thoughts –
no, it's Infinity, no, it's both – cause my mind to do exactly that.

Aren't we all supposed to be unconditional love? I ask once
my heart has slowed back down to normal.

*In reality, that is true. The difference is that while most
humans still have to work at remembering it, Maverick and the
rest of his kind are incapable of forgetting it. They are the living
embodiment of limitless, undiluted, unconditional love. Your
course of action is wise.*

To ask the Drifters to take in Maverick's brother and sisters?

I sense their agreement. I try to decide who, exactly, was
sending the thoughts and I can't; it isn't possible to separate
Amarilla from Infinity. I realise I've just experienced the mental
equivalent of what I saw when Infinity's eyes watched me through
my aunt's. I smile, pleased for my aunt as I understand.

As I begin to walk the deserted cobbles of Goldenglade, a
female voice shouts out of an upstairs window. 'PLEASE GO
AWAY. WHOEVER YOU ARE, WE DON'T WANT YOU
HERE. WE CAN'T HAVE YOU HERE.'

I look up, but I can't see anybody.

'Mummy, who is it?' says a child's voice. 'Can I go and see?'

'Shhh, if we all stay inside, he'll go away.' The woman speaks
loudly, to make sure I can hear her.

'I'm going to go down and meet him, and you can't stop me,'
says a boy, his voice breaking mid-sentence into that of a man.
When he continues, he sounds like a boy again. 'Let go, Mum,
you can't just keep telling me it's for my own good that I can't
leave the village and I can't speak to the Pedlars and Heralds
when they come, because I know it isn't. LET GO!'

A door slams, footsteps thump down stairs and then the front
door is flung open.

'JAKE!' the woman screams, but her son runs down the

cobbled path of their front garden, jumps the wicket gate and lands in front of me, breathing hard. His black hair is cropped close to his head and although his vest and shorts are clean, his hands and knees are dirty and he has dark shadows beneath his eyes. He's tall and lanky, a teenager in the process of becoming a man.

I grin at him. With Maverick in my arms, I'm Aware of how much Jake loves his parents and younger sister and how hard he tries to do as his parents tell him. But he feels trapped and isolated in the shell that his parents have made him build around his mind "for his own protection". He feels the human collective consciousness pulling him to be Aware that he's one with all of us and that he doesn't need to feel alone. His soul prods him to follow his feelings, but his parents' warnings that he will lose himself if he feels at one with everything, that he will forget who he is and who they are, that he, Jake Bakerson will no longer exist, scare him witless. With teenage hormones rampaging through his body, adding extra confusion, he's tearing himself apart.

'Who are you? Have you come to help me?' He casts anxious looks back at his house. Then, he sees Maverick asleep in my arms. 'What's that?' He reddens as his voice breaks again.

'I'm Will and this is Maverick, my pup. I found him and his litter mates in the woods. They've lost their mother and they won't survive on their own. I can feel someone waking up in my back-sack. Do me a favour and pick out the one who's awake before she wakes the others?' I turn around so that Jake can see Maverick's sister attempting to climb out of my back-sack.

'It won't... bite me?' Jake says.

I chuckle. 'If she's anything like Maverick here, she'll be more likely to lick the skin off you. That's a sign of affection, by the way. Go on, hurry up, before she jumps out and hurts herself.'

I feel the load on my back lighten slightly just as Jake's

mother appears at the front door. 'What on earth? Flaming lanterns, Jake, put that down and come here, right now.'

I feel her exhaustion. She's tired of fighting her soul and the collective consciousness while trying to pretend to herself that it is for the best. She's tired of trying to find ways to convince the son who doesn't believe her any more. She's tired of feeling afraid.

I turn to Jake to see that he's smiling at the grey ball of fur in his arms, who is wagging her tail frantically as she licks his face.

'Put her down for a minute so she can pee, otherwise this will get messy,' I advise and he immediately does as I suggest. The puppy squats and a small puddle appears at Jake's feet. He laughs delightedly as she jumps up at him, demanding to be picked up again.

Jake's mother walks uncertainly down the path towards us. As her son's laughter intensifies, a tear runs down her face. 'Jakey?' she says, but her son ignores her. 'I haven't heard him laugh since... actually I can't remember,' she says, without looking at me.

I want to hug her and tell her that it will be okay, but I'm Aware that my sympathy won't be welcomed or even tolerated. I'm also Aware that I can be of most help here by making my presence as brief as possible. 'I don't want to bother any of you. I'm just here because I have some puppies who will die if I don't find someone to raise them. This was the closest village, so I was just wondering if any here would take them in?'

'Puppies? Wild dog puppies? You have to be joking, they'll hunt our livestock.'

'Not if they grow up knowing that their food comes from their family, they won't. If my pup's anything to go by, all they'll want is love and friendship. And judging by the effect that pup is having on Jake, I'm pretty sure she'll give back far more than she needs from you.'

The woman looks at her son and a faint smile softens her face. 'The Dawsons are having as much trouble with Lia as we've been having with Jake. They might take one. The Mitsons possibly will too. How many are there?'

'Four. If you'll keep the one Jake's holding, that's just one left without a home.'

'The Woodcocks. I'm pretty sure they'd be interested once they see what's happening to Jake. Bring the pups inside. I'll empty the potato box and put a blanket in it, they can go in there while I sort out which one goes where.'

'I know you don't want me here, but I need to know that the pups definitely have homes before I leave,' I tell her.

She looks as if she will argue, but then turns to Jake. 'Take that puppy with you to Dawsonhouse, Mitsonhouse, and Woodcockhouse and ask any adults who are there to come over here, straight away. Then come home. Okay? Jake?'

Jake nods and walks off, smiling as he talks to his puppy.

'You think they'll come, knowing I'm here?' I ask.

'When they see how Jake is behaving, I'll be surprised if they don't come at a run,' she says. 'Are the puppies eating solid food, or will they need milk?'

'They're eating solid food. They ate the meat I gave them this morning while it was still warm and then they tucked into some bones. Once they're older, they'll probably want to go hunting with you all, then they can help to feed themselves.'

The woman nods. 'Maybe Jake will agree to go back to school if the puppy goes with him. Do you think it will have the same effect on the others who are struggling too?'

I shrug, biting the inside of my cheek hard to stop myself from telling her what I know. The dogs will definitely help the children to be calmer than they have been, but they aren't the fix that this woman hopes they will be. Telling her that won't help. I frown as

I realise yet again the effect the puppy in my arms is having on me. Since when have I been the one who is calm, rational and able to put what's best for someone else before what I want to say? I smile and bury my face in his fur as he sleeps, breathing in his scent along with the extra calm it gives me.

'May I... may I stroke him?' the woman asks.

'He doesn't know you, so maybe not while he's asleep. Feel free to take the next wriggler and cuddle her though, before she jumps out.' I turn my back for her to lift the next waking puppy out of my back-sack.

When I turn back to her, the puppy is in her arms, yawning. She strokes the puppy's head. 'She's so warm and... comforting. How are you doing that to me, little one?' she asks the puppy. 'How is it possible?' she asks me.

I try to find words that are true but that won't freak her out, as any answer that comes from my Awareness is likely to. 'It's just part of being a dog,' I say eventually.

She frowns at me thoughtfully and opens her mouth to say something but then hears running feet behind her. She turns, just as two teenage girls almost collide with her in their haste to reach the puppy in her arms. One of the girls holds a finger out to the puppy, who sniffs and then licks it. 'This one's yours, Brionie, I can feel it.' The girl gently takes the puppy from the woman, places her in her friend's arms and then turns to me. 'Where are the others?'

I'm Aware that this teenager is stronger willed than the others in the village, the one closest to knowing her own mind and leaving. I like her instantly.

'They're in my back-sack. They're just waking up, so put your hand in slowly and see who wants to come to you.' I know exactly which of the two remaining pups it will be.

I hear snuffling and then a squeal of excitement as Maverick's brother claims the girl. His squeals are matched by hers as she lifts him out and holds him to her. 'He needs a wee,' she says and puts him on the ground, where he instantly proves her right. 'Brionie, put yours down too, she won't leave you. If her tank's anywhere near as full as this little lad's, she'll be desperate,' she bosses her friend. Once her puppy is back in her arms, she holds out her hand to me. 'I'm Lia, and I'm going to call my puppy Breeze, for the one that blew you into Goldenglade.'

Like Jake and Brionie, Lia is haggard and dirty, despite the cleanliness of her clothes. Her brown hair hangs in tangled bunches but her green eyes are bright with determination. I'm Aware that she has incited her friends to follow her lead as she defies her parents by refusing to wash, so long as they continue to insist that having barriers imprison her mind is the only way to be safe. Everything about her is screaming that they're wrong. She's begun to experiment with dropping some of her barriers, but she's too scared to drop them all. She has, so far, stopped short of running away to find help, but she's threatened it and is very close to following through on her threat.

I shake her hand. 'Hi, Lia, I'm Will. Thanks for taking Breeze, I know he'll be safe with you.'

'You do?' Her eyes bore into mine. 'You do,' she tells me and pulls me to one side. 'You have to take me with you. I knew help was coming and then you brought Breeze to me.' She giggles as he nibbles her ear. 'I feel better already. Please, take me and Breeze with you?'

I look round to where more people are arriving and either staring at me or fussing Brionie's puppy, and then turn back to Lia. 'I know you won't freak out if I tell you that I know exactly how you've been feeling and how you're feeling now. Lia, you've done amazingly to push your folks to the stage they're at now, and that's why you have to stay here with them, for now.'

Lia opens her mouth but I hold a hand up. 'Let me say what I need to before your parents get here. I'll come back and I'll bring the help that you and your people need. Breeze and his sisters will help you all to feel better until I do. Believe me when I tell you that if you leave your parents now, they'll sink down to a level where they can't be helped. If you stay and keep Breeze with you, you'll be able to stand it until I get back, and then you won't need to leave your family at all, because we'll help all of you. Stay and raise Breeze and help your friends raise his sisters. Take them to school with you and let them make it bearable for the rest of your friends, and I promise you, Lia, I'll be back. Promise you'll stay until then?'

'When will you be back?'

'I don't know, exactly, but it'll be as soon as I can. Stay?'

Lia kisses Breeze on the top of his head, and he yaps playfully and tries to grab hold of her nose with his teeth. She laughs and puts a piece of her pullover in his mouth for him to chew on. 'What are you doing to me, little pup? I can't believe I'm saying this, but okay, I'll stay. You have to get back as soon as you can, though, Will.'

'Lia, come and show us your puppy? Please? Darling?' The man expects to be disobeyed.

Lia looks straight into my eyes as she passes me to go to her father and although there is still defiance in her gaze, there is also softness there, pleading me to do as I have said I will.

I nod.

~

'So, Brionie has Snow, she called her that because she's mostly white. Lia has Breeze, after the wind of summer that blew us into Goldenglade, apparently. Jake has Grey, named because Jake has even less imagination than Brionie, and a boy called Toby has Joy. I'm glad he didn't just go with the trend and call her Blackie. I like her name the best, apart from yours, obviously. Maverick, are you listening to me? You can't be falling asleep again already?'

My dog's acorn-brown eyes gaze sleepily up at me as I carry him in the sling that Lia rigged up for me before she let me leave Goldenglade. He's trying to stay awake, but now that his belly is full again, his eyes are closing of their own accord. I stroke the white stripe that runs the length of his nose, between his eyes to the back of his sleek, black head.

'Well, at least this is more comfortable than carrying you in my arms. I just have to find where I dumped the contents of my back-sack, and then we'll make our way back to Rockwood. Why am I talking to you like this? I'm not used to chatting. It's all down to you, little guy. I can't wait for you to meet my family, they'll love you, especially my sisters. Mum will just want to look after you, in fact you'll find yourself in the bath if I let you out of my sight. Dad will think you're amazing because you're calming me down enough to be Aware. Then he'll get all nostalgic because the last one to do that for me was Candour. I still miss him. But now, I have you. I can hardly believe it, but here you are.'

Maverick snuggles down into a ball and with a sigh, falls fast asleep.

SEVEN

Amarilla

—————

*R*ight. The litters are finished and loaded. Justin and Marvel have the tents, Vic has the food, I've got the cooking and hunting gear, you've got all our clothes, Am, Holly will have all the blankets and ground sheets, and Will can take everything that falls into the miscellaneous category, including his puppy.' Rowena checks us all off on her fingers as she tells us for the hundredth time what she has allocated to the litters we will each be dragging behind us. 'Vic and Holly are down the road at Holly's mother's so we'll just yell for them when we're ready to go. Can't your sister persuade Will to get a move on, Am?'

'Err, no. You have met my nephew, Ro?'

'Yes, and I know he won't be told what to do, I was meaning more of a polite request. Some of us aren't getting any younger.'

'I think that's obvious, going by the amount of stuff you're insisting we take with us,' Marvel says. 'I mean tents? Blankets? It's already summer and the weather's only going to get warmer and drier. We can pick up food from villages or hunt and gather it as we go, I really don't see the need for Vic to have to drag a whole litter full of it. We were gone for months when we went off in search of the Kindred and we just had a couple of saddlebags each of gear. I mean, a whole litter's worth of clothes…'

'It can still get cold at night and the blankets are to sleep on top of, as well as to keep us warm. I'm not sleeping on the hard ground any more, Marvel, if I do I won't be able to walk the next day. And need I remind you that last time, we had to shelter from a monsoon under nothing but waterproof sheets for days on end…'

'We created that monsoon! We're not going to be doing anything that crazy again, especially now that Sonja isn't here to talk us into it,' argues Marvel. 'Jus, help me out here, mate?'

Justin shakes his head with a smile. 'After all this time, Marv, you still bother arguing?'

'It defies belief, doesn't it,' says Rowena. 'Anyway, Am, about this nephew of yours. I know he's enjoying getting to know his dog and everything, but I'm sure you could get him to listen to you if you let him know that there are people waiting for him to get back so that we can help him do what he's been waiting his whole life to do?'

Marvel grins and shakes his head as he looks at me expectantly, to see if I can do what he can't, and win an argument with his partner.

'I've no intention of trying to hurry him,' I say. 'For the first time since Candour passed on, Will has a way of being Aware for decent amounts of time. That won't go on for much longer because Maverick's growing fast and soon won't need to be carried for such long periods, and then Will is going to find it very hard being alone in his head for more of the time again. And as you said, Ro, he's enjoying feeling their bond growing and strengthening. Of all people, we know what that's like, how precious the early days with a Bond-Partner are.'

Rowena's eyes fill with tears and without another word, she nods.

Marvel slaps his knee. 'The emotional angle. Now why have I never thought to try that?'

'Maybe because the only thing you can be emotional about is ale?' Rowena retorts, and we all laugh.

It is five days before Will and Maverick arrive in Rockwood and then a further day before Will knocks on my front door. I open it to find him clean, shaven and carrying a back-sack full to bursting. He is wearing a large sling on his front which I assume is for carrying Maverick.

The pup is a total delight. Mostly black but with a white stripe down the middle of his face, and with a white chest and feet, he bounds around my legs, trying to grab hold of my boot laces with his teeth. When I crouch down beside him, he stands on his hind legs and smothers my face with warm, wet licks. I smile and the grief that has had me in its grip all morning subsides, allowing me access to Awareness and to the part of me that is Infinity. My relief is enormous, even as I know that it is unlikely to last long.

I stand back up and hug Will. 'He's a tonic, isn't he? I'm so happy for you.'

Will hugs me back with an enthusiasm I haven't felt from him since he was small. 'Thanks, Am, just... well you know, without you, I'd never have found him. Thanks.'

He hugs Justin and shakes hands with Marvel and then Rowena, who says, 'We're all packed and ready to go when you are, which by the look of you, is some time in the next few minutes?'

'Errr yeah, about that,' Will says. 'Thanks very much for

the offer of coming with me, but I think Maverick and I will just go on our own. I can be Aware when I'm touching him, so I'll be able to find the horses and stay in touch with you to learn what you think I need to, Am, and we'll be able to move much quicker by ourselves, being, well you know, younger and everything. I really have to be as quick as I can, so that I can get back to Goldenglade with the horses before Lia and her friends decide they can't wait any longer.'

Justin glances quickly down at Will's hand to make sure he isn't touching Maverick, and then his words brush my mind. *Rowena, don't say anything. Let Am handle it, okay?*

There is fury in Rowena's eyes as she looks from Will to me, but she gives an almost imperceptible nod. I try hard not to smile at the mirth I can feel Marvel just about holding in, and ask Will, 'What do your mum and dad think about the idea?'

'They think I'm being unwise and impetuous as usual, but they said if it's okay with you, then it's okay with them.'

Out of habit, I almost go to check in with Infinity, but then I remember – I feel – that she is part of me and I already know what we think. What we know. I smile as I never could have on my own. 'Then thanks for coming to say goodbye. When you need help, you know where I am.' I hug him again.

Rowena hugs him stiffly and I see Justin's and Marvel's mouths twitch as they line up to say their goodbyes. Will scoops Maverick up in his arms and is gone.

Rowena waits for all of about five seconds after the front door has closed. 'HE THINKS WE'RE TOO OLD TO GO WITH HIM? THAT WE'LL SLOW HIM DOWN? WHO, BY THE WIND OF AUTUMN, DOES HE THINK HE IS?'

Justin, Marvel and I all chuckle.

'I imagine you're going to tell me why you've just let Will

relieve us of our adventure, before I have to go delving around in your mind to find out for myself?' Rowena asks me.

'Now that Will has Maverick with him, he has a way to find the answers he needs. We need to let him do exactly that, otherwise this whole undertaking will be one long battle.'

'We're still going then?' Rowena says.

'Yes. No need to unpack the litters,' I say.

Marvel says, 'Flaming lanterns, if Will thought we were too old to keep up with him before, he's going to go nuts when he sees what we're going to be dragging with us.'

There's a hammering at the front door.

'He's a fast learner, I'll give him that,' says Justin.

I open the door and Will storms in. 'I can't find them, even with Maverick's help, I can't find them.'

'Who?' says Justin.

'Stop teasing, Jus,' I say and turn to Will. 'You can't find the horses in your Awareness. What did you try?'

'I drew Candour to me so that I could feel his essence and then I reached out until I was Aware of essences that felt similar, but they all shrank away from me. I tried to follow them, but they dodged me, somehow. So, I tried again and found another herd, but the same thing happened, and then the same with another three herds. How are they avoiding me? Why can't I pin them down?'

Infinity glares out of me. 'Were you a horse, would you like to be pinned down?'

Will takes a step back. 'It freaks me out seeing Infinity looking out of you, and now she's flaming well talking out of you too.'

'Would you answer the question?' I say.

'Well, no, of course I wouldn't like being pinned down, but I didn't mean it like that, I just want to know why they won't let me pinpoint their location.'

'Why would that benefit them?' I ask.

'Err, well I'm not sure, but I need their help.'

'And what about what they need?'

'I didn't get that far, I've already told you, they disappeared so fast I couldn't find out anything about them.'

'Which tells you what?'

Will looks into my eyes defiantly. 'How would I know?'

'Pretending that you don't know merely delays the discomfort you'll feel when acknowledging the truth. It doesn't remove it.'

'Aaaaagh for the light's sake, you sound like Candour. He used to talk in riddles too,' says Will.

Maverick whines and Will immediately looks down at him and sighs. 'Sorry, little pup, I didn't mean to raise my voice.' He puts him on the floor and looks at me. 'Sorry, Am.'

'No problem.' I wait.

Eventually, he sighs. 'Okay, well I guess the horses don't want me to find them. They don't even want me to contact them. But why? What's wrong with me? They've always helped people in the past.'

'Some of them have. One of them still does, you see her in my eyes and you hear her in my voice. But wild horses have no need to be anywhere near us. We helped them to achieve perfect balance so that they could clear the negative effects of their eons of servitude to humanity. Why would they want to expose themselves to us again?'

'Because we're asking for their help?'

'And how did you ask?'

'You know I didn't get that far,' Will says.

'Yes, you did, actually.'

'NO I DIDN'T!' Will clenches his teeth and then breathes out deeply as he sees Maverick snuggling up to Justin, having peed on the floor in fright. 'Oh, Mav, I'm sorry. Am, help me, please, I need to keep calm so I don't keep upsetting Maverick, but I don't understand.'

'As soon as your essence touched that of the horses, they knew all about you, including what you want from them. Their response speaks for itself.'

'So, they won't help me?'

'They already are helping you,' I tell him.

Will takes off his back-sack and sinks dejectedly into one of the comfy chairs by the fireside. Maverick jumps onto his lap and licks his face. As Will strokes his dog's head, my nephew gradually calms and relaxes. I feel the touch of Will's mind on mine and allow him to search for the answers he needs. The wilfulness that blinds him in so many ways makes him able to see with astonishing speed and clarity when combined with his Awareness.

'The horses are avoiding my mind because there's something about me that's repellent to them. But they won't avoid yours. Your mind is as much Infinity as it is you. I need your help to find the horses and get near enough to prove that I'm worthy of their help. Will you help me please, you and Fin?'

'Always, Will.'

EIGHT

Will
―――――

I wasn't wrong, having my aunt and uncle and their friends along is definitely slowing me down. Maverick doesn't mind, it just gives him more time to explore as the rest of us walk – no, forgive me, stagger – whilst dragging our completely impractical and ridiculously heavy litters behind us. It's only been a few hours and I'm already wondering who's going to drop first.

When Maverick eventually tires, he clambers up to the top of my litter and snuggles down into the bed I've made for him, before whimpering his dreams to the rest of us. When he wakes up, he makes us all laugh by sitting up and surveying his surroundings from his position of height, before climbing down off the litter and tearing around as the rest of us continue our trudge.

When we eventually stop to camp for the night, everyone else does the work setting up camp and cooking dinner, while Am takes me and Maverick to one side. She lays a blanket on the ground and gestures for me to sit on it. 'I'm thinking that this will be the best time of day for us to work together, when Maverick is ready for another sleep and before you're too tired,' she says and Maverick duly proves her right by climbing on my lap, curling up and instantly falling asleep.

'Great, are you going to teach me how I can get the horses to trust me?' I say.

'No, they'll do that. I'm going to begin helping you to be Aware of the future and the past.'

'That just seems ridiculous.'

'It won't be easy to begin with, just being human makes it difficult to grasp the fact that time isn't linear – that it's all happening now – but if I can do it, you certainly can,' Am tells me.

'But how can all of time be happening now? My life has been one long chain of events, occurring one after the other. And what do you mean, if you can do it, I can? NOBODY apart from you has ever seen the future.'

'Nobody else achieved perfect balance as young as you and I did, Will. We both achieved it when we still had the openness of mind that goes with youth – you far more so than me, since you were still a small child. Achieving perfect balance whilst so open had the effect of locking that openness, making sure that we will never lose it as we age. And openness is a very powerful trait to have. It will allow you to be Aware of a huge amount all at once, giving you the ability to grasp concepts that others can't, like the fact that although events seem to occur one after the other, they are in fact all occurring simultaneously, like sheets of paper stacked in a pile, instead of side by side in a row.'

'But I'm Aware at the moment. If I'm as open-minded as you say, why can't I grasp what you're saying, right now?'

'Because you aren't as Aware as you need to be. Maverick calms you down enough for you to access your Awareness, but your personality still dominates you, as it always has. You need to be more centred. Every time Maverick helps you to be Aware, you need to focus more on your Awareness of All That Is than on your personality, until you are influenced by the two in equal measure. Then, your mind will be in a position to accept what I've told you.'

'And I'll be able to do what you can do.'

Am shakes her head. 'You'll be able to do far more. As the son of a Horse-Bonded father and a mother open enough to be the first non-bonded to achieve Awareness, you have a unique heritage. Combine that with having achieved perfect balance at such a young age, and the result is what you possess – the potential for unlimited open-mindedness and therefore unlimited Awareness, something which has never occurred before. Once you can stay centred so that your personality stops getting in your way, your open-mindedness will allow you to develop abilities that have, up until now, been considered impossible. You will know that all time is now and you will have the ability to be Aware of any of it that you want. That's your potential, Will, but for now, you just need to work on being more Aware, more of the time. Maverick is your key to doing that. He's also the key to me being able to reliably help you.'

Am strokes Maverick's head as it rests on my knee and I feel the sadness that weighs her down, slowly lifting. Then she smiles as she reconnects with the part of her that is Infinity.

'Okay, let's get to work on helping you to be more centred. Most people tend to be overly distracted by what they feel in their Awareness, so it's a case of giving them exercises to refocus their attention in their physical environment. With you, it's the other way around. I want you to immerse yourself in your Awareness. Focus on Maverick. Know everything he is and everything he has ever been, until your Awareness of him is as much of you as the irritation you've been feeling all day.'

I do as she says. Love. That's who Maverick is. Warmth floods steadily through me, until it takes up as much of my mind as my impatience to get on and find the horses. Interesting. My desire to find the horses no longer feels so urgent. It's something I'll do, but there are other things that need my attention too. Shock hits me like an icy gust of wind and I'm Aware of Amarilla and Infinity steadying me. Their confidence that I will easily accept ongoing, rapid changes to my thought processes now that Maverick is here to help me, is total and absolute. I find myself beginning to relax again.

You are doing well. Regain your centre, I am told.

I'm amazed at how easily I find it. I've undergone hours and hours of wasted instruction over the years, but it's so easy now that I have Maverick.

Now reach out further in your Awareness. Point in the direction of the nearest rabbit you can sense while saying out loud who is speaking over there.

'Marvel and, uh… hold on…'

Your personality took priority. Regain your centre and remain there so that you are able to utilise your personality and Awareness equally and at the same time. How old is the tree behind you and how many flowers has Marvel just given Rowena?

'Six yellow flowers and, err… um… err…'

At the same time, Will. Try again.

By the time I've been able to describe the pattern on Rowena's shirt while knowing whether the bees swarming in the distance are on their way to or from their hive, and have been able to count the birds flying overhead while knowing whether the badger creeping through undergrowth a short distance away is hungry or full, I'm exhausted.

'Well done. Tomorrow, we'll move on to you answering questions about what you can feel in your Awareness, whilst holding a conversation. Dinner's ready by the smell of it, let's eat,' Am says.

'I need to hunt fresh meat for Maverick,' I say.

'Marvel or Vic will have done that by now, come on, you need to eat before you sleep, which by the look of you, won't be long.'

I've always felt comfortable around Amarilla and Justin, but I surprise myself by enjoying the company of their friends too. We sit cross-legged around the campfire on blankets on top of waterproof sheets – about which Rowena is teased nonstop – eating beef and vegetable stew, and they make me laugh as they tell stories about the last time they travelled as a group, more than twenty years ago.

Maverick is having a great time leaping around us all, tossing twigs into the air and then catching them and chewing them into little pieces, before presenting them to each of us. When he's tired himself out, he curls up in my lap and I find myself Aware of something strange. It's as if the air around us is thicker than usual. It whirls around us all with intent and purpose and makes my head spin. Power. That's the only word I can find to describe it. There is power being generated by us all being together in one place.

I see Amarilla watching me with a smile. *Look deeper,* she and Infinity instruct me.

I concentrate on the vortex of energy and realise that I am at the centre of it. Not only that, but Infinity's discarnate energy is making it spin even faster than it would by our group's existence alone. My mind is too overloaded to be able to grasp exactly what's happening, but I'm suddenly very grateful for the company of everyone who is sitting, laughing and chatting, around me.

Do not try to understand. The more you try, the more you contribute to the belief that you do not already know. Everything will become clear. The thoughts of my aunt and her soul mate are gentle and reassuring. I feel a hand on my shoulder and this time Amarilla speaks quietly into my ear. 'You need to sleep, Will. Holly has made your bed up in your tent, come on, you and your pup have done enough for one day.'

She gently lifts Maverick from my lap and he snuggles into her arms with a sigh. She strokes the top of his head and kisses it, before holding out a hand to me as she used to when I was a child. I find myself taking it and allowing her to pull me to my feet.

'Sleep well, Will,' says Vickery. 'We'll try and keep Marvel quiet so he doesn't disturb you.'

'While he's awake, anyway. Once he's asleep and snoring, I'm sorry, but there's nothing I can do, short of suffocating him. I almost resorted to that once you know...' Rowena's voice fades behind me as I shuffle after my aunt, to the edge of the firelight. She passes Maverick to me and then holds a tent flap open for me.

'Sleep well. We'll wake you at dawn, if Maverick doesn't first. Night, Will.'

I reach for her arm as she turns to go. 'Am... you and Infinity... you know... thanks.'

I feel emotion surge through her and for the first time in my life, I fully realise that I'm not the only one who feels things so strongly that nothing else can get in. My mention of Infinity has sparked a yearning in my aunt. All she wants to do is to go to her Bond-Partner, to see her grazing in the moonlight, to feel her warmth as Amarilla puts an arm over her back and leans against her, to discuss how things are going and to hear Infinity's reassurance that everything is okay. Even though Am has spent the evening feeling happy and complete in their oneness, it only took the unexpected mention of Infinity's name for my aunt's grief to kick back in and block everything else out. I can't see Am's face, but I know she's crying. She pats my hand and then pushes me gently into my tent. I hear her walk further into the darkness and then I feel all of her hurt and sorrow as she releases it into the night. I'm just about to go to her when I hear someone running past my tent. As always, Justin's got this. I put Maverick down on a blanket and curl up around him.

A shrieking female voice wakes me. Others roar with laughter as I open my eyes and realise that it is morning and Maverick has gone. I leap out of my blankets and stick my head out between the ties holding the tent flaps together. Rowena is dripping wet and chasing Marvel around the campfire in her small clothes, while Maverick leaps up, trying to lick the water off of her as she runs. Marvel, bare-chested, his greying hair wet and uncombed, is laughing as he keeps just out of his partner's reach. Justin, Vickery and Holly are doubled over with laughter and Amarilla is smiling, her head poking out of her own tent in the same way that mine is. I rub my eyes, wishing I hadn't seen as much of Rowena as I have.

'I only wanted a handful of water to splash my face with, I'd have got my own to wash properly in, you horrible man,' Rowena says breathlessly.

'You always say that, and then you change your mind, go for the full wash and make my water all soapy. I said you could use the first bucketful, but you told me no, and to go ahead. So, if you then come barging in while I'm washing, you can't complain if I decide to speed the process up by giving you the whole bucket in one go.'

Rowena comes to a stop and puts her hands on her hips. 'You just wait, Marvel, I'll get you back when you're least expecting it…'

'I'd forgotten how entertaining you two are when you're pretending to argue,' Vickery says, wiping tears from her eyes and yawning.

'Lucky you, Vic. Am and I have never been able to keep them away for long enough to forget,' Justin says. 'Morning, Will, sleep okay?'

I nod with a grin and realise that I feel... different. Well rested, with a steadily rising impatience to get going, but somewhere deep inside, it's as if something is in a slightly different place from where it was before.

'Don't think on it too much, Will, it's all good,' Am calls out softly to me. Even from here, I can see Infinity in her eyes and I remember all that happened yesterday. I grin at her and nod before retreating into my tent to get some clothes on.

Maverick has eaten and had a sleep by the time we have packed up our litters and struck camp, so he's ecstatic that we are on our way again. He runs off madly in a circle and then slides to a halt in a play-bow in front of me, his eyes bright and full of mischief. I bow back to him and stamp a foot forward, pretending that I'm going to chase him. It's all he needs to dash off madly, before circling back to repeat the game.

I love watching him run. He holds his tail up gaily in the air as his sleek body streaks across the scrubland, jumping the dense tussocks of grass when he sees them in time, and stumbling over them when he doesn't. When he's worn himself out, he climbs up into his bed on my litter and pants hot breath on the back of my neck. I don't mind at all that he adds to the weight I'm dragging, I'm already finding it hard to remember life without him.

We traipse after Amarilla as she follows her sense of the nearest wild horse herd in her intermittent Awareness. None of the others reach out to the horses, although I don't think the horses would recoil from them as they do from me. They know that the horses will be disturbed the least by Amarilla's mind, shared as it is by Infinity, so they don't even allow themselves to wonder where we're heading. I find their self-control over the top and baffling when I'm alone in my head, but as soon as I touch Maverick, it makes sense. It's confusing to have two opposite opinions that change places in an instant according to whether or not I'm in contact with my dog, but I'm beginning to find that just having him near me keeps me calm enough to tolerate the confusion. It's as if the world around me that used to seem so contradictory and unfair, has slowed down to wait for me to either understand it or at the least, realise that it doesn't matter when I don't.

I am the least tired of the group by the time we stop to set up camp for the night; I'm by far the youngest and since I've never been able to use my Awareness reliably or concentrate enough to be any good at the Skills, I've always earned my keep by chopping logs, hauling feed and bedding for livestock, loading and unloading carts – all of the hard, manual work that nobody else wants to do. As a result, I'm fit and strong. I feel bad that I get to sit down to "work" with Amarilla when everyone else has to persuade their ageing, aching bodies to collect firewood and water, put tents up and make beds before they can sit down, especially when I learn that Marvel and Vickery were up before dawn, hunting for us all.

We all have our roles to play. Guilt has no part in these proceedings, I am informed as soon as Maverick has settled in my lap and worked his magic on both Am and me. I'm Aware of amusement as my teachers remember discussing this subject many times before.

I look over at my aunt and see, for the first time since Infinity passed on, a fierceness in both sets of blue eyes that look back at me; Amarilla's grief is slowly passing. Now that she's having a bit longer at a time to get used to the new relationship she has with Infinity before grief swamps her again, there are moments when she and Infinity are more equal partners in the mind and body that they share. It makes it even harder for Amarilla every time grief kicks back in and she loses her sense of Infinity all over again, but slowly, she's getting there.

I feel their impatience to get on and I grin.

Smiling suits you, Will. It is not impatience we feel so much as...

Call a spoon a spoon, it's impatience, Justin interrupts. *You called it impatience when it was Infinity cajoling you, Am, and it's impatience now that the two of you are about to cajole Will. Sorry, Will, this won't happen again, my mind was just passing and caught the lie you were just about to be told.*

I look up to see Justin grin as he catches the beaker that Am has just thrown at him.

'Now, where were we,' my aunt says to me. 'I know, I was just about to ask you to describe your sisters to me in turn, in the minutest of detail, while telling me the age of every bird in the vicinity. Go!'

NINE

Amarilla

*A*s the days go by, the change in Will is greater than he realises. His mind is so busy catching up with itself that even when he shocks himself with a new thought pattern or a new realisation, he has only the briefest time to notice before his mind is speeding onwards, deciding what it means and where it fits into his idea of himself.

It has been barely more than a week since I started coaching him, yet he is now centred from the second he touches Maverick, and I'm running out of exercises to help him stay there that he can't complete. He has accepted the fact that I'm leading him towards the horses and that when we reach them, he'll learn how to get them to trust him. That has meant that he's stopped obsessing about the goal of our mission and has focused all of himself on the help I've been giving him, which is remarkable in itself.

He still feels uncomfortable, though, when he sees the others setting up camp while he sits in the shade with me. One evening, Vickery notices. She rubs the small of her back, groaning, as she straightens after bending down to knock in some tent pegs. It is only when Maverick curls up in my nephew's lap and Will becomes Aware that Vickery is play-acting for his benefit, that she winks at him and grins. I'm delighted to see him stick his tongue out at her and then chuckle to himself. I knew that Will's personality would lighten following his bonding with Maverick, but that doesn't make it any less heart-warming to witness.

'Before you ask,' Will says as soon as we settle down to work one evening, 'that buzzard up there is carrying half a baby rabbit back to her young. She didn't kill it herself, she found it, but it's not long dead. Marvel and Rowena are the far side of that tent, arguing about which vegetables to put in the stew but Holly has already decided, and is peeling carrots and potatoes. Justin is meant to be fetching water but he's skinny dipping...'

Tell-tale. The mention of Justin's name draws his attention to us.

'...and there are five birds sitting on that branch, twenty sticks of assorted sizes on the ground between us and that tree, and you have run your fingers through your hair three times since I mentioned that Justin is skinny dipping.'

I laugh. 'Show-off. I get it, being centred is easier for you now. We'll move things on.'

Will nods. 'It'll be cool to be Aware of things going on in the future, but why are you so adamant that I need to be? I mean, you hardly ever tell anyone what you see, so it doesn't seem to be that useful? Uh-oh, Infinity is glaring at me out of your eyes as if she wants to burn a hole through me. Am I going to wish I hadn't asked?'

I smile, remembering the look in my horse's eyes that Will describes and then I feel a pang of sadness as I wish I could see it for myself... then I get lost in a whole load more sadness. Again. I just can't seem to help it.

Will shuffles closer to me on his bottom, so that I can reach Maverick. I stroke the pup's head and he stirs. He licks my fingers sleepily and then rests his head in my hand and goes back to sleep with a sigh. It may only be a little puppy sigh to him, but to me, it's a reminder of how easy it is to be at peace. I feel myself calming and growing stronger. I push back at the sorrow holding me down, until I come back to myself. To ourselves.

'Thanks,' I say to Will, and gently lower Maverick's head to rest on his leg. 'Where were we?'

'You were going to tell me why it's important for me to be Aware of the future.'

'That's right. Although it's just as important for you to be Aware of the past.'

'Why?'

Because it is there that you will find the answers you will need.

'Answers to what?'

To the questions you will have.

Will is silent. I can feel his personality trying to assert itself and demand a full explanation, and he is only just about managing to remain Aware, despite Maverick's presence. Without him, this conversation would have been pointless. I wait.

Eventually, Will takes a deep breath. 'You and Infinity think you've given me the answer to my question and you've got no intention of letting me know any more, so I guess I just have to sit with it for now.' He looks over to where Marvel and Holly are jumping around and waving to get his attention. When they see that they have succeeded, they give him thumbs up and wide smiles, before carrying on with what they were doing. Will smiles and says, 'Clowns,' but I feel his gratitude for their support.

'What I want you to practise doing from this point onwards, Will, is being centred every second that you are able. Whenever Maverick is resting or asleep, whether you're eating, walking, doing chores, even sleeping, be in contact with him and be centred. Then, when you start to see glimpses of events that are unrelated to your present life and situation, notice them. That bit is important – notice the glimpses but don't focus on them, or they'll slip away.'

'How do you know I'll have these glimpses?'

'The openness of your mind guarantees it, so long as you are sufficiently Aware.'

'Why do I have to wait to see them? Can't you just teach me to be Aware of them at will?'

'When your mind has reached the state necessary for you to be Aware of any time of your choosing, I'll help you to do exactly that, but in order to get to that point, you need to do as I suggest.' Immediately, I sense Will's impatience and irritation at my response.

Regain your centre. Infinity's discarnate energy powers our words into Will's mind and then increases the speed of the energy that swirls around him. His eyes widen slightly and then he takes a deep breath, relaxes and centres himself… and immediately sees a glimpse of himself and Maverick walking amongst a herd of horses. I feel his excitement as he attempts to capture as much detail from his vision as possible. I am tempted to intervene, but he has to learn. The fragment of the future fades away despite Will's furious attempts to grab hold of it with his mind.

'AAAAAAAAAAGH!' Will holds his head with both hands.

Maverick jumps with fright and leaps from Will's lap, leaving him alone in his head.

'AAAAAAAAAAGH!' Will shouts again and Maverick runs as fast as he can to Holly, who bends down and takes him up in her arms.

'A lesson does not always make sense until you do the opposite of what you were told to do.'

Will looks at me with fury in his eyes, which quickly soften. 'How do you and Infinity look out of your eyes and say really unhelpful things that somehow seem helpful?'

I manage to swallow down the hurt that wants to take me over at the mention of Infinity, and laugh. 'It's always been one of Infinity's talents. It's infuriating, isn't it? Now, are you going to make it up to Maverick for scaring him half to death?'

'Maverick, come here, mate,' Will calls. His pup makes us all gasp by leaping out of Holly's arms, twisting in the air and somehow landing on his feet, before launching himself at Will and licking my nephew's face all over. Will chuckles. 'I'm sorry for frightening you again, little guy. Not that you're bothered, you really are the most goofy puppy, aren't you?'

Maverick leaps off his lap and play-bows. Our session is over.

'Remember, Will, be centred as much as you can and notice, just notice, what you see,' I say.

Will raises a hand to me as he shoots off after his dog. 'Got it, Am, I'll try.'

'Do not try. Do.' The words Infinity told me so often are as much a part of me as she is.

Justin catches my eye and blows me a kiss.

Holly sits down beside me and puts an arm around my shoulders. 'I know she hasn't moved on in the way our horses all have, but it's hard for you all the same,' she tells me. 'You're doing great. I know you have Justin, but sometimes I'm just going to need to give you a hug.' She pulls me to her and I rest my head on her shoulder.

'I'm glad you guys are all with us. As it turns out, it's not just Will who needs you,' I say.

'It never was, sweetie,' Holly replies.

TEN

Will
___

I am back to carrying Maverick in his sling when he wants a rest, instead of dragging him on my litter, so that I'm in contact with him as much as possible. I've climbed hills in the heat and had my litter pull me down the other side. I've walked through forests and had my clothes snagged on twigs, bushes and undergrowth. I've been part of a human chain passing the litters across a shallow river while Maverick leant out of his sling, barking with excitement and catching splashes of water in his mouth. I've even crossed a makeshift bridge across a ravine whilst carrying a wriggling, whining Maverick, and I've managed to stay centred the whole time. But when my mind sees something that, without Am's teaching, I would have dismissed as a daydream, I can't help being fascinated. I try to just notice these glimpses of other times, but in trying, I seem to focus on them even more and then they disappear and I can't even remember what I saw. I'm getting better at keeping my frustration to myself so that I don't scare Maverick, but I lose my centre every time it happens and it takes me a while to get it back.

When I tell Am what's happening, she just grins and tells me that as soon as I stop practising how not to be Aware of other times, I'll find it easy. She's such a bloody infuriating person/horse-person/person-horse, whatever it is that she and Infinity are these days.

As I drag my litter up yet another hill, Maverick runs across my path, grinning from ear to ear due to the large stick in his mouth. I can't help smiling, in spite of myself. He shows everyone else his prize before returning to me and throwing it at my feet. He looks up at me expectantly, wanting me to throw it for him. He could end up with splinters in his mouth or the stick down his throat, so I look around for something else. When he sees me pick up a fir cone, his stick is forgotten. I throw the cone and he spins on his heels, leaps over a clump of ferns and dashes off after it. That game sees him through the rest of the day. When he needs to rest, he's careful to not let go of the cone until he's safely in my sling and can drop it where he can pick it straight back up as soon as he is awake. His constant requests to have it thrown for him are exhausting, but I know I'd feel even more tired than I do, without him.

When we finally stop for the night, I ask no one in particular, 'How much longer are we going to be walking before we reach the horses, anyway?'

'It's hard to say. I don't know this area, so I don't know if we're going to come across any more obstacles,' Am says, 'but if we walk at a steady pace, I'd say, maybe a week or so?'

'We're not walking at a steady pace, though, are we? We're plodding at snail's pace and that's when we're actually moving and not either setting up camp or taking it all back down and packing up. We'd have a good few more hours of travel in the day without having to do that,' I reply.

'Yes, we would, if we were in a hurry,' says Justin.

'But we are in a hurry. The horses return with me and Maverick to help the Drifters, that much I've managed to see, so we need to hurry up and find them. I'd be able to see a whole lot more, like how I get them to agree to it, if I could just have some more help to do it.'

'What help is it that you need, Will?' Am's tone is mild, but Infinity stares out of her eyes, daring me to challenge her.

I try to not shout because Maverick is nearby, but it's hard. 'I keep telling you. I'm seeing bits of what I think are the future, but I need help to stop them slipping away.'

'No, you don't.'

'YES, I DO!' I see Maverick cowering and my temper evaporates. I crouch down and he slinks up to me. I stroke his head and he jumps into my arms.

No. You do not. The potency of my teachers' thought almost knocks me onto my backside.

Everyone but Amarilla suddenly becomes very busy with the chores of setting up camp. She motions for me to sit and I find myself obeying her.

You do not need help to stop your visions from slipping away from you. That is not what you have been asked to practise.

'I know I'm meant to just be noticing them, but I can't do it, I've tried,' I say.

Trying to do something merely reinforces the falsehood that you cannot already do it. Know you can do it.

'Just know I can do it? When I've already failed so many times?'

You have failed at trying. You have tried to merely notice the fragments of time to which your soul guided you and therefore reinforced to yourself that you cannot already do it.

'Why is it so important to just notice them, anyway?'

Because focusing on them is not possible.

'It isn't?' I say weakly.

No. Because time is not linear. Your mind can accept that fact but your brain cannot. It can only process thoughts and images one after the other, in linear form. When you focus on something, you involve your brain and it will try to force something that is non-linear into the form with which it's familiar. The event will seem non-sensical and your brain will dismiss it. You must notice and accept with your mind, and only allow yourself to think about it – only allow your brain to become involved – once you have seen all you need to see.

'But how will I know when that is?'

Relax. Allow yourself to know and you will know. Allowing rather than forcing is not something that comes naturally to you but you will learn. Infinity's influence on their thoughts is strong and I find myself accepting their observation.

My days slip into a pattern. When I wake in the mornings, Maverick is snuggled up to me. I centre myself and then use the time before everyone else wakes to practise just allowing thoughts to enter and leave my mind. Every now and then, I see the future. Maverick and I are always surrounded by horses, sometimes walking, sometimes resting and on one occasion, approaching Goldenglade. That is as much as I can see. I just can't seem to stop myself from being too interested in my visions and the moment I pay them too much attention, they vanish.

I trudge along behind the others all day, with Maverick's antics making me smile when he's awake and his presence easing my mind when he's asleep in my sling – although for how much longer I'll be able to carry him I don't know, as he's growing like a weed. I swap between being centred and being frustrated at my lack of progress and as the evenings approach, I'm annoyed far more often than I'm centred. I try and smile at my companions' attempts to cheer me up, but I always find myself going to bed at the earliest opportunity, desperate to escape the battle between my brain and mind by going to sleep, knowing that my best chance of progressing will be to start all over again when I wake up the following day.

'You're getting quite a tan, there, Will,' Justin informs me as we sit around the campfire one evening. 'I should think Lia will approve when you get back to Goldenglade.'

I scowl at him. 'Who cares what Lia approves of? Besides, I can't do the whole seeing into other times thing well enough to know how I get the horses to go back with me, so we'll probably be stuck out here, wherever here is, until we're old and grey.'

'Everyone except you is already old and grey, mate, so on that basis, we'll be heading back pretty soon,' says Marvel.

'Speak for yourself, Marvel.' Vickery gathers her long, blond hair and flicks it behind her shoulder.

'There's grey in there, Vic, it's less noticeable because you're fair, but it's there.' Marvel's eyes twinkle like Maverick's do when he's daring me to play with him.

Vickery stands up and goes over to stand in front of Marvel. 'Find one. Just one.' She bends over so that her hair falls down in a curtain in front of him. Maverick dashes behind the curtain and Vickery squeals as he licks her face.

Amarilla sits down next to me. 'What do you look like in the visions you see?'

'Like I do now.'

'And Maverick?'

'He's a bit bigger and... gangly. Like I was when I was a teenager.'

'And the weather?'

'There are no clouds in the sky, the sun is high and the grass is long and dry. Oh, okay, I get your point. It's still summer. We'll be heading for home within the next month or so. I just can't see how I get to that point, though. I can't discipline myself to just notice the glimpses I get of the future, so they're gone almost as soon as they arrive and I have no idea how I get the horses to help me.'

Maverick chooses that moment to land in my lap. He sits on my legs, yawning, and puts his head on my shoulder.

Discipline has no place here.

'But I have to practise allowing myself to notice what my soul nudges me to notice, and that takes discipline,' I reply.

Who does the disciplining?

'I do.'

Then who does the allowing?

'Ummm, well it should be me… dammit.'

You see the problem.

'Yes, oh wise ones, I see the bloody problem,' I say. 'Disciplining is kind of the opposite of allowing in this scenario.'

Your personality tries to disguise its wilfulness but force is force, no matter how it is labelled. Do not be upset with yourself. Each mistake you make takes you closer to being the person you have seen yourself become.

'I get it. I just wish there was a shortcut to being that person, one that doesn't involve being wrong all the time.'

But then you would be of no use as a teacher. You cannot teach what you have not learnt.

'I never said I wanted to be a teacher.'

But you agreed to it, just as we and Maverick agreed to help you.

I sigh. My soul agreed. My soul has a whole flaming lot to answer for.

ELEVEN

Amarilla

We are not far from the horses now. I haven't disabused Will of his recent notion that he needs to see the future in order to understand how to gain the horses' trust and help, even though I know he won't be in a position to do the former until he's done the latter. I've prepared him as best I can. When he's in contact with Maverick, he is centred most of the time, and when he loses his centre, he's better at getting it back. His mind is primed for the teachings of the horses.

I need to forewarn Justin and our friends of our proximity to the horses, so that they have time to prepare themselves. I play with Maverick, knowing that he will lift me away from the sadness I've been feeling for the past few hours, back to the place I share with Infinity. As always when I find my way back there, the shock I felt at losing my sense of her and all else is replaced by warmth and a feeling of completeness, laced – however the rest of me tries not to allow it – with trepidation at the knowledge that at some point, grief will take it all away from me again.

I wait for Will to retire early to bed, as has become his habit.

Once I know he's asleep, I touch the minds of my friends gently and briefly, sharing with them what I know of the herd of some forty horses. A smile shapes each of their faces and their eyes go distant as they remember the last time we were amongst wild horses. I feel Verve drawn to Vickery's thoughts, his presence comforting her as she yearns for the past. Gas arrives with Justin, whose smile becomes even wider and warmer. A tear rolls down Holly's face as she remembers riding Serene in perfect balance whilst wild horses shuffled for position in order to watch. Serene is with her by the time the memory comes to an end, and I feel their mutual delight. Marvel puts an arm around Rowena's shoulders as Broad and Oak join them in their thoughts, and she hugs him back.

For a moment, I miss hearing Infinity in my mind. I miss the reassurance with which she would have infused me had she been in her body. I miss the sight of her grazing in the evening sunshine, batting flies with her tail and wrinkling her nostrils at the herbs or grasses she didn't like. I miss the whiskers of her soft, pink muzzle that used to tickle my face as she breathed warm air down my neck, and I miss scratching her withers while she groomed me back. My lips begin to tremble as I sink back down into sorrow, but then warmth floods my being again as Infinity pushes back. I smile. My grief is weakening and I am strengthening.

Marvel clears his throat. 'We're a soppy lot, aren't we? Who would have thought that being close to horses again would…' his voice wavers and he clears his throat again.

'Remind us who we are?' finishes Rowena.

Marvel nods. 'Yes, exactly.'

'Except in this scenario, we are merely the wind beneath Will's wings. When he realises he can fly on his own, we'll be redundant. A load of old has-beens,' says Rowena.

'I prefer to think of it that we'll be free to sit back and watch it all happen around someone else for a change,' Justin says. 'Apart from Amarilla and Infinity, that is, they'll have a whoooooole load more work to do.'

I feel our friends' instinctive attempts to probe Justin's mind for more information. It's a bit like watching water dashing against rock as he clamps down the relevant areas of his mind to prevent them all from gaining access. He holds up his hands. 'All in good time, people, all in good time, the future will only distract you.'

Rowena scowls. 'Why will it distract us and not you?'

'Because I, my friends, am magnificent. More to the point, though, I've been subjected to what Amarilla calls "training", but is actually scolding, for more than twenty years, and am therefore immune to being distracted by the bits of the future she's told me about. You lot have escaped the "training" and are therefore completely unprepared for the scenes that I am carefully, and not without substantial skill, hiding from you...' Justin stops talking as a pullover lands on top of him and unfolds to hang down over his face.

'Now that we have that cleared up, are you going to let Will approach the horses tomorrow, Am, or is that yet more information we aren't trusted to know?' Rowena softens her words with a wink.

'That's why I wanted to let you know we're this close, while Will is asleep,' I reply. 'My feeling is that we should let Will take charge of events now, but I wanted to check that you all agree? It will mean following and supporting him whether we think he's right or not and that isn't going to be easy on any of us when there are horses involved.'

'I agree,' Vickery says immediately. 'The only reason we all achieved perfect balance with our horses was because we had exactly the kind of support from each other that Will needs now.'

'Agreed,' says Justin. 'Let the fun begin.'

'I'm not sure I'd call it fun, trusting an angry young man to lead us into goodness knows what kind of a mess, but whatever, I'm in,' Rowena says.

'Add that to travelling with an angry old woman and the immediate future doesn't look too rosy for any of us, but count me in too,' Marvel says.

'Just a straightforward yes from me, Am,' says Holly. 'I'm looking forward to seeing what happens.'

I nod. 'Then we're going to need to brace ourselves.'

The morning sun warms the top of my head as I hang the water pot over the fire. I realise that I'm able to enjoy the feeling; for the first time, I have woken from flying the oneness with Infinity and managed to hold at bay the heartbreak of remembering that I face another day without her physical presence. She knew I'd come to terms with it, and at last, I'm beginning to feel that she was right. As always.

Birds chatter to one another from their perches on nearby branches, or dart around above me at breakneck speed, snatching insects out of the sky. I choose a swallow and ride with her as she homes in on an insect no less focused on his business than she is, and then pursues him with astonishing agility. My mouth opens in wonder at her prowess as she plucks her prey from the air and then moves on to her next target without pausing to think. She is, like all of her kind, completely, absolutely, in the moment, unhindered by the distractions of thought.

A familiar darkness enters my Awareness and I am already

looking over to Will's tent by the time he exits his tent, shaking his head with frustration. Maverick bounds around him. He feels Will's frustration and everything about him wants to offer comfort. He is a reminder of who we all really are, even for those who struggle to remember. I see it every time Will looks at the unadulterated adoration in his dog's eyes and then calms as somewhere inside, he remembers that he is part of All That Is and as such has worth, whoever he is and whatever he does. Will bends down to accept Maverick's attentions and then smiles. I feel my nephew's frustration lighten and then dissipate entirely.

'Morning, Will, you're just in time to help me with breakfast.'

Will looks around. 'We're the first up? That's unusual.'

'Thanks for being too polite to say that it's me being up first that surprises you.' I grin and bend down to fuss Maverick.

'Why are you up so early?'

'Call Maverick to you and see for yourself.'

Will does as I suggest and a smile steals across his face as he picks up the images I place at the forefront of my mind. 'We're close to the horses!'

'Yep, you'll be able to see them later today. We'll come with you and give you any help you ask for, but aside from that, we'll follow your lead.'

He nods enthusiastically and I wonder when he will remember that he has no idea how to get the horses to accept his presence when they won't even tolerate the touch of his mind. Then I remember that this is my nephew. His thoughts race ahead to everything he wants to happen, and plans form and solidify within his mind, emptying it of all else.

'We'll have breakfast, pack up camp and then go to where the horses are,' Will says. 'I won't even try to contact them with my mind, and once they can see for themselves that I pose no threat, hopefully they'll let me approach them.'

'We'd best wake the others, then, hadn't we?' I say.

I can feel Infinity's stare burning out of my eyes as we watch Will rushing from tent to tent, shouting excitedly that today is the day he will get to meet the horses. We will stand back from the proceedings for a while. Maverick has created the environment needed for Will to be able to learn. Now it's up to Will to decide whether he'll allow the horses to teach him to be the person he was born to be.

TWELVE

Will

I could really do without my travelling companions, today of all days. They dawdle along without a care in the world and at this rate, it will be evening by the time we reach the horses. Amarilla has pointed me in the direction I need to head and the way looks clear – no woodland, no water, no ravines to slow us down, just hilly scrubland dotted with bushes, boulders and the odd tree. I want to get a move on. For once in my life, I would like to do things at my own pace. But wait a second, there's no reason why I can't – Am said that they'll all be following my lead from now on. I turn to my companions and wait for them to catch up.

'I'll go on ahead with Maverick, I think, that way I'll have more of the day to work on the horses,' I tell them.

Amarilla, Justin and Holly nod immediately and Marvel and Vickery are only seconds behind.

'We'll see you sometime later then,' Amarilla says.

Rowena frowns and I think she's going to say something, but then she nods curtly.

'Great, see you later, come on, Maverick.' I clap my hands and Maverick barks and leaps on ahead. We quickly leave the others behind us and by the time the sun is high in the sky, they are dots in the distance behind us. They'll stop for lunch soon, I know, but I'll eat on the move and Maverick can eat while he's resting in his sling, which by the look of him, will be very soon.

I'm just licking the last traces of rabbit jerky from my fingers when I top the brow of a hill and see the horses. I drop the traces of my litter and smile. They are little more than dark spots spread out across a distant hillside but I want to shout out loud at the sight of them. I just manage to stop myself so that I don't wake my sleeping puppy. I leave my litter and hold Maverick firmly to my chest as I run down the hillside, my attention solely on avoiding tripping over the numerous tussocks of grass. I can't risk falling and hurting Maverick, not to mention increasing the time it will take to reach the horses.

I'm gasping for breath and pouring with sweat by the time I reach the brow of the next hill. The horses have disappeared. I spin around in disbelief. Where have they gone? I can't see them to either side and they couldn't have come around behind me, so they must have gone further on ahead of me. Dammit, there's another hill to climb up and down before I even get to where they were, but there's nothing for it. Good job I'm fit.

When I reach the hillside where the horses were grazing, I see patches of grass that have been nibbled down low, whole sides of bushes that have been stripped and flattened areas where the horses have obviously lain to rest. I come across an area littered with dung and am impressed by the horses' use of a latrine area. As I climb further, uncomfortably hot now under the summer sun, I see gouges in the ground and realise that they are hoofprints. The horses must have been moving at speed in order to mark the hard ground like this. I continue my pursuit of them. I'll probably see them once I reach the top of this hill – maybe they're just down the other side.

I'm thirsty but I pick up pace again. I'll stop to drink once I'm near the horses. I have to get near them so that they can see I mean no harm.

I follow the hoofprints and flattened grass to the brow of the hill and am rewarded by the sight of the horses almost at the top of the next hill. To a horse, they stop grazing and lift their heads to look in my direction. Then they are off and within seconds have disappeared again over the brow. I want to shout out in frustration, but again, my peacefully sleeping puppy stops me. I stamp my feet and then spin around and kick the nearest bush. I'm so dizzy, I almost fall over. I pull my water flask over my head and drink half of its contents, leaving the other half for Maverick. He yawns and reaches up to lick my chin. I'm relieved he's awake, we'll be able to move so much quicker if I'm not having to carry him.

I lower him to the floor and pour water into my cupped hands for him to drink. Then we're off. The urgency of the situation takes me over and I don't watch my footing as carefully as I did when I was carrying Maverick. I catch my foot on a bramble that stretches out of sight through the long, stalky grass, and take a header down the hill. I sit up, spitting dirt out of my mouth and feeling like howling, but Maverick bounds around me excitedly, play-bowing in response to the exuberant play-bow he thinks I have just performed. The fury that was about to explode out of me melts away and I slap both hands to the ground and make as if to chase him. He tears off, barking with delight and by the time he returns, I'm brushing myself down ready to go again.

I jog down the remainder of the hillside and across to the next hill which is, thankfully, a far gentler slope. I pass hoofprints that show the spins the horses performed in their rush to be off, and again follow the gouges in the ground left by them as they tore up the hill at speed.

When I reach the top of the mound, I can't see them anywhere. There is a rustling and growling coming from a bush just off to one side as Maverick pulls at one of its branches, and there is a bird of prey circling above, making its distinctive "ki" noise, but other than that, everything is still.

Then, I catch movement in my peripheral vision. The horses are moving at speed in the distance off to one side, heading back in the direction from which Maverick and I have just come. They disappear down a dip and then reappear for less than a minute before cresting a hill higher than the one on which I am standing and disappearing down the other side.

'AAAAAAAAAAAAAAAAAAGGGGGGHHHHH!' I drop to my knees and pound the earth with my fists until they bleed. Then I sit on the ground with my head in my hands. I feel helpless and furious, just as I always have. I thought things would be different now, but they're exactly the same. Nothing goes as I want it to – whatever I do, I just end up feeling like this.

My hands hurt as a tongue gently licks them. I drop them away from my face and Maverick shrinks back away from me. My anger oozes away and is replaced by guilt, sorrow and love for the beautiful dog who comforts me no matter how much of a git I am.

'Come here, Mav, I'm sorry,' I say, holding my hands out to him.

He slinks towards me on his belly and licks my bleeding fingers again. I stroke his head and he creeps onto my lap.

I don't dare reach out to the horses in my Awareness, but I don't need to; they've left something of themselves lingering in the ether. I sense the instinct that runs through each and every one of them to avoid energy like mine. They won't tolerate the touch of my mind on theirs, my physical presence or even my gaze – to them, they are the same.

I am surprised to find that I'm not offended. I haven't bothered to try and centre myself, so my response doesn't come from any kind of balance on my part, but more because I can feel the horses' complete lack of agenda. Their actions aren't personal, in fact there's no conscious thought whatsoever involved on their part, any more than there is on mine when keeping a comfortable distance from the flames of a fire.

There's something about the horses' energy that makes me want to be different from how I am. To be accepted by them. I have no idea what to do about it. I'm not a bad person. I would never hurt anyone, in fact the whole reason I'm here is because I want to help the Drifters, which is more than anyone else has tried to do, so what is it about me that the horses can't stand? What's wrong with me?

There is nothing wrong with you, I am informed by Amarilla and Infinity. *Indeed the aspect of you that repels the horses is the very trait that will enable you to be who you will be. But you must use it differently. You will become the force of nature you have always sensed yourself to be, but not by forcing your nature as you have always had the tendency to do.*

I'm tired. Way too tired to try and make sense of riddles, I reply.

Retrace your steps. Dinner will be ready for you by the time you reach camp.

I get to my feet, gently tipping Maverick to the ground. He bounds off to fetch the stick he managed to wrench from the bush, and then dashes back, throwing it at my feet.

I'm knackered and sore but his energy gives me a lift. I grin at him. 'I'm not throwing it, Maverick, it'll hurt you. Here, what about this?' I pick up a clod of earth and throw it as far as I can.

It'll break apart on landing but Maverick will enjoy the chase and subsequent hunt for its parts.

It seems like forever before I see a flickering campfire, surrounded by tents. Maverick runs on ahead of me and I hear Holly squealing from her tent when he bursts in on her. He emerges, his whole body wagging along with his tail, and throws himself at Justin and Marvel as they stand by the fire, before dashing off to find the others.

Amarilla appears from behind Holly's tent. 'Right on time, Will, dinner's almost ready... er, you're probably going to need to wash first?'

Rowena appears from behind her. 'Well, I must say, the family resemblance is even stronger now, you look just like your aunt did after her first horse-hunting mission, only without all the pus. Ow! Elbow me all you like, Am, it's true. No, wait, you didn't have dirt around your mouth as Will does, I'll give you that.'

Justin brings a bucket of water over. He slaps an arm around my shoulder and guides me to my tent, grinning. 'Ro's right, you know, you do seem to have inherited your aunt's tendency for calamity where horses are concerned, it's actually quite endearing.' He hands me the bucket. 'Get yourself cleaned up and then Am can patch you up before dinner.'

My knees, nose and chin are just grazed from my tumble down the hillside, but the self-inflicted wounds on my knuckles and fingers are deep, full of dirt, and very painful now that they have my full attention. As I sit in the entrance of my tent, gingerly trying to clean my injured hands, I curse myself for being such an idiot.

Amarilla puts her herbal pack and a bucket of clean, steaming water on the ground beside me and then kneels down. She takes my hands in her own and inspects them.

'Ouch,' she says. 'I know it'll hurt even more, but I want you to put your hands in this clean water and swirl them around a bit to clean off the soil you've managed to loosen. Then I'm going to pack the clean wounds with healing unguent and poultice the wounds that are still dirty. It will mean having to bandage your hands afterwards, I'm afraid.'

'Sure, whatever.' I do as I'm told and then hold out my hands again. As soon as the healing unguent is applied, the pain in my hands decreases. Then it gets worse as Amarilla prods her poultice into the deepest wounds.

'You don't need to feel embarrassed, you know,' my aunt tells me as she bandages my hands. 'You've heard the tale of my antics when Infinity tugged me – by the time Rowena and Oak found me, I was unconscious, my clothes were shredded to the point of indecency, I was, as we've just been reminded, exuding a not insignificant amount of pus, and I stank to high heaven. By comparison, you've looked after yourself pretty well.' She looks up at me with a grin and I can't help but smile.

'I feel daunted,' I say.

Am looks at me thoughtfully. 'It's easier to change than you think, and you've already begun.'

'But I don't know what to do.'

'It's not about doing, so much as being. I know you're tired, but remember what we told you earlier. Just remember it. The horses will help you to understand what it means.'

'Something about being a force of nature?'

Amarilla nods. 'You'll become the force of nature you have always sensed yourself to be, but not by forcing your nature as you have always had the tendency to do. Being, not doing. Now, come and have dinner.'

THIRTEEN

Amarilla

It has been a highly enjoyable week for all of us except Will. While he and Maverick have been absent from camp during the day, the rest of us have spent our time keeping track of him in our Awareness while taking our time over camp chores, playing cricket with a bat, stumps and ball secretly packed by Rowena in the "miscellaneous" litter, and lazing around in the sunshine, relishing the easy company of old friends.

Our camp is at the foot of a hill, out of which flows a stream of deliciously cool water. A dead tree, apparently felled by lightning, lies nearby, conveniently providing a never-ending supply of wood for the fire. With our tents, blankets and ample clothing supply, we have never camped in such luxury, as we are frequently reminded by a very smug Rowena.

Will has been up at dawn each morning, sometimes having seen visions of himself with the horses, sometimes not, but always with fresh determination. He's eaten what we have prepared for him, accepted a satchel with his and Maverick's food for the day, and then left with his dog in whichever direction I have pointed out to him. He's tailed the horses relentlessly with no improvement in their acceptance of him and has returned in the evenings looking more and more dejected by the day.

We have fed him, tended his wounds, aired his tent, kept his bedding and clothes washed and, occasionally, made him smile. That is all we can do.

'He's not looking quite as bad as Aleks did at his worst, but he's not looking great, is he?' Vickery says one morning as we watch Will stride off with purpose, Maverick by his side. 'He's lost weight and those shadows under his eyes are getting darker.'

'He's lost weight because of all the running around he's doing,' Justin says. 'He just can't seem to stop himself.'

'It's hard to reconcile the centred version of Will with the person he's insisting on being at the moment, isn't it,' says Holly. 'He's centred when he wakes up and before he can think too much, but as soon as he gets glimpses of his future self with the horses, or even worse when he doesn't and he panics, he's like a man possessed.'

'That's exactly what he is. His personality is taking up all of him again,' says Rowena. 'He's stressed, so it's easier for him to be the way he's always been, even when it's getting in his way and stopping him solving the problem that's causing him to be so stressed in the first place. It's fascinating.'

'And familiar,' Marvel says. 'Let's not pretend we haven't all got in our own way. None of us struggled once we were Aware, as Will is, though. Oh, except for you, Am, it was quite some time before you found it easy being centred, wasn't it? You'd be off with the fairies for months on end and then suddenly be back with us and on one mission or another, and nothing could get in your way…'

I hold my hands up, laughing. 'Okay, I see the parallel, Will is quite clearly struggling because he's related to me.'

Justin hugs me. 'Your missions didn't exactly end badly though, did they? Pushing your students to achieve perfect balance until Quinta did it, then going off to find the Kindred. Nothing wrong with a bit of determination, even if you did leave me behind when you went off gallivanting with this lot.'

'Your loyalty to Am is, as ever, cute, Jus, but gallivanting?' Rowena says. 'We made friends with a Kindred, we helped an injured horse to heal and then helped all of the horses to achieve perfect balance. If anyone was gallivanting, it was you – drifting in right at the end once the hard part was done...'

'Swinging the balance so that Mother Elder accepted me and then helped the others to accept us all,' I interrupt Rowena with a grin.

'Oh, you two are impossible when you're all loved up,' she says, smiling back at me.

'Maybe we should try that?' Marvel says and then burps.

The rest of us laugh at the revolted look on Rowena's face until eventually, she joins in.

It's been three weeks now and the horses have finally worn Will down. He is forced to sit and contemplate at the boundary that they don't allow him to cross; a non-physical boundary whose existence Will has learnt the hard way. Any attempt by him to ignore it and get closer to the horses results in them leaving the vicinity at full speed. And they will leave every bit as quickly if Will has even the tiniest thoughts of how else he can get the horses to accept him.

Yesterday, Will thought of just giving up and leaving the horses alone. To a horse, they stopped grazing and turned to watch him. He wondered if, finally, they might let him approach. They left at a gallop, leaving a cloud of dust in their wake. For the first time, Will didn't get to his feet and immediately follow. When he did finally follow their tracks, he caught sight of them far sooner than he expected to. He sat down at the boundary they have taught him to respect and when Maverick settled in his lap, for the first time whilst in the horses' vicinity, he focused on finding his centre. One of the horses turned and began to graze in Will's direction, effectively moving the horses' boundary a little closer. Will stood up, excitedly hoping that this was the breakthrough he had been looking for... only to see the horses' heels disappearing into the distance. When he returned to camp, he was lost in thought.

Not wanting to interrupt his deliberations, none of us said a word to him during the evening, but each of us hugged him as we went about our usual routine of tending to him and Maverick. He acknowledged all of our attentions briefly with an exhausted smile, before losing himself once more in his thoughts. When I saw his eyelids drooping, I motioned to Justin and we hauled him to his feet and took him to his tent. He was almost asleep as Justin pulled off his outer clothes and laid a blanket over him. He was sound off by the time I knelt down to tuck the blanket tight around him.

'We're all proud of you, Will,' I whispered. There was a snuffling in my ear and then a tongue licked the side of my face. I chuckled softly and stroked the furry head that snuggled into my neck. 'And of you, Maverick, where would we all be without you?'

Maverick curled up next to Will, his head on Will's chest. I left them to sleep.

~

'I wonder whether it'll be today,' Vickery says as we sip tea, delaying the end of breakfast and the chores that await us all.

'No, Will being Will, I think he'll need a bit more hiking around before he fully gets it, but it won't be long, now,' says Holly.

'Agreed,' says Rowena. 'The way he needs to be for the horses to tolerate him is the last way he'll choose of his own accord, so he'll need to well and truly prove to himself that it's the only way before he'll accept it.'

'He's a strong-minded lad, isn't he?' Marvel says.

'Yep, and when he can balance that with the level of openness and Awareness he's capable of as a result of his heritage and early experiences, he'll be a force to be reckoned with,' Justin says.

'He'll be the force of nature he has always sensed himself to be,' I murmur and a shiver goes down my spine.

FOURTEEN

Will

I am shattered. I envy Maverick's energy as he tears around in front of me, his tail wagging in frantic circles as it always does when he's found a fresh scent to follow. The sun is just cresting the hill in front of us, its deep orange rays reminding me of the heat it has flung down on me day after blisteringly hot day. I don't feel as if I have the energy to follow the horses if they keep galloping off again today, but I suppose I'll end up finding some every time I break the rules that I'm still trying to figure out.

Everything I've done or even thought of doing so far has pushed the horses away from me, and that has only made me more and more desperate for them to accept me. I can't figure out how they can frustrate me to the degree that they do and yet still exert such a pull on me that I can't let go of the need to be near them. This has gone way beyond just wanting to get them to trust me so I can ask for their help with the Drifters. Being with the horses is something I need to do for me.

In my exhaustion yesterday, I thought about giving up, and weirdly, the horses were suddenly interested in me instead of repulsed. Since they won't let me reach out to them in my Awareness for any answers, I have tried and tried to work out for myself what changed, but I can't put my finger on it, despite something jogging my memory every time I think about it, as if I already know the answer. When I decided to focus on centring myself to see if I could remember what I think I must know, I saw one of the horses move closer. I thought I'd cracked it, that they'd finally accepted that I'm no threat and would let me near, but then they left again.

Today, I'll work on being centred again and I'll see what happens. Maybe nothing. Maybe what happened yesterday was just coincidence and the horse moved closer to me by accident. I know I don't believe that, though. I definitely made headway yesterday and hopefully I'll make more today. One thing is for certain – it's getting too hot to be doing much running around, especially for Maverick.

When I see the horses on a distant hillside, I know how much further I'll be able to move towards them before they won't let me get any closer – the light knows, they've hammered the message home enough times. Maverick has finally slowed to a walk and is panting, so he'll be glad of a drink and a rest.

Once I'm at the boundary over which I mustn't cross, I drop my back-sack and fish out the shelter that Justin has cobbled together for me out of sticks and some cloth. Maverick flops down in the shade gratefully as soon as the shelter is up. I crawl in beside him with a bowl and pour him some water, which he laps up before lying down on the ground beside me. I take a long swig of water myself, and then put my hand on Maverick's side as he falls asleep. I glance up at the horses and see that they are grazing peacefully. I focus on the sound of Maverick's quick breaths and count them while reaching out to my family in my Awareness. My sisters are still asleep but my parents are awake. They instantly feel the touch of my mind on theirs and I feel their relief. They don't ask me anything, they already know. They're proud of me! That's new. When I am as Aware as I am conscious of my physical surroundings, my parents retreat from my mind, leaving a sense of love and pride behind them. Now, to stay centred and see what happens.

Two of the horses, still grazing, move closer. My heart leaps and although I manage not to repeat my mistake of yesterday and get to my feet, I see all of the horses raise their heads in my direction. I focus on breathing deeply while keeping my mind focused in my Awareness. I know that Maverick is dreaming contentedly, yet the herd of deer who caught his scent as we made our way here are still moving purposefully further away. The rabbits that graze nearby are bolder, reassured by the safety of their nearby burrows. I watch as the horses lower their heads back down to graze and the closest two continue, very slowly, to move along the valley floor towards me. Another three leave the herd and begin to follow and I am unable to prevent a surge of excitement. It's working! Maybe once all of them have realised they don't need the boundary anymore, I'll be able to approach them. The horses all raise their heads immediately. I can just make out their ears pricked in my direction before they perform the spins I've seen so many times before and gallop off.

I punch the ground, creating new wounds where the previous ones have barely finished healing. It's all I have the energy to do. I feel like crying as I haven't cried since I was a kid. Instantly, Maverick wakes, sits up and licks my face before he has even had time to yawn. I bury my face in the fur of his neck and sob.

'I can't do it, Mav. Just when I think I've got it right, I get it wrong, yet again. And there's no point asking the others what to do because Amarilla will just answer me in riddles and everyone else will tell me to ask Amarilla. You're the only one who really helps me, but it's not enough, I can't do this.'

Maverick pulls away from me, licking his nose and yawning. Then he reaches forward and licks the tears from my face. When he finally stops, he just sits there, watching me. I almost can't bear the adoring, expectant look in his bright, brown eyes. He is waiting for me to decide what to do next. Will we play? Eat? Move on? Whatever I decide, he has complete trust in me that it will be the greatest, most fantastic and enjoyable thing to do. And somehow, I find it impossible not to believe him. I rub his chest and he throws himself onto his back, wriggling in delight. I can do this. We will follow the horses again, and I will carry on trying to figure out what I am still doing wrong.

Being. Not doing, I am advised.

Am?

No response.

Infinity?

They don't answer, but I feel their attention on me. They are waiting. Being, not doing. The words seem to pulse in my mind and I feel Infinity's energy powering them, giving them a life of their own. They are the key to… everything. Being, not doing.

All of a sudden, understanding floods through me as I remember what it is that I know. I don't have to work out what I'm doing wrong, I have to work out how I am BEING wrong. I have to be the force of nature I know myself to be, but not by trying to force nature as I always do. Allowing, not forcing. Being not doing. It's all the same. My mind races. Being centred draws the horses closer to me, but any attempt or thought of approaching the horses – of doing something – pushes them away. Being not doing. Everything makes sense when I relate it to those three words that continue to pulse with Infinity's discarnate energy.

I pour more water for Maverick and when he has drunk enough, I pack up the shelter and we move on. Maverick is delighted, as always. He tosses a sprig of heather to himself and then runs off, tail aloft, with his prize, only to return and run across my path, proudly displaying it before tearing off again. I smile. It's down to him that I've made it this far. Without his constant companionship and his abilities to lift me when I'm down, comfort me when I'm miserable, trust me when I don't trust myself and calm me when I want to rage, I would still be incapable of being anyone other than who I was.

I walk quickly along the valley floor, keen to get the shelter back up and Maverick out of the sun. As we round the base of a hill, I see the horses dotted across a hillside in the distance. There is an enormous horse chestnut tree nearby. I decide not to get as close to the horses as they will let me; Maverick and I can take advantage of the tree's shade while I practise being how I think I need to be.

I sit on the ground and Maverick settles beside me. I find my centre and then stay there. I don't know how much time passes before Maverick suddenly gets to his feet, his hackles up and his tail held stiffly as he stares into the distance. I look up to see that the wild horse herd is on the move again – towards us! Maverick begins to whine and looks anxiously from the horses to me. I stand up and scoop him up in my arms.

'It's okay, little guy, I've got you,' I tell him, watching the horses streak across the scrubland towards us. I'm flooded with Awareness of them as one big mass of pure, unadulterated consciousness, living in the moment and responding with total honesty to everything that presents itself. My forceful nature has repelled them up until now but when I didn't even try to get close to them, when I relaxed my will enough to stay centred, they sensed the part of me that is like them. They are curious.

As I watch the horses get closer to me, my chin drops. They aren't galloping so much as... flowing. The whole herd appears to be suspended from the air by invisible strings, their hooves touching the ground merely by chance. It seems impossible that animals of their size can move so lightly, yet I know that neither my eyes nor my Awareness deceive me.

The herd is led by a tall, black mare. As soon as I single her out from the others, I am Aware of her essence becoming more defined within the collective consciousness of the herd, as if my observation of her as an individual has caused her to be exactly that. She immediately slows herself and her herd to a halt, as one. She is close enough that I can see her ears flickering between me and the rest of her herd as they fan out either side of her. Chestnuts, greys, browns, blacks and one skewbald stand ready to turn and run at any moment. The horses' ears are pricked, and their eyes are wide and bright as they stare at me standing with Maverick in my arms, both of us watching every tiny movement they make.

I grew up around the bonded horses of my father, aunt and uncle, so the sight of a horse in perfect balance is familiar. The sight and feel of a herd of wild horses who have never compromised anything of themselves in order to be acceptable company for humans, however, is new to me. Their wild, undiluted reactions to everything around them are of an honesty and strength I have never come across before – and yet relate to. Their pull on me has intensified with their closeness and I can't help taking a step forward. The horses, as one, move backward several steps, never taking their eyes away from me. Several of them snort.

If they won't allow me any closer, how will we move forward

from here? I wonder to myself. I realise my mistake even as I think the thought. To a horse, the herd sits further onto its haunches, spins and blasts away from me with breath-taking elegance and speed.

I feel a profound sense of loss as I watch the herd become a distant mass, and then separate out into dots as the horses settle down to graze. Why did I have to go and stuff it up by thinking of what to do? Why can I not just be?

You can. The horses just proved it to you. Will, you're doing brilliantly. Remember that you already know that you can be how you need to be. You've seen it. Infinity's discarnate energy makes the words spin, so that I can't dismiss them.

I lower Maverick to the ground and retreat further into the shade of the tree, dragging my back-sack along the ground behind me. I feed Maverick, fill his water bowl and then eat my own lunch, feeling too weary to even try and think of anything other than the words that Infinity has fixed into my mind.

I don't remember falling asleep, but I find myself waking to the sound of Maverick barking. I leap to my feet and reach for my bow and arrows; if there are wild cats around, they'll select a lone pup as an easy target, regardless of whether he's with a human. The sight in front of me causes me to drop my hunting gear instantly. The horses are back. They are the same distance away as before, and grazing.

I call Maverick and as soon as he is close enough to touch, I centre myself and then enclose him in a net of reassuring energy, the same way my mother used to do for me when I was little. He calms straight away and stops barking. For a second, I'm surprised that the horses weren't disturbed by his noise and what I'm sure would have been sudden movement when he woke to see them there, but then I feel their acceptance of a baby animal calling to his parent.

I sit down and lean against the trunk of the tree, stroking Maverick's head and thinking as I watch the horses graze.

Being, not doing. You already know you can be how you need to be. You've seen it. Infinity fuels the words, making them pulse with the total, absolute confidence that Amarilla and Infinity have in me.

I remember all of the visions I have seen of myself walking amongst the horses and I know they are right. I know I can be how I need to be. I relax. Being, not doing. Being centred, not using it as a means to then do what I want. Panic seizes me. Having ideas and plans and acting on them, forcing them through, that's who I am. But if I want to feel relief from the frustration of not being accepted by the horses, I have no choice other than to change the way I relate to the world. Panic turns to shock as my decision takes hold in my mind. I begin to shiver uncontrollably.

Hoofbeats approach and Maverick snuggles up close to me and whines. I wrap him in my arms and get to my feet, my legs trembling as the tall, black lead mare stops an arm's length away.

Her nostrils flare and relax as she takes in my and Maverick's scents. She raises and lowers her head to make sense of the sight of us up close. Maverick whines anxiously again as she shakes her head to dislodge the flies clustering around her eyes. I stroke his head with a shaking hand and turn away from the mare so that my body shields Maverick from her. He quietens.

Being, not doing. The words spin with Infinity's energy, penetrating my shock and reassuring me that my inability to think what to do is a good thing. I feel warm air on the back of my neck and turn my head slightly to see that the mare has moved closer. I feel my shock begin to subside, as if she is drawing it out of me and into herself with each inward breath. I regain my centre and am Aware that the mare has no thoughts of reassuring me, she is simply drawn to an imbalance that can be corrected by her energy.

I am overwhelmed by the power of one who is completely without judgement or agenda, one who lives in the moment, responding purely and honestly to what is around her. I find myself drawn to accept her way of being, knowing it is how I want to be. How I can be now that she has shown me how. How I am.

FIFTEEN

Amarilla

I look around me to see that Justin, Holly, Marvel, Rowena and Vickery have all forgotten the various chores they were doing and are standing around with their mouths open. I can't stop smiling.

'Blimey,' says Vickery eventually.

Rowena jumps and murmurs, 'Thunder and lightning.'

Marvel just shakes his head.

'After everything we've been through, I didn't think much could surprise me, and then Will goes and does that,' says Holly. 'And Infinity too – I mean, flaming lanterns, did that really all just happen?'

'Knowing he's capable of being that open is one thing, witnessing it was just… I mean the speed he accepted change once he realised…' Justin disappears into his thoughts again.

'He's done it,' I say. 'I think we'd better pack up camp.'

~

It is evening and the heat of the day is finally, blessedly, decreasing by the time we crest the last hill and see the horses grazing in the valley below. Some of them raise their heads briefly in our direction, but our presence is no surprise and they accept it without discomfort. Grief grips my throat at the memories evoked by the sight of the horses, and I'm not alone. The six of us stand close together, remembering the horses we have known well and loved, and those we met only briefly, yet who still left their imprints on us. Before long, we're all smiling at the miracle of horses, past and present.

We watch Will as he walks freely among the herd, a nervous Maverick staying close to him. I love Will's manner. He asks nothing of the horses at all. He doesn't offer a hand as invitation for any of them to sniff and greet him, he doesn't even look at them directly, but simply allows both his gaze and Awareness to drift, taking in whichever aspects of the horses present themselves. He bears no intention whatsoever that would disrupt their peace.

Every now and then, one of the horses lifts a head to watch Will or sniff his scent as he passes. A couple of them extend their noses towards him and both times, he stops, his body turned slightly away as they approach. He allows them all the time they need to inspect his person, and makes no move to touch, or even look directly at them. When they wander off, he continues his stroll.

A grey mare approaches Will and after spending some time sniffing him with her neck outstretched, she moves closer and nudges him gently. He makes no move until she wiggles her upper lip on his shoulder and nudges him again. He accepts her invitation to groom her and lifts a hand to stroke and then scratch her withers. She wiggles her upper lip more strongly and works her way up to his neck and then his head. He copies her, scratching her neck and then her face. She lifts her head over his and nuzzles his other shoulder. He obliges her request to swap sides, and scratches the newly-presented side of her withers. Will's blond hair is a tangle of grass and saliva by the time the grey mare is satisfied and moves off to graze again. He couldn't care less. His joy is infectious and we all laugh out loud with delight.

I'm glad you finally made it, Maverick and I are starving. Will's thoughts dance into our minds with an uncharacteristic humour and cheer.

'Cheeky git,' Marvel says. 'Hang on... Will's Aware and he isn't touching Maverick.' He slaps his forehead. 'Of course! The fact he's been using an energy net to reassure Maverick while he's been wandering among the horses should have given it away.'

'Now he's as the horses are, he's centred all the time,' murmurs Holly thoughtfully, 'and the level of Awareness he has... well it feels like it's...'

'Vast. Unprecedented,' Justin confirms. 'He reached perfect balance when he was so young, and combined with his heritage and upbringing, that means his mind is open to an extent that no one's ever managed before. Now he's given up the need to force his way through life, he's open to his Awareness without limit. And even being Super-Aware as he is, he can stay centred – that will of his that we've all had reason to curse, is strong enough to keep him in balance.'

'He's magnificent, isn't he,' says Vickery.

'Shall we go down and see him, rather than just standing up here, staring at him?' says Rowena.

I'll come up to you, Will tells us. *You've all had to take turns dragging my litter as well as your own. Sorry.*

As soon as Will turns in our direction, Maverick speeds on ahead of him. When the pup reaches us, his tongue is lolling and he is panting hard, but nevertheless, he greets us all as if he hasn't seen us in weeks. By the time Will arrives, Holly has found a bowl and Maverick is happily lapping water.

Justin is the first to pull Will into a hug, telling him, 'Awesome, mate, just awesome.'

'I'm not going to lie, you took us by surprise with the speed it all happened at the end there, but we knew you could do it, even if we can't see what Am can.' Vickery holds her arms open and wiggles her fingers for Will to go to her.

Marvel slaps him on the back as Will passes him. 'Do you know, Ro went quiet for nearly ten minutes while you were doing your thing? I mean how often does that happen?'

'So did you, Marvel, in fact your mouth was open for so long, I'm surprised the flies missed it,' I tell him with a wink at Rowena.

'It's his breath. No living creature would approach that willingly,' Rowena grins. 'Come here, Will. What you just did, I mean, the way you just changed like that, it was gobsmacking.' She hugs him fiercely and then looks around at the rest of us. 'Haven't you all missed this? Being right in the thick of it again? I mean the last twenty-odd years have been great and everything, but to be right at the forefront of change again, with this vortex of energy spinning around us with even more force than Amarilla's did – no offence, Am…'

'None taken.'

'…and Will right at the centre of it all, poised to move forward in ways I can't even fathom, it's all so exciting. Come on, I can't be the only one who's missed it?'

Marvel puts an arm around her. 'Do you know, I was only thinking the other day that we were due for one of your motivational speeches, Ro. Now those, I HAVE missed.'

We all laugh as Rowena swats him.

Will accepts a congratulatory hug from Holly and then looks at me. 'Thanks, Am, for what you and Fin did for me. I get it now, why she left, I mean the sheer power of her now – I couldn't have done this without her helping me the way she did, she's... well, she's...'

I try to smile at him but am unable to stop my lower lip from quivering. 'Infinity. Yes, she is.'

For the first time, Will is fully Aware how difficult it was for me to stay in my body when Infinity left hers. The look of tenderness in his eyes brings it all flooding back again and as my Awareness winks out, Justin moves towards me. Will reaches me first and enfolds me gently in his arms.

'I know you don't need me to be sorry for being such a massive pain in the arse when you've had so much to deal with, but I am,' he says. 'And I may have changed, but I still need your help and I'm still capable of being that massive pain in the arse, I mean, I'm still me, aren't I?'

'Yes, you are. You're everything we knew you would be and everything we all love,' I whisper. Then I take a deep breath, pull away from him and say, 'Now are you going to show us the best place to set up camp before we all collapse with exhaustion?'

Will releases me and grins. 'Sorry, yes, down there by that big tree, and this time, I'm helping.'

'We wouldn't dream of disagreeing with anything you say, magnificent one,' says Rowena.

I laugh. 'Get used to that, Will, I can tell you from experience that she won't let up.'

'Get used to them agreeing to do what I say? No problem, so, Ro, if you could dig an oven and bake one of your cakes, that would be great. Vic, your priority is to make that amazing sauce you make from your herbs, ready to go with the venison that Marvel hunted this morning. I'm sure you and Holly are going to love cooking it over the fire that Marvel will light and then tend, in between trips to get water. Am, Justin and I will put the tents up and make the beds. Oh, and, Holly, if you could slice some venison off for Maverick before you cook it, that would be great, he's one hungry pup.'

There is a stunned silence and then Marvel says, 'Okay, so Will may be related to Amarilla, but they are two veeeeeerrrrry different people. Rowena, did you hear me? Next time you decide to tease Will, make it "I" rather than "we", got it?'

Everyone laughs and then Will grins at me and winks. 'See, Am? That is how it's done.'

After dinner, as the sun finally sinks behind the hills, and Will and Maverick settle down for a well-earned snooze, the rest of us visit the horses. Many of them are standing nose to tail, flicking flies from one another's faces as they rest. Some of them are lying down, either perched on their elbows, dozing, or sleeping flat out. A few are still grazing and two are grooming one another. None of us make any attempt to hide our emotions at the sight, smell and sound of the horses, so familiar, so evocative of our own beloved horses.

The herd mostly experiences itself as one huge being of many parts. It responds instinctively, either as a whole or via one or more of its pieces, to whichever energy patterns present themselves, as has already happened with Will – and as is now demonstrated by our presence.

Each of us is approached by a single horse. Out of the corner of my eye, I watch a dark bay mare canter towards me, slow to a trot and then halt abruptly next to me. Through my tears, I smile with appreciation of her warmth and gentle beauty. She extends her neck and the black, velvety skin of her nose touches my cheek as she breathes in my scent. She sniffs all the way down my neck and arm, and nuzzles my hand. I gently stroke her muzzle with the back of my finger and turn towards her slightly. She moves a little closer and I stroke her sleek, glossy neck. She is beautiful. But she isn't Infinity. Infinity is with me. As soon as the mare feels me come back to myself, to ourselves, she wanders off to graze.

I smile after her, knowing that she doesn't need my gratitude, but feeling it nevertheless. I look over to Justin and our friends and see that they also now stand alone, their tears replaced by smiles now that they, too, have been comforted into remembering that the loss they were feeling was, in reality, imaginary.

As I snuggle up to Justin for the night, I wonder how long it will be before Will realises how easily he can be Aware of the past and future, now that he no longer has the tendency to try to force it. He doesn't keep me guessing for long; dawn hasn't even broken when Justin and I are woken by a furry mass hurling itself on top of us and licking our faces as if our lives depended on it, followed by Will's apologetic, 'Knock, knock,' from outside.

'Ow, Maverick, you're standing on my hair,' I tell him sleepily. 'Will, you'll have to come in, I can't move until your dog does.'

'Is there anyone else wanting to come in, seeing as this is clearly the place to be at... whatever time this is?' Justin mumbles.

'It's just me, everyone else is still asleep.' Will crawls in. 'Oops, sorry, whose foot is that?'

'Mine. As soon as Maverick lets me sit up, there'll be room for you to sit there.' I rub my eyes and yawn.

'Maverick, come here,' Will says.

The weight holding my hair down disappears, and then before I can move, lands on my stomach. 'Oooof!'

'Sorry, Am, there isn't room for him to go around you,'

'You've noticed that, have you?' Justin says.

When I can finally sit up, my eyes make out the dark shape of Will clutching Maverick as he settles down in front of me. 'So, what did you see?' I ask him.

'I should've known there'd be no surprising you, see for yourself.' Will places his vision at the forefront of his mind.

The wild horses are with him and Maverick at Goldenglade, as he has seen before. This time though, the vision continues into various scenes of the horses moving as one being and then occasionally interacting with people. But not in the way that our bonded horses did. These horses stay as a herd at all times.

'There's no sense whatsoever of individual horses choosing individual people to bond with. The wild horses aren't going to be giving up anything of themselves like the bonded horses did,' Will tells us. 'They'll carry on living as a herd in perfect balance, and they'll help the Drifters purely as a consequence of who they are, just like how they helped me. And they don't even need to be asked. They've picked up the imbalance in humanity from what I know of it, and when we leave here, they'll come with us because allowing their energy to show the imbalance how to correct itself is the natural thing for them to do. Pure and simple.'

I nod. 'And while you were perusing the future, did you come across the potential obstacle to the horses bringing balance to the Drifters?'

Justin speaks before my nephew can answer. 'Hold on a second, Will, you can not only see the glimpses of the future that flash into your mind unbidden now, but you can also go looking for others at will? Already?'

'Well, yes, I mean once the glimpses arrived in my mind, it was easy to let them play out and then I found I could be Aware of any other related scenes that I wanted to see.'

'Jus, you knew he'd be able to do this,' I say.

'Yes, I know, you saw it, but it's the speed he's changing I can't get over. I mean less than a day ago, he couldn't even be Aware without Maverick but now he's Aware to an extent that even with all our experience, we can't fathom, yet effortlessly keeping himself centred – and now he's not only seeing and interpreting glimpses of the future but he's finding them in his Awareness at will? I mean you can't even do that, Am.'

'What can I say? I'm a great teacher,' I tell him with a chuckle.

'You can't, Am?' Will says.

'Hmmm?'

'You can't see the future at will?'

'Nope. You're capable of a lot more than I am, Will, as I told you before. You have the openness of mind to be able to accept limitless Awareness and all that entails. I was older when I achieved perfect balance than you were, so I don't have the openness that you do. I can see what my soul nudges me to see, but that's it.'

'You saw enough to know what to teach me so that my mind was prepared for the horses to be able to get through to me, though,' Will says thoughtfully. 'You weren't joking, you are a great teacher.'

'I was joking, as it happens, we all know who's behind everything I do, but thanks. Anyway, back to my question-that-wasn't-really-a-question-because-I-know-the-answer. Did you see the complication that could prevent the horses from being able to help the Drifters?'

'No, I only thought about them actually helping, so those were the aspects of the future that I saw.'

'Okay, well I've buried the answer in my mind deeply enough that you won't pick it up by accident and I'm now preparing to be amazed at the speed you'll find it in the future for yourself. I just want the problem, Will, not the solution, at the moment. You'd better brace yourself too, Jus, you're still not over everything he's done so far.'

'Hmmmm, I see it,' Will says.

'Seriously? Flaming lanterns, I couldn't even follow what your mind just did.'

'Shhh, Jus, let him finish,' I say.

'It's me. I'm the complication. I saw one of the Drifters asking if I'm Horse-Bonded. The Drifters know it was down to the bonded horses that we all became Aware in the first place and if they believe I'm Horse-Bonded, they'll think I've brought a herd of horses to force Awareness on them somehow. Thunder and lightning, it was hard enough for me to learn from the horses, and I wanted to – if the Drifters won't go anywhere near them because of me, it will be impossible. You don't want me to find the solution?'

'Yes, I do, but not from looking for it in the future – you've seen enough of it to know as much as you need to for now, any more will be a distraction from the present. It's the past where I want you to look.'

'The past? Why?' Will says.

'Because the person who can help you there also needs your help, as do the rest of us. Without it, the Horse-Bonded will never have existed.'

SIXTEEN

Will

I can feel that Aunt Am is serious but I don't know what she's talking about. 'You're blocking me from knowing what you mean,' I say. 'That's impressive.'

'Everyone else should be a part of the conversation. Plus, thanks to Maverick, I have dirt in my hair and I need to deal with that now that it's getting light enough to see where my hairbrush is,' Am tells me.

Justin laughs. 'You may be well past the point of needing my counsel on most things, Will, but when it comes to your aunt's personal hygiene, I can advise you with total confidence not to get in her way.'

'Okay, so when will you explain, then?'

'Over breakfast will be fine,' Amarilla says.

I sigh. 'Come on then, Maverick, we know when we're not wanted.'

'And yet you've waited until now to consider acting upon what you know. Fabulous, I may even get back to sleep.' Justin yawns.

'Grumpy old git,' I mutter as I leave the tent, smiling at his, 'I heard that.'

I busy myself stoking the campfire and then adding sticks to it until it's hot enough to boil water for tea and porridge. Once the boiling pot is in place over the flames, I allow my buckets to bang against one another as I pass the tents to fetch water from the stream. When I'm back in camp, I set out our wooden bowls and drop a spoon into each one from a height, with a grin. Maverick barks excitedly as he watches the spoons drop, thinking the game is for him.

'Atta boy,' I whisper to him as heads begin to poke out of tents.

'Will? Is that really you sorting breakfast?' Vickery rubs her eyes. 'I can't believe it, aaah, you want us all up, now it makes sense.'

I broadcast the reason and there is silence, even from Rowena. The heads all disappear and then reappear attached to their bodies, as everyone except for Amarilla and Justin comes to sit around the fire.

'Somehow, despite all of your noise, Justin is asleep and Am is ignoring you.' Rowena yawns.

Marvel reaches across to put his hand over her mouth. 'You're welcome,' he says to the rest of us and then yells, 'JUS, GET OUT HERE. IF I'M UP THIS EARLY ON MY MORNING OFF FROM HUNTING, YOU SHOULD BE TOO.'

The water boils and I pour some into the teapot and add oats to the rest.

'IT'S WORTH BEING UP JUST TO SEE THE EVIDENCE THAT WILL KNOWS HOW TO MAKE BREAKFAST,' Marvel adds.

Rowena scowls. 'Can't you just go and get them, instead of deafening all of us?'

I look down to where Maverick is nudging a ball of moss at my foot, and grin. 'Maverick will get them.' I pick up his newfound toy and take it with me to Amarilla and Justin's tent, with Maverick bouncing excitedly at my side. I hurl the moss ball between two of the ties that hold the door flaps together, and Maverick barks and tears in after it. I'm already laughing by the time Amarilla giggles and Justin starts cursing.

The ties are undone and Justin appears in his small clothes, scowling. When he sees me doubled up, his irritation fades and his mouth twitches into a grin. 'I think I preferred you when you were angry and misunderstood,' he says. 'Alright, you win, I'm coming. I can't speak for Am though, I think she's stolen your dog.'

I peek into the tent to see Maverick wriggling delightedly on his back, his tail wagging furiously as Amarilla, propped up on one elbow, tickles his tummy. 'You're supposed to be herding her out of there, not colluding with her,' I tell him.

'So, I'm still standing out here in my smalls,' Justin says.

I grin. 'Sorry, I'll just move.'

'Will, it smells as if the porridge is burning,' calls out Rowena.

'Well, someone could always stir it,' I say, running back to the campfire.

'Seriously, Will, if you think you got away with giving out orders last night, now is the time to realise how little you know Rowena,' says Marvel, and Rowena smiles her satisfaction.

'Fair enough.' I focus on Rowena briefly and find that I know all there is to know about the journey her soul has travelled through all of its incarnations.

Marvel, Rowena, Vickery and Holly all stare at me.

'It's a good thing I'm not a private person,' Rowena says eventually and everyone laughs.

'I'm sorry, Ro, I didn't realise I could do that until I just did.'

She holds up her hands. 'It's okay, Will, really, I get it. When I was first Aware, I remember being mortified at the feeling of invading people's privacy while I was experimenting with what I could do, and my capabilities aren't even a fraction of yours. I mean the speed you just did that! We learnt from the Kindred how to transfer huge amounts of information at once, but that's information we already know, you just thought of me and you... what was it you did, exactly? It felt as if you just attracted everything about me to you, like iron filings to a magnet.'

'Imagine being exposed to Will's abilities in the middle of the night, when you're not even sure whether you're asleep or awake. That's even more confusing.' Justin pretends that he means the glare he gives me as he sits down on a log next to Holly. His dark brown eyes draw me in and then, just like that, I know all of him, just as I know Rowena.

'Dammit, sorry, Jus, I can't seem to help doing it.'

Justin laughs. 'And you shouldn't try. None of us have any secrets from one another, except the parts of the future that Am and I keep hidden so they don't distract from the present. You can know all of that for yourself now, but as with everything else you know, it's up to you what you do with the information. You can sift through it, analyse it and let it distract you from the present, but my advice would be to let Amarilla and Infinity guide you through it, and only focus on things when they prompt you to. They've had a long time to figure it all out and they've already proved that they know what they're doing.'

I nod. I might now be, to quote Amarilla and Infinity, "the force of nature I sensed myself to be," but I'm inexperienced and I know it. I feel like a toddler who has just learnt to walk and needs something to hold on to while getting used to it. 'Okay, but while I'm waiting for Am's guidance, I think I'll just focus on when you were learning to ride Gas. I mean, you really were shocking, weren't you?'

Everyone laughs.

'And yet, he was one of the first Horse-Bonded to achieve perfect balance, and one of the best instructors,' Amarilla tickles me in the ribs as she passes behind me to sit with Justin.

'Only one of the best?' I begin to tease and then get a sense of immense, all-consuming peace as I sense who else is in her thoughts… and just like that, everything of Adam and Peace is known to me, as if I have always known them. I smile as I realise that in reality, I have, and then frown as I realise that I didn't know that before. I pull myself back to my surroundings.

'And just like that, he's back with us,' says Holly.

'Okay, that's enough of everyone being astonished at what Will can do, any more of this and he'll start thinking he's special,' says Amarilla and winks at me, knowing that I instantly know Infinity's views on the matter.

I grin. 'She gave you a hard time, didn't she. If she hadn't though, you would never have been the second catalyst.'

'The what?' Vickery says. 'Hey, wasn't Will meant to be doing that?' she adds as Holly hands her a bowl of porridge and a mug of tea.

'Yes, he was,' Rowena says, 'every bit as much as he wasn't meant to be using the information he picked up from Justin before time.'

'Amarilla was just about to explain it all, I just brought up the subject,' I say.

Rowena rolls her eyes. 'Oh, you're impossible, and it's our fault you're like this, fetching and carrying for you as we did, so that you could go off chasing the horses while they drummed some sense into you. We've created a monster, that's what we've done, everyone.'

'Well then, according to your memories from a few weeks back, that makes you a redundant old has-been,' I say.

Marvel slaps his knee. 'I think you've met your match, love,' he tells Rowena before crumpling up with laughter.

Everyone joins in, including Rowena. I knew she would. She's bossy and grumpy out of habit and because it's the role everyone knows, loves, and expects her to play, but she's fully Aware of who she really is and when the character she chooses to play is challenged, the warmth, loyalty, compassion and humour that are the roots of her personality in this lifetime, shine out of her.

She picks up on my thoughts. 'Rumbled,' she grins. 'So, Amarilla is the second catalyst, and you're the third, eh?'

I laugh again. 'Now who's picking up information and using it inappropriately?'

'What can I say? You're an open book. Am, are you ever going to tell us why Will so rudely woke us this morning, or am I going to have to sift through Will's thoughts in an even less appropriate manner?'

'First, you can tell me how you managed to block me from knowing that you and I are the second and third catalysts, when I picked it up so easily from Justin,' I say to Amarilla.

She smiles. 'Just a little trick I learnt from Mother Elder when she blocked me from my Kindred friend, Fitt.'

I chuckle as I become Aware of how she did it. 'There was no block, it was just a suggestion of one that your mind made to mine – you tricked me!'

'Yes, I did. And when I do it again, you won't believe the block that I suggest to you, but you'll choose to respect it and divert your thoughts, as you've already agreed to do. You've adjusted incredibly quickly to your capabilities, but your inexperience could still leave you open to being distracted from the present by the past and future,' she says. Two pairs of blue eyes stare at me and I find myself nodding.

'Okay, so you're the second catalyst, Am, I'm the third and

there's someone in the past who needs our help. Yours, Infinity's and mine, not just mine alone. With the utmost respect for the suggestion of a block you have in place, I know that the person we need to find is the first catalyst. And if he needs our help, shouldn't we hurry up?'

SEVENTEEN

Amarilla

owena's right, you're impossible,' I say to Will, and
of course he knows I don't mean it. 'As for your
suggestion that we hurry up, your supreme level of Awareness will
allow you to know that...'

'There's no rush because time is all happening now and
always will be – until time is no longer needed,' Will finishes
for me.

I roll my eyes and sigh, but Will is no more convinced by my
theatrics than he was by my words. He winks at me and grins. I
shake my head and smile back.

'Okaaaaaaay, seriously now, are you going to tell us what
you're gibbering about, or are we going to have to continue
trampling around in your minds in order to fill in the blanks?' asks
Rowena.

'I'm still trampling,' says Holly. 'They're talking about Jonus,
the first Horse-Bonded. He was the first catalyst.'

'Yes, he was,' I say, 'but he won't be, without our help.'

'You're planning to influence the past as it's happening,' Holly says thoughtfully. 'What does he need you to help him with?'

'Accepting what's happening to him when he's tugged and then sees his horse for the first time, for a start. He's been suffering the effects of food deprivation for long enough that it will be easy for him to add hallucination to his list of symptoms.'

'But we know that's what happened from the Histories. We know he thought he was going nuts when he felt Mettle tugging him, but once he eventually gave in to being tugged and actually found his horse, everything turned out fine,' says Vickery.

'The Histories gloss over the struggle Jonus had before they turned out fine, and they don't mention the help he had, other than from Mettle, because he never told anybody,' I say.

'What, that he had help from the future? Flaming lanterns, I'm not surprised he kept that to himself. It must have been hard, though, I mean that's some secret,' Marvel says.

'Mettle counselled him well,' I say.

'And he was ahead of his time, as Amarilla was and as Will is now,' says Justin. 'It takes a certain type of energy to be a catalyst, that's why they can help one another.'

'Like resonates with like,' murmurs Rowena. 'So, you two will find Jonus in your Awareness of the past, because he has the answer to Will's problem, and you'll help him to be the first Horse-Bonded?'

'Yes, only it'll be Will who finds Jonus. I'm open enough to see the future and past that my soul – or in this case, Will – draws to my attention, but I can't go looking for specific people or events like Will can.'

'I wish I could do what you two can,' Rowena says.

'Do you think your attention will need to be in the past for long? I mean how does it work?' Marvel asks.

'I'm pretty sure Will could do what needs to be done in the

blink of an eye, but my mind will limit us, so it will be a case of Will finding the right point in time and then allowing me to set the pace. We'll need to bring our attention back to our bodies at regular intervals to eat and drink, though,' I say.

'I have a question,' says Rowena. 'How will you be able to help Jonus? I mean, he isn't Aware, so he won't be able to sense either of you.'

'Not without help, he won't, but he's Horse-Bonded,' says Will.

Rowena frowns. 'Well, how will that help? I mean none of us could hear anyone other than our own Bond-Partners before we became Aware.'

'Amarilla could, Diligence got through to her,' says Justin, 'and with Jonus being a catalyst like her, he has the same openness to change. If Mettle can get through to him, then so can Infinity.'

'But Infinity is…'

'Amarilla,' Will finishes for Rowena. 'Exactly.'

There is silence. Justin smiles at me as our friends consider what we have told them.

'Right then, we'd better get you two comfortable, hadn't we?' Rowena says eventually. 'Marvel and Justin, you'll need to get Will's and Amarilla's blankets and put them ready in the shade of the tree over there so they can lie down while their attention is elsewhere. Holly, give them another helping of porridge each, we don't know when they'll be eating again and then you two,' she looks pointedly at Will and me, 'will need to make sure you have a good, long toilet break.'

'Seriously, Ro?' Marvel looks over at us both apologetically.

There's no need. Will and I both know that Rowena is disappointed at not being able to help us with what we will do in the past, and in need of feeling involved in some other way.

I love you, Ro. She knows it, but I tell her anyway.

She comes to sit next to me and puts an arm around my shoulders. 'I'll know what you're up to in the past, so you behave yourself, okay?'

I put an arm around her waist and hug her back. 'I have no clue why you think I wouldn't.' We lean our heads together and chuckle.

When Will and I have eaten as much porridge as we can, drunk plenty of water and then taken our toilet breaks as instructed, we lie down on our blankets under the large and plentiful leaves of the horse chestnut tree. Maverick lies down between us and snuggles up alongside Will, his head on Will's hand. Instantly, I am reminded how much I miss the physical reassurance of my Bond-Partner. No. This can't happen now. I reach for Maverick and his tail thumps on the ground. He licks my hand and then crawls over to me, nestling between my body and my arm, his head on my shoulder. I stroke him as tears run down my face, tickling as they come to rest in my ears. Maverick shifts to lick the tears he can reach and then rests his head back on my shoulder. He is just there. Warm, comforting, loving. Everything is okay. My tears slow and then stop and I breathe in and out deeply. I turn my head to see Maverick's eyes closing and I feel his peace… and everything else. I am ready.

'Good luck, you two,' says Justin and kisses my forehead. His words are echoed by everyone else, and Will and I grin up at them and then turn to one another.

'Ready?' I say.

He nods. 'Ready, boss.'

Okay, Will, you need to find the aspects of our two energy patterns that resonate purely as a consequence of us being catalysts. Take your t…

Got them, he tells me.

They are the reference points that we have in common with Jonus. Focus on them and think of the one who resonates with us.

Okay, got him too.

Be how the horses are. How you are now. Pick up where there is an imbalance in Jonus's life that our energy can correct. As your attention is drawn to that moment, I will allow mine to be drawn to it along with yours.

We observe a tall, stooped, extremely thin man wearing dirty rags. He has long, straggly brown hair tied back in a tail and he is standing at the side of a river, shaking his head. His hands are trembling as he holds them over his mouth to stop himself from screaming. He is looking along the riverbank to where a tall, muscular, grey stallion with a long, white, wavy mane and impossibly dark eyes, watches him. It is only the calm reassurance with which the horse is infusing him, that stops the man from turning around and running for his life. The horse twitches an ear as he senses our attention and we are Aware of his immediate acceptance.

Will weaves a net of soothing energy around the man and it has an immediate effect. He stops trembling and drops his hands from his face. Then he frowns in bewilderment.

Jonus, you've done amazingly well. You've had the courage and strength to leave the city in which you grew up and you've found others in the same position, with whom you've built a community. You've done all of this by following your intuition. Don't stop now. Infinity's discarnate energy powers my thoughts so that, even as they arrive gently within Jonus's mind, infused with my love and admiration for all that he has achieved, they swell, leaving him no room to panic, or to think of anything else. *The horse in front of you has called you to him because he can help you. You're perfectly sane. This is merely a new experience on top of all of the others that have exhausted your body and mind. Be calm and trust your instincts. The future depends on it.*

Jonus stands motionless, his eyes darting left and right. *My thoughts are recognisably human and the familiarity of their construction reassures him, even as Infinity's discarnate energy gives them an intensity that he can't ignore.*

Be calm and trust your instincts. Infinity's energy swirls the thought around soothingly within Jonus's mind and he begins to relax. He watches the grey horse move to the river to drink his fill and then graze the river bank. It is late summer and vegetation is plentiful, so the horse moves slowly, selecting his preferred varieties of grass and herbs.

Be calm and trust your instincts. The words fill Jonus and he begins to live them. He takes a step towards the horse and is ignored. He waits a while and then takes another few steps. The stallion continues to graze. He waits until Jonus is a body length away before lifting his head. Jonus jumps backward and turns, ready to run.

Be calm and trust your instincts. Infinity makes the words pulse in a rhythm, pulling Jonus back to himself. He turns back to the horse.

'Um, hello?' Jonus says and then shakes his head and says to himself, 'I can't believe I'm talking to a horse.' He takes a deep breath and then lifts his chin. 'What happens now? Are you going to say something in my head too?'

The horse lifts his head and peers along his nose at him as he places his thoughts in Jonus's mind. *When it becomes necessary. First you must tend to your body so that you are in a better position to listen.*

Jonus steps back so quickly that his heel catches on the ground and he sits down with a bump. He leaps to his feet in panic. 'So, you are in my head now too. Who was it before?' he asks the horse.

Two who would help you. Tend to your body, the horse tells him.

Tend to my body? Jonus's thought is tentative.

Immediately. Your scent is unwholesome and you require nourishment.

Jonus directs his thoughts to his horse more confidently this time. *Well, tell me something I don't know. I can't remember the last time I wasn't hungry, and I don't have time to wash. I'm up at dawn trying to find a better way to rebuild all the shelters before the weather turns, and I don't stop until it's dark. I eat what I'm given, and it's never enough, but that's the same for all of us. This year's crop is pitiful, so we're probably going to starve during the winter, anyway.*

There are brambles full of blackberries in the grass over to your right, there's a tree dripping with plums in the near distance and that river is full of fish, I tell him.

Jonus holds his head in his hands. *Who are you? It's hard enough hearing the horse in my head, but at least I can see him. I don't even know where you are.*

There'll be time for that later, I reply. *For now, do as you have been advised and take care of yourself.*

Okay, I'll find the fruit, but I don't know how to get the fish from the river. We've all tried, but they move too quickly.

You've been trying to spear them and that isn't the easiest way to catch fish, it takes a lot of skill and practice. Eat some fruit and then I'll teach you to catch them with your hands. I've added making fish nets to the list of things you need help with, as well as smoking fish to store for the winter, but first things first.

Jonus finds the brambles, and loses himself in eating blackberries until there are only red or green ones left. He stands up and shocks himself as he asks in his thoughts, *Where is the plum tree?*

The tree is the other side of those bushes in the distance. It's a young tree so you'll reach its fruit easily. And don't worry, you'll get used to things that you thought were impossible rapidly beginning to feel normal.

Jonus obediently begins to walk to where I have directed him. *How do I know I haven't just gone mad?* he asks me.

What does your instinct tell you?

There is a pause and then Jonus replies, *It tells me that I can trust you, whoever you are, and that I can trust that horse. All the times I cried and wished that help would come, somehow, I knew it would. But I never dreamt it would come in the form of something pulling at my mind, driving me crazy until I had to follow it to a horse, of all things. I mean, I've only ever read about them and there was no mention of them talking to people in their minds and telling them what to do. And then there's you. I don't even know who or what you are, but I'm doing what you tell me and it feels like the right thing to do...* He takes a deep breath. *Be calm and trust my instincts, I think that's good advice.*

It is. I can tell you from plentiful experience though, that receiving good advice can be very wearing at times. You have my sympathy in advance, I tell him, Aware of Will's amusement.

If you can show me how to survive, I'll take as much advice as you can give me.

Right then, eat your fill of plums and then take off your shirt and fill it with as many as you can. Then we'll go back to where your horse is grazing, you can get a fire going and I'll teach you to fish.

My horse?

In as much as you are his human, yes. He's your horse, your teacher and your friend. You have the beginnings of a bond with him that very soon, you'll treasure above everything else. He'll teach you, and through you, your people, how to stay on the path you've all chosen. In time, other humans will be selected by horses so that they can help too. You are the first of the Horse-Bonded and those that follow will need you to help them understand what is happening to them, just as we're helping you.

I feel Jonus's excitement as he peers around the bushes, back to where his horse is grazing. *We have a bond. Does that mean I'll never have to feel alone, ever again?* he asks.

I feel a sense of a circle closing as Infinity and I allow our thoughts to settle in Jonus's mind. *He is here. You are here. Everything is as it should be.*

EIGHTEEN

Will

*H*orses are awesome, we all know that, but this stallion has blown me away. His grey coat is dappled with white patches in such a perfectly uniform pattern that I can't find even one that looks out of place. His white mane and tail are in direct contrast to his almost black eyes, which glisten with a gentle knowing. He's in his prime, yet has been living amongst a bachelor herd of horses, not even trying to win himself a herd of his own. As soon as he sensed the time was right, he left the herd to come and find Jonus.

Already, the stallion's essence has changed. Unlike the wild horses that he's left behind, he is constantly Aware of himself as a discreet individual. He is equally Aware of his oneness with the rest of his kind, but in order for him to focus his thoughts enough for Jonus's mind to recognise them as communication, and for Jonus to be able to relate to him as teacher and partner, he has had to know himself as an individual first. And now that Jonus has responded to his horse's call and accepted the touch of his mind, the bond that has begun to form is changing both of them. Jonus can only change for the better. His horse, however, will need to be every bit as strong as he looks, not to be brought down by Jonus.

The man is on the brink of insanity, and not just because of the extreme hunger and stress he has suffered for the past few years, but because of who he is. I've read the Histories. I've written essays on aspects of it and memorised pivotal moments, as all children of The New do, but nothing could have prepared me for what I feel from Jonus. He's sensitive, determined, clever and brave, but there's an undercurrent of fear and something that is so foreign to me, it takes me a minute to find the word for it. Violence. I don't mean the concept of causing physical damage. When I shoot a deer for everything its body will provide, I've caused physical damage but there is no aggression, no thrill, only a mutual respect and acknowledgement between prey and predator that we've played our parts in the dream. But the energy that this horse is exposing himself to in the most intimate way by bonding with Jonus, is the capacity to hurt others out of a desperate need to lessen fear, with a feeling of immediate thrill that fades to an even greater fear and self-loathing.

I carry on sifting through everything I know, and I gradually begin to realise how much I have to learn about people. My admiration for the horse who has given up so much of himself to help the man whose energy I can't stand, is slowly added to by admiration for the man himself. He's a product of where he grew up, yet he turned his back on everything he was taught, everything that was familiar, to focus on the parts of himself that hinted at a better way. He listened to his inner self and chose difficult and unknown over easy and familiar, and is still trying to do it, even though he's starving and his community is failing. I now understand why the horse has chosen him; their courage and determination are equally matched.

I pause in my thoughts to witness Jonus lying on his stomach in some reeds, peering into the river while Amarilla teaches him how to tickle fish. The enormity of what he and the other Ancients did in leaving behind the safety of everything they knew for a future that was unknown and couldn't even be imagined, hits me again and staggers me. I've read about why they did it, but it's only now that I'm Aware of Jonus in his entirety, that I can fully understand it.

I witness Jonus growing up as all of the children of The Old did. His mother fed him his rations of the sterile, nutritionally balanced but almost tasteless meals. She took him to his allotted play sessions, where he was taught how to interact with other children of the same race, religion and social standing. She put him to bed when the voice of the building supervisor came through the apartment's speakers to tell her it was time, and she got him up when instructed in the morning. She put him in front of the wall screen when it buzzed for his preschool education and then when it made a pinging noise, for his daily entertainment. After each screen session, she made sure that he rested for the advised time for his age.

When Jonus was old enough to go to school, his mother saw him to a waiting passenger vehicle outside their building each morning, entered the destination, waited while it scanned his eyes and hair and then kissed him goodbye to enjoy a safe, structured day at school. When he reached the school building, his eyes and hair were scanned at the entrance and his attendance logged. His departure was recorded in the same way, and his mother alerted to expect him home, provide him with food and ensure that he did his homework before the instruction came to put him to bed.

At weekends, she accompanied him to his youth interaction sessions, where his training to socialise appropriately with other children of his age continued. Occasionally, it was the turn of all the children in their building to walk to the sessions for extra exercise. Otherwise, they went by passenger vehicles, to give the children of different buildings, and therefore different religions or races, their turns to walk. There was never any opportunity for people of differing views or heritage to meet and come into conflict.

For the most part, Jonus was considered a satisfactory child. He disappointed, however, when it came to speed of compliance. There was often a delay between the passenger vehicle door opening and its sensors registering the presence of the expected passenger, because Jonus would pause to watch a bird flying high in the sky, to feel raindrops splashing on his skin or to smile as the wind ruffled his hair. The interval between him leaving the vehicle and having the eye and hair scans at the entrance to the school building was also often recorded as too long. He was always at the back of the group when they walked to youth interaction, because he would stop to investigate an insect that had landed on him, watch leaves that had blown into the city from far away, swirling around in circles, or just stop and breathe in the fresh air. Whenever the alarm in the living room went off, warning his parents that Jonus was no longer in bed, they would find him at the window, staring at the moon and stars.

As he got older, Jonus received increasingly threatening verbal warnings by the school, the building supervisor and, finally, his parents, to follow the rules. He found himself becoming more and more frustrated. Who cared if he didn't get the compulsory eight hours of sleep, so that he could concentrate optimally on his studies and avoid being fractious due to insufficient rest? Who cared if he were twenty seconds late getting into the passenger vehicle because he stopped to enjoy the feel of the sun on his face? Just about everybody, it seemed. Other parents made sure to be there to back up his mother as she insisted that her son move from the building to the inside of the passenger vehicle without pausing. Yet more were waiting for him at the other end of his journey to escort him promptly into the school building. He was suspended from a youth interaction session every time he left his bed during the night. And when he still resisted the rules that kept him from the only snippets of pleasure that felt real to him, the beatings began. No deviation from the model that would ensure he became a safe and pleasant citizen, was tolerated.

By the time Jonus left school at eighteen, he had learnt how to appear biddable on the outside, whilst seething on the inside. He was one of the few who weren't trusted to attend the postgraduate fair alone, so at his building's allotted date and time, his father escorted him, muttering about how little point there was, when no institute of advanced study would take such a troublemaker, and the chances were that none of the trade organisations would either. Jonus couldn't find a way to care; it all seemed so pointless and he couldn't believe that no one else appeared to think so. How could he be the only one to see that the "safety and comfort" guaranteed at every turn just served to suffocate him and crush his very soul? Why didn't anyone else appreciate the beautiful colours that nature had instilled into the few animals that couldn't be prevented completely from coming into contact with him? Everyone else swatted at any insects that came near them, without ever stopping to wonder at the speed at which the tiny beasts could fly, or envy them their freedom.

He stood in line at the fair, waiting for his eyes and hair to be scanned so that when he entered the hall, lights would automatically flash above any institutes or trade organisations that had registered interest in him. When his turn came, he was surprised to see two lights flashing, one above the booth for the refuse department and one, surprisingly, above the booth for mechanical engineering. Without a word, his father took his arm and steered him straight towards the representatives for the mechanical engineering trade organisation.

'He'll do it. Where do I sign?' Jonus's father said to one of the two women sitting behind the desk.

'What will I have to do?' Jonus asked.

'You'll do as you're told, young man, and sign where I do,' said his father.

As one of the women began to type into a computer, the other said to Jonus, 'In a nutshell, you'll learn to service and fix machines. We have a particular lack of vehicle engineers at the moment, no one seems to want a job that might involve them spending time outdoors, for some reason.' Jonus saw a ghost of a wink that he immediately thought he must have imagined.

He signed the computer screen to enrol as a mechanical engineering apprentice, and shook the womens' hands. The woman who had spoken to him took his hand in both of her own and made sure he felt the piece of paper she was pressing against his palm, before she let go. 'We'll see you bright and early tomorrow morning,' she told him, 'when you will begin your education as a vehicle engineer. Congratulations, you will have what I know is going to be a very satisfying life. Goodbye, Jonus. Mr Blair.' She nodded her head to Jonus's amazed father.

Jonus put the note into his jacket pocket and didn't risk reading it until he was in bed.

You will be among friends, so don't mess it up by being rebellious. Get to work on time and do nothing to arouse suspicion. Swallow this when you've read it, we're trusting you.

Jonus read it over and over, trying to decide what it meant. Friends? He'd never had any of those, not really – as soon as he began to show tendencies of non-conforming, other children gave him a wide berth. He barely slept for wondering what would happen the following day.

His parents lectured him over breakfast about the fact that he wasn't a child anymore, and needed to make sure he rested enough to be alert and ready to learn, rather than going to work with bags under his eyes as he was clearly planning to that morning. He listened in silence, as always.

His father saw him to a passenger vehicle, watched him enter his destination on the navigator panel and stood watching until he was on his way. Jonus's heart leapt. He would be among friends.

He arrived at an enormous, grey skyscraper that looked identical to all of the other buildings in the city, apart from the plaque over its front doors that said MECHANICAL ENGINEERING. Once he had been scanned, he entered the building to find the woman who had passed him the note the day before, waiting for him by the reception desk. She wore the same burgundy trousers and pullover that everyone else in the department wore. As Jonus shook her outstretched hand, he thought she looked tired.

'I'm Freya,' she told him, 'and you will be apprenticed to me. We'll get you your uniform and then we'll get started.'

Jonus opened his mouth to speak, but closed it again as Freya shook her head almost imperceptibly. He followed her to a storeroom where he was given three sets of clothing, and directed to a changing room. When he emerged, wearing one of his uniforms and carrying the other two along with his normal clothes, Freya said, 'Leave them in the cubicle and collect them on your way out this evening,' and promptly left the storeroom.

Jonus ran to catch the door before it closed, and followed her.

She led him to the lifts and then selected -20. As the lift began to drop, Jonus stole a look at Freya. She was younger than he had first thought, about thirty, he decided. She wore a wedding ring but none of the others that would have been given to her had she had children. That was strange. Even if she were infertile, she should have had children by now, via incubator. He decided that she must be a widow.

The lift doors opened and a vast workshop stretched away before them. Freya marched off in the direction of a wall of lockers, inserted a key into one of them and extracted a tool kit. 'You'll get one of these once you know what all the tools are for,' she told Jonus. 'For now, you'll be handing me what I need, when I ask you for it. We'll be servicing those PVs over there, but we're on call to go out to any vehicles, passenger or otherwise, that need attention in situ. When we get call-outs, I always use them as a chance to do spot checks on the rails in that area, it's no good waiting for sensors to tell us everything. Prevention is always better than cure, I think, don't you?'

Jonus couldn't decide whether or not she had winked at him again, but thought it best to assume not. 'Err, yes, I guess so.'

Jonus had spent less than two hours learning about the inner workings of passenger vehicles, when a voice from the speaker on the side of Freya's tool box announced that her arrival was expected within fifteen minutes at a vehicle whose eye scanner was giving conflicting information to that of its hair scanner.

'Okay, leave everything here, there'll be a tool box on the back of the bike,' Freya said, and made off in the direction of the lift.

Jonus felt a thrill at the realisation that he would get to go on the back of one of the attendance bikes that he had seen from time to time from the safety of his passenger vehicle. Since the standard vehicles all ran on rails, gridlock occurred when one was halted for any reason, so the quickest way for the engineers to reach them was by motorbike. Only engineers qualified to supervisor level and above were considered of level enough character to ride them and take a pillion passenger safely, so Jonus thanked his luck that he was apprenticed to Freya.

They didn't go very fast, but Jonus couldn't remember ever having felt so happy as they wove in and out of the various transport vehicles rattling along on their rails. To be moving so freely, able to change speed and direction, was something foreign to Jonus and yet somehow, he felt as if he were remembering how good it could feel, as if somewhere deep inside, he knew of it and had missed it.

They passed a stationary line of vehicles, both passenger and freight, all with their passengers and contents locked inside, as was regulation when they were forced to make unscheduled stops. Thirteen minutes after receiving Freya's summons, they arrived at the front of the tailback, where they found a passenger vehicle with its door opened upwards. Its prospective passenger stood underneath the door, sheltering from the drizzle that was just beginning to fall.

'The PV door won't shut until the eye and hair scans match, which you'll know if you've ever tried to use one with a faulty scanner,' Freya said as they dismounted the bike. 'Leave the tool bag there, just bring a screwdriver and a torch for now.'

Jonus followed Freya as she motioned for the waiting woman, who was wearing the green of a scientist, into the PV, and then followed her.

'Shine that torch up there where the sensor is, in case anyone is watching, we don't have long,' Freya said in a low voice, to Jonus. 'What did you use, Sula?' she asked the woman.

The woman held up a short brown hair. 'Got it at work from one of the wild cats they've captured for the Enforcer experiment.'

'Nice one. The computer can't connect the reading from the

hair scanner with what it expects from your eye scan, or with its records of anyone else either, so it's registering as a fault,' Freya replied. 'We'll say it was a faulty sensor. Jonus, I'm going to the bike for a replacement sensor, and while you're taking the front panel off the hair scanner, you can get to know Sula, your future wife.'

Jonus dropped the torch. 'My what?'

Freya grinned and disappeared.

Sula said, 'We've been watching you. You don't belong here, and you know it. We can help you, but we need your help in return.'

'I don't belong here?' Jonus asked and then immediately confirmed, 'I don't belong here. No, I absolutely don't. I want to go where the birds and insects go when they fly away from here, I want to be free like they are. I want to get wet when it rains and then let the wind dry me. I want to feel the warmth of the sun on me for more than a few minutes at a time, I want to see other animals for real, not just in story books, and I want to feel something natural under my feet, something that is any colour except grey. I want to go to sleep and wake up without a buzzer. I want to walk and run in the fresh air, in circles, zig-zags, any way other than in straight lines. I want to live how I know I'm supposed to live, in a way that feels worth living, not like… this.' He flushed red. 'I'm sorry. I don't know what came over me.'

Sula took his hand. 'We know. You're not the first. We can help you to leave.'

'I can leave? Really? And you can help me? Where would I go? Actually, it doesn't matter. I've got a better chance of survival out there. If I stay here, I'll just shrivel up into nothing. But what about you? You know how to get out, yet you stay? Who are you, anyway?'

'We are the Kindred,' said Freya, climbing back into the PV, 'and yes, we choose to stay. We watch for those who will never cope with living the way we are all forced to, and we help them to escape. We collect or steal food and clothing and we give it to the elderly, so that they can live as long as nature intended, rather than, when they are considered a burden to society, being slowly starved to death with ever-decreasing food rations, or frozen to death by "faulty heating". And it looks as if we're going to have to try to find ways to protest against the government's new plans, as our sources are giving us information that is increasingly troubling.'

'Our numbers are increasing,' Sula said, 'but those of us who are single can't do what we need to whilst living with parents, we need our own apartments. Only married couples are given apartments, but if a spouse dies, the widow or widower can stay on.'

'So, you need spouses,' Jonus said.

'Husbands, to be precise. We're all female,' said Sula.

'Really? Why is that?' asked Jonus.

'Men can't seem to stay under the radar when they rebel,' Sula inclined her head towards him.

Jonus nodded. 'Point taken. Is it only men that you've helped to leave, then?'

Freya shook her head as she removed a perfectly-functioning sensor and handed it to Jonus. She took a new one out of her back pocket and began to install it. 'We've helped single women, couples, whole families sometimes, actually. They give us everything they can't take with them, and we store it and then give it to those who need it. Unfortunately, the government takes their apartments, so we're particularly happy when a single man needs to leave, even though it's more complicated.'

'Because…?' Jonus said.

'Because with everyone else, we just sneak them out. We've

become good at that. When it's a man who is leaving though, we need him to leave a widow who can remain in her apartment, so we have to fake his death. It's riskier, not just for the man departing, but for the widow he leaves behind. We're getting pretty good at that too though, now that there are more of us and we've infiltrated more departments. With Sula being a scientist, your departure will be the easiest yet.

'You met today while you were helping me repair her PV. You'll put in a request to court her, and one of our girls will process your request. Sula is four years older than you, but that will be entered into the system as a positive, since her age, experience and profession will make her the perfect candidate to kerb your tendency for independent thought. In six months' time, you'll propose to her and she'll accept. You'll be married the compulsory four weeks after engagement and you'll be awarded an apartment. Sadly, Jonus, your health will deteriorate at some point after that. Everyone will say how fortunate it is that your wife was able to diagnose your condition so rapidly, and was so conveniently placed to administer your treatment – which of course, will fail. You'll be dead within six months of marriage and your young wife, in her grief, will not be talked out of performing one of the tasks she has been given by this wonderful government of ours, even though the corpse in question is her husband. It will, of course be an empty coffin that is cremated and you will be outside the city gates and free to do… whatever it is that everyone does once they're out there. Questions?'

'How do I know you're who you say you are? How do I know you won't kill me for real in order to get an apartment?'

Sula grinned. 'That's the first time anyone's accused us of being murderers. Secret police or informers attempting entrapment, yes. Murderers – that's new. I'm going to say to you what we've said to everyone else we've helped even after they've accused us of having ulterior motives. You've all had one thing in common; you've all talked about knowing this way of life isn't right, knowing that you want things you have no experience of, but knowing you want them anyway. And if you know those things, you can know what you need to about us. Freya can't prolong fixing that panel back on any longer, so you need to leave. I won't see you again unless you put in a request to court me, which I really hope you do. Goodbye, Jonus.'

Jonus shook the hand that Sula offered him and stepped out of the PV, followed by Freya. As they reached the motorbike, the passenger vehicles were already beginning to move.

'We'll do a rail inspection while we're here. Leave the tools, it's just your eyes you'll be needing,' said Freya and motioned for him to follow her with a tilt of her head.

When they reached a stretch of rail that was clear of vehicles, Freya stepped between the rails and beckoned for Jonus to walk alongside her. She pointed down at the rails as if showing him something and said, 'I'm sorry I've been rushing you around, I was worried you would try to speak in the wrong place. All tool boxes have microphones and speakers so that we can communicate with our managers, so don't say anything other than would be expected in normal conversation when you're near one. Also, don't mention any of this when we're at work, even if there's no one nearby. You won't be able to do it without looking furtive and someone will notice. That will mean you'll be watched closer than just by me – yes, I've been told to monitor you closely, and not just how well you learn and work, but your attitude and behaviour.'

'And I suppose the beatings will start again if you report that I'm falling short,' said Jonus.

'Beatings, followed by worse if you continue to exhibit deviant behaviour. You're not a kid anymore, Jonus, and you won't be treated with the leniency they award to under-eighteens.'

'Leniency? I'm covered in scars and my jaw is held together with wire,' said Jonus.

'Believe me, in their eyes, they've been tolerant with you so far, but their paranoia is getting worse and if they achieve what they want to with the Enforcer experiments, then heaven help us all. That's for us to worry about, though, you'll be long gone. But, you have to be a model citizen if you want to get out of here. I need to know now that you'll do exactly as we tell you. We've trusted you not only with the fact that the Kindred exist, but with my and Sula's identities, because we know you're struggling and we know we can help. But if you can't tell me that without reservation, you'll do what we say, then we'll have no choice but to leave you to your fate and hope that you don't take us down with you.'

Jonus was quiet for a few minutes and then said, 'Okay, I feel as if I can trust you. I'll do exactly what you say, when you say. I'll get you an apartment and anything else you want, in exchange for my freedom.'

Jonus was as good as his word and so were Freya and Sula.

Understanding sweeps over me as to why the ancestors of our modern-day Kindred named themselves after the organisation of women to which Freya and Sula belonged. Any of these women could have left the cities and saved themselves in the same way that they saved so many others, but they stayed to resist a regime rooted in madness, to provide help to those who needed it, and to give hope. They were strong, brave and compassionate. They perished along with everyone else of The Old, but their legacy, the chance for humanity to begin anew, lives on.

As Jonus jerks my attention back to his present situation with a shout of delight at the capture of his second fish, I realise that he's younger than his appearance suggests. The sadness and longing of his early childhood have combined with the fear, violence and anger of his teenage years and the hardship of the last few, to produce a young man who looks more than ten years older than his twenty years. And his life isn't going to get any easier. Jonus is the first of the Horse-Bonded. His horse will set him the task of starting the people of The New on the path of advancement that we are still walking, which will feel as overwhelming to him as trying to single-handedly change the course of a river. But he doesn't just have his horse at his back. For now, at least, he has Amarilla and Infinity. And he has me.

NINETEEN

Amarilla

*J*onus has done well. He's cooked and eaten one of the fish he caught, and has set another three to smoke over the fire while he bathes in the river. Together with the plums he collected, that means he has enough food for both an evening meal and breakfast in the morning. That should give him a bit of space to come to terms with the new developments in his life.

Jonus returns naked from the river and lays his newly washed clothes on the stones that surround his campfire. There is heat in the sun, but he's shivering. He rocks from one foot to the other and alternately holds his hands out to the fire and then rubs his arms.

Okay, I'm fed and washed. Now what? Jonus thinks to his horse, who is standing, resting a leg, his eyes closed.

'Errrr, horse?' Jonus calls out.

The stallion sighs deeply, opens his eyes and then bends his knees and lies down. He lowers his nose to rest on one of his forelegs and closes his eyes again. Jonus begins to walk tentatively towards him.

'I've done what you told me to do, so what next?' When he receives no response, Jonus continues, 'So you pester me until I leave my people, who probably think I'm dead now by the way, I spend two days trying to find you, I do everything you tell me and now you're just going to sleep? What am I supposed to do?'

Will blasts his way through the link that Infinity and I have established with Jonus. *You can start by appreciating that the advice he's already given you was for your benefit rather than his, and leave him to rest. He's had a much longer journey to get here than you have.*

Jonus jumps, blushes and instinctively covers his private parts. Then he scowls. *You're not the one who was in my head before, who the hell are you? And why are you in my head, anyway? You and the other one? How many are there of you? Where are you? Can you see me?*

We can see you in the same way that you can see your friends in your mind's eye when you think of them, I tell him. *There are three of us, although two of us are one. I am Amarilla and just as you are the first Horse-Bonded, I am the last. My Bond-Partner is with me and her name is Infinity. It's through her that we can communicate with you, since your mind is open to her in the same way as it is to your own horse. The third of us, who just blasted his way into your mind so rudely through Infinity and me, is Will.*

I just made a point that needed to be made, Will informs us.

And now that you have, do you think you could give Jonus some space? I ask him.

So, let me get this straight. Not only can I hear my own horse in my head, but through another horse, who I can't even see, I can somehow hear two people as well? And you can see me in your mind's eye? So why can't I see you? Jonus asks.

You can. I will show you what the three of us look like. I show Jonus an image of Will, Infinity and me standing together.

He gasps. *She's beautiful. And strong. She holds herself as if she knows everything and is frightened of nothing. And those eyes...*

Amarilla and I aren't bad, either. Will's amusement makes Jonus smile.

You two are related. What are you? Mother and son?

Aunt and unruly nephew, I reply. *Will's only a little older than you, Jonus, and he's here to learn, which he seems to have forgotten.*

Are you going to have a horse too, Will? Are you learning what it will be like to be Horse-Bonded? Jonus asks. *No, wait. Amarilla, you said you're the last Horse-Bonded. So, there will only be two of us? But you said before that others would be chosen by horses, and I would need to help them adjust to being Horse-Bonded, the same way you're helping me?*

Thousands of Horse-Bonded will follow in your footsteps, many of whom you will help, I tell him. *All of them will have the honour of being chosen by horses as their students, and will keep humanity from reverting to the ways that you and your friends had the courage to leave behind. That is your future and our past.*

Your past? What do you mean?

It will serve you better if you can arrive at the answer to that question by yourself.

Jonus's mind spins as he tries to understand. Then he feels his horse's calm confidence that he will find the answer for which he's looking and he slows his thoughts and thinks through what he has been told. Finally, he volunteers, *You're communicating with me from the future. How is that possible?*

It's possible because we all succeed, Jonus – you, me and Will, I tell him. *You persuade your people to accept that their survival depends on what the horses can teach them through you and the Horse-Bonded who will follow. In so doing, you propel them forward into a time of peace and happiness. When the time is right, Infinity pushes me to realise the full potential of humanity and ensure that others strive for it too. Will is the product of that process and has abilities of which all humans will someday be capable, one of those being the ability to access other times in his mind. He has brought me back with him to find you and since Infinity is wherever I am, here we all are.*

But why? You said Will is here to learn, but if he's this superhuman of the future, what can he possibly need to learn from me? Can't the horses teach him whatever it is? Jonus asks.

Infinity helps him when necessary and a herd of wild horses has shaped him in ways you aren't in a position to imagine, but at this point in time, Will is in a similar predicament to that in which you will soon find yourself. We are here so that he can learn from you as you learn from your horse, and so that we can help you in return. All of the Horse-Bonded who will come after you will know what is happening when they are tugged by their horses and will readily accept the touch of a foreign mind on their own, as a result of your experience. It was necessary for us to be that support for you.

Jonus considers what I've told him and then directs his thoughts back to me. *So, without me being the first Horse-Bonded, they won't exist, you and Infinity won't bond and help Will to be who he is, and he won't be able to bring you back to ensure that I become the first Horse-Bonded. It's a circle, isn't it?*

Brace yourself for the answer to that one, Jonus, Will advises and I feel his glee.

The kind, gentle thoughts of the grey stallion enter Jonus's mind. *For it to be a circle events would have to occur in a linear manner and time is not linear. The future has already happened at least as much as the past is yet to come. Everything happens simultaneously and events in apparently different time frames can be influenced by one another. Rest now and allow your newfound knowledge to settle.*

Okay, well I would rest, but I'm cold and my clothes are still too wet to put on, Jonus replies.

My body will provide yours with heat. We will rest together.

What, like lean against you, you mean? Jonus asks.

Stating that which is obvious merely prolongs your discomfort, his horse tells him.

Will is Aware of my thought to leave the two of them and before I can frame another, we are back in the present.

'Awwww, hey, Maverick, I missed you too, ewwww, your tongue went in my mouth and I bet you've been licking your boy bits, calm yourself down.' Will sits up and rubs his dog's ears affectionately. He turns to look down at me with a grin. 'How cool was that?'

I sit up to see Holly sitting cross-legged at Will's feet and Justin doing the same at mine.

'Very,' says Justin.

'Totally,' says Holly. 'I mean the two of you and Infinity just made sure that the Horse-Bonded exist, that we all had the amazing time we did with our Bond-Partners, that we're even sitting here right now…'

'Don't go there,' Will wags his finger at her and then continues in a high-pitched imitation of me, 'it will only serve to distract you from the present.'

I grin. 'You did brilliantly, Will, even if I wasn't expecting you to pitch in quite so soon.'

'Do you mean to say, to actually sit there and say, that you didn't know that was going to happen?' Will opens his mouth wide in mock astonishment.

'I see glimpses, but you know I don't see everything like you can. I did, however, know that you and Jonus would hit it off.'

'I would say more bounce off one another than hit it off…'

'You're twin souls, Will, and if your situations were reversed, you'd have lived each other's lives in exactly the same way,' says Justin.

'If you say so,' Will grins and gets up. 'I'm going for a run with Maverick, and then I'm going to spend a bit of time with the horses before we go back. I felt kind of sad being with that amazing stallion, he's so weighed down with life, compared with how horses are now.'

As we watch Will jog away with a delighted Maverick bouncing up and down by his side, I realise how hungry I am. 'We've missed lunch and it's mid-afternoon, so time passed at the same speed for us in the past as here – I guess because that's what my mind can cope with. I'm limiting Will.'

'And as Holly just said, Will wouldn't be who he is if you and Infinity hadn't got through to Jonus like that,' Justin says.

I nod. 'But we wouldn't have been able to if Maverick hadn't helped me back to myself, and we only just made it back here in time before I lost myself again. I just can't stop missing Infinity. I'm with her in the oneness when I'm asleep, her thoughts are my thoughts, her words come out of my mouth and I feel her as part of me when I'm not sad, but when Jonus was being counselled by his Bond-Partner, it brought back so many memories of her being here as she was. And when he was invited to curl up with his horse as we all used to do with ours…' I bite my lip as my voice begins to waiver.

'We know. We all feel that way, only for you it's more raw. That's why Ro and Marvel have been making a surprise for you.' Holly points to where my friends are pouring water into what looks like a shallow dip that has been dug in the ground and lined with a waterproof sheet.

Justin takes my hand and pulls me to my feet. 'You need to eat, but first, look in the mirror.'

By the time we reach the pool of water, the ripples have stilled. I smile and then can't see for tears as I recognise the eyes that look steadily back at me from behind my own. I can't touch Infinity as my humanity craves that I do, but the sight of her soothes me. I wipe my face as her past accusation reverberates through me. *Give a human the chance to be overly emotional and she will surely take it.*

Everyone is Aware of it and we all laugh together.

'Thank you, all of you,' I tell them.

'No problem,' says Rowena. 'Now come and eat. Vic went to put the soup on to warm when we felt you coming back to yourselves, so it should be nearly ready.'

Marvel shakes his head. 'No problem, says my dear Rowena, having stood guard over a water bucket and a waterproof sheet, while she watched me dig the dip.'

'Which would have been a hole big enough to bury yourself in, if I hadn't been supervising. A shallow mirror was required, and a shallow mirror we produced, it really was no problem, Am.' Ro squeezes my hand. 'I'd shout for Will, only it feels like he needs time on his own with Maverick and the horses.'

I nod. Since Will is capable of so much, it's easy to forget how recently he became the person he is, and that he's still human. Having subjected his mind to the energy of Jonus and his Bond-Partner – similar enough to that with which he's familiar that he related easily to them, but different enough to be unsettling – time with Maverick and the horses will ease him back to himself. I smile at the perfection of it all.

TWENTY

Will

_A_marilla thinks it's her mind that limits the speed we can do what we need to in the past, but now that we've returned our attention to the present and I've had some time with Maverick and the horses, I've realised that I have limits too. I can take us to the past and help Amarilla and Infinity to do what they need to do there, but I can't be there for too long at a time; I need to be with my dog and my herd so that they can remind me who I am when the fear and misery of The Old threatens to knock me off-centre.

I'm fully Aware of the perfection in the journeys that everybody makes as they find their way to balance. I see the inevitability of it all. The Ancients have to be given the space to live the lives they have agreed to live, to play the parts they have agreed to play in this dream of ours and I will, in turn, play my part by taking Amarilla there. But it's hard being exposed to the energy of the past without being affected by it. It's violent and fearful and… separate. There's nothing more harmful than believing one is alone, as Jonus always has. He thinks he has to prove himself worthy to be part of his new community when in fact his worth has never been dependent on anything – but I can't tell him that. He wouldn't believe me and anyway, that's not my role there.

No. It is his horse's, Amarilla and Infinity agree. *You are wise to recognise how your inexperience at being who you now are leaves you vulnerable. We will be sure to return our attention here at regular intervals so that Maverick can remind you that nothing has changed and the horses can remind you of yourself. We will visit the past when you are ready and not before.*

I am ready when I wake the following morning. I sit up and Maverick rolls over, wriggling on his back as he does when he wants a tummy rub. I make a fuss of him and silently thank him for the millionth time for being there. For being a never-ending source of fun, love and companionship. For only ever seeing the best parts of me, so that I remember they're there.

We go outside to relieve ourselves and then I give Maverick some meat, pour some water into his bowl and some into the boiling pot, and poke the fire back to life. It is barely light when Amarilla sits down next to me. I hand her the mug of tea I have just made and pour myself another.

'I'm ready,' I tell her.

'I know. Here, we made these last night.' She hands me a sandwich and a small cake.

'I checked in with the Drifters at Goldenglade last night,' I say and she immediately picks up on what I saw.

'Hmmm. Maverick's brother and sisters have calmed things, but Lia's increasingly impatient for you to return. You know this doesn't change anything, though.'

'I do. I can't return there before I know how to get them to accept the horses' help. Don't worry, I'm not going to take the answer from what you know, or by looking into the future for it. Even if we didn't need to visit the past for Jonus, I've realised from our last experience there that I have more to learn there than just what you told me I could. I have to learn to be who I am, regardless of what's going on around me, regardless of the energies, the pressures or the situation.'

'There's no keeping anything from you, is there, even when I try to hide it behind something else,' Amarilla says.

'Nope. Do we wake the others before we go?'

'No, they'll be up soon enough and Maverick will watch over us until then. Here, I saved a bone for him so he has something to do while we're gone.' She tosses me a raw bone still covered in sinew and I hand it to my elated puppy. 'Here, wash your hands in this.' She pours warm water to the ground in front of me. 'Ready?'

'Yes. Are you going to boss me around again this time?' I ask her as she hands me a blanket.

'Probably. Isn't that what aunts are supposed to do?' She puts an arm around my waist as we walk over to the base of the horse chestnut tree.

I put my arm around her shoulders and hug her to me. 'No, you're supposed to be on my side when my parents boss me around, but I suppose, seeing as they aren't here...'

'Marvellous, just remember you gave me your permission,' she says, smiling as she spreads her blanket on the ground. I put mine next to it and Maverick immediately lies on it and sets about his bone.

'Oi, cheeky,' I say and he wags his tail. I grin and squash myself onto the blanket next to him.

'Ready when you are,' Am says.

I find Jonus as soon as I think of him. When I am drawn to the moment when he next needs us, I find him on his way back to his community, his horse at his side. He is clean, breakfasted and wearing only his boots and trousers. His shirt is slung over his shoulder, full of plums and apples, and he carries a whole load of smoked fish, speared on a stick.

Our friends have returned, his horse tells him.

'About time,' Jonus says loudly. 'I have so much to tell you. My horse's name is Mettle! He showed me his essence, I mean, who he is inside, and it was just amazing. Then he told me to choose a word to call him that described what I saw in him. He's so strong and determined, so the word just came to me. Mettle. That's his name. And he's kept me warm every night. He grazes until it's dark and then he lets me lean up against him when I sleep, and when I wake up in the mornings, I'm warm and I feel like I've slept for a week. I NEVER sleep that well.

'We've kept having to stop so that Mettle can graze, so it's taken a while to get back to my village, but that's okay, because we've been getting to know one another. We're nearly there now. Why have you been gone so long? Mettle just said you would be back when you were back, but if you'd come back sooner, you could have been teaching me how to make nets to catch fish, oh and how to hunt better? I'm not very good at that, either and I don't think Mettle will be able to help with it, you know, with him not needing to hunt. But, anyway, there'll be time for that, won't there? I mean you guys can teach me that once we're back at the village? I've been practising catching fish, look at all these I'm bringing home, and this was just what I could carry. If I go out with a basket, I could bring back loads more.' He finally pauses for breath.

So, what was it you wanted to tell us? I ask.

Jonus stops walking in surprise. *Are you... joking?* he replies finally and then jogs to catch up with his horse.

What gave me away?

Well, it was the fact that... are you joking again?

I allow my amusement to flood through the link to Jonus provided by Infinity and Amarilla, and they add theirs.

Jonus laughs. *Thank you, I hardly ever do that and it feels... nice.* His gratitude is accompanied by a feeling of happiness that is so uncertain, it's heart-rending.

I'm afraid you've just given Will an open invitation to tease you, Amarilla tells him.

That's okay, he made me laugh and I can feel that he cares. I've never had a friend like that before.

You've never had a friend who could tell you a decent joke, have you? I ask him, though I already know the answer.

Nope, never.

Flaming lanterns, okay then, prepare to split your sides...

Flaming lanterns? What is that? An attempt at swearing? Do you not know how to swear properly, Will? I can teach you the mother of all curses...

There'll be time for all of that once you've introduced Mettle to your community, Jonus, Amarilla interrupts.

Jonus looks up to see that he's now within sight of the ramshackle collection of shelters that he calls home, and villagers are gathering to watch his and Mettle's approach. I'm Aware that a few are relieved that he isn't dead, some are angry at his unexplained disappearance, and others are either awestruck or fearful at the sight of Mettle.

'JONUS HAS A BEAST WITH HIM! IS THAT... IS THAT A HORSE?' one of the men shouts.

'HOW DID YOU CATCH IT?' shouts another.

'IS IT FOLLOWING YOU, JONUS? HOW DID YOU MAKE IT DO THAT? CAN YOU MAKE IT PULL A CART?' a woman shouts and other voices join hers.

'CAN YOU MAKE IT DRAG LOGS FROM THE WOODS?'

'WE SHOULD EAT IT.'

'NO, WE NEED TO CATCH ANOTHER AND BREED MORE.'

'WHERE IS THE CATAPULT? IF JONUS CAN KEEP IT WALKING IN A STRAIGHT LINE, I'LL SORT THIS, IT WON'T KNOW WHAT HIT IT.'

Jonus's anger at Mettle being referred to as "it" turns to rage at the suggestions of what to do with him.

You must remain calm, Mettle advises him. *They will respond far better to your composure than to your anger.*

Remain calm? Are you kidding me? They want to kill you. It'll be them who doesn't know what hit them in a minute.

Mettle infuses Jonus with confident, relaxed assurance that he can do as he's been advised, but it isn't enough. All of the hurt, anger and helplessness that Jonus managed to contain within himself during the beatings of his old life, blast out of him like a storm unleashed. Infinity's discarnate energy is there in an instant, powering Mettle's love and assurance to the forefront of Jonus's mind. Jonus frowns and shakes his head as his rage begins to subside. He looks at his horse in wonder. *How are you doing that? How are you making me feel as if it will all be okay?*

It is impossible for me to make you feel anything. I am merely showing you how I feel and you have chosen to trust me, Mettle tells him.

But how can you feel so unafraid, so... loving when they're threatening you like that?

It may seem as if they are threatening me but that does not make it so. I am in no danger.

But what if I can't stop them hurting you? Jonus asks and then feels Mettle's amusement as his horse spins on his haunches and gallops away, then circles back, jumping the low bushes and boulders in his path as he heads straight for the villagers. Those at the front of the group move backward, pushing the others behind them. Just as they are beginning to turn and run, Mettle slides to a stop in front of them and snorts loudly. The villagers flee, screaming, to their hovels. Mettle sits down onto his hindquarters with an ear-piercing whinny and paws the air with his front legs. Doors slam, one so hard that it falls out of its frame onto the pathway.

Jonus, who has watched Mettle's display in disbelief, now looks at his horse with reverence as he canters back to him and takes his place at Jonus's side.

There will come a time when you trust without question that my counsel is well considered, Mettle advises.

Errr, okay, so I'll try not to get angry, Jonus replies.

You'll find that trying not to get angry isn't the same as not getting angry, I've often made that mistake myself, I tell him.

Will... Amarilla warns me.

Either Mettle will tell him in riddles, or you'll jump in which means that Infinity will tell him in riddles and either way, he won't get it. I'm just telling him in plain language that he can understand. Jonus, you're welcome.

Jonus is holding his head, trying to grasp what he's been told in time for when the villagers pluck up the courage to venture back out of their homes. Then he feels his horse's confidence and patience, and he relaxes. He rubs Mettle's neck. *Okay, so I'll just explain who you are and how you can help them, and they'll respond well if I stay calm.*

They will respond better. They are unlikely to respond well, warns Mettle just as the first heads poke back out of their doorways.

'You can come back out, my horse won't harm you,' Jonus calls out.

A few of the villagers venture onto the pathway between their homes. 'How do we know you can stop it? You didn't have any control over it just then,' a woman replies, her voice unsteady.

Jonus is taken aback by the notion that he should have control over his horse and then he's shocked as he realises that only a few days ago, he would have felt the same way. He sees the villagers in a completely new light and his mind spins as he tries to make sense of how he can have changed so much in so little time.

Amarilla's thoughts settle gently in Jonus's mind. *When I was first bonded with Infinity, a friend told me that the first few months of being newly bonded are like being blindfolded and spun around until you don't know which way is up and which is down. She was right. As time goes on, you will get used to the fact that nothing is as you thought it was. Just follow Mettle's counsel, take each moment as it comes, and in time, everything will feel less confusing, less overwhelming and eventually, completely normal.*

Jonus nods and breathes in and out slowly. Then he stands tall and says to the villagers, 'First of all, my horse is a "he", not an "it", and his name is Mettle. Second of all, I don't need or want control over him. He's here to help.'

'Help? Is that what you call it? If I hadn't run, he would have trampled me to death,' a man says.

Jonus manages to keep his voice even. 'If you hadn't run, you would have seen that he stopped well short of you. He wasn't trying to hurt you, he was showing me that I don't need to worry about his safety.'

'How can you possibly know what he was doing? He's a mindless beast, and a dangerous one. The sooner we knock him senseless and slit his throat, the better,' the man retorts.

Calm, Mettle reminds Jonus.

Jonus grinds his teeth and breathes slowly until he is composed enough to speak. 'Mettle is just about as far from being mindless as it's possible to be. He knew who I was before he even saw me. He tugged at my mind with his, until I followed my sense of him and found him. And I'm so glad I did. He's incredible. He knows things that can help us to survive and he's willing to teach us all.'

There is silence, and then laughter breaks out. Scared, tired, disbelieving, hysterical laughter. It's a horrible noise that only gets louder as more of the villagers come out of their homes and join in.

Remain calm. All is well, Mettle tells Jonus.

Jonus manages to maintain his composure as he raises his voice above the laughter. 'I know it sounds weird, but look, you can see that Mettle is with me of his own accord.'

'Weird? He knows it sounds weird, did you hear that?' a woman shrieks and the laughter continues.

They're not going to listen to me, Jonus observes.

You have done well for your first attempt. We will leave now. Mettle turns to walk back the way they came.

Jonus picks up his fruit and fish and jogs to catch up with his horse. *We're leaving? But I didn't manage to get through to them. They don't believe me that they need your help.*

At this moment they need my absence. A mind can only cope with so much when it is tired. When it is scared it can manage even less. We have given them as much as they can process for now. When they are ready we will return.

How will we know when they're ready? Jonus asks.

I will know.

Oh. Where will we go now?

We will know when we arrive.

'AND WHERE DO YOU THINK YOU'RE GOING, JONUS? YOU'RE MEANT TO BE HELPING US TO REBUILD THESE SHELTERS,' a man shouts.

'Let him go, we've got enough problems without a nutter and a dangerous animal making things worse,' another says.

'But he's one of us. Jonus, come back,' a woman calls out.

Jonus stomps along beside Mettle in angry silence.

Aim for woodland and I'll teach you which vines to take down for fishing nets and which make the best ropes, Amarilla suggests. *By the time the villagers are ready to listen to you, you'll have a whole host of things to show them that will make their lives easier. They'll think the two of you are a lot less crazy and dangerous then.*

But it won't have been from Mettle I learnt those things, it will have been from you, Jonus tells her.

You'll know that, but they won't.

I can't lie to them. We all agreed that we would never lie to one another, Jonus protests.

It would be inadvisable to inform your friends of the help you are receiving from the other catalysts. In time they will accept me but any attempt to convince them that you are also receiving help from the future will undermine what we do here, Mettle counsels.

So, you're telling me to lie.

I am advising you to be of help to your friends in a way that they can accept. Otherwise it is not help but self-gratification.

But surely I have to stick to the moral code I've agreed to? Otherwise what does that make me?

Mettle has no intention of discussing the subject any further, so I pitch in. *It makes you helpful. Someone who puts his friends' welfare before his own peace of mind. You're going to need to get over yourself, mate.*

You don't need to lie, Jonus. Just tell them Mettle's advice when they're ready to hear it, and let them assume that everything else you know has come from him too, Amarilla suggests.

It's still not being entirely honest though, is it? Jonus replies.

You either trust Mettle's advice or you don't, it's up to you, I tell him. *If you decide that you don't, do me a favour and make sure I'm here to witness you telling your friends about Am, Infinity and me, would you?*

So that you can laugh at me?

Well... yes.

Oh, stop it, Will, Amarilla reproaches me. *Jonus, in the early days of being Horse-Bonded, I sometimes took my time following Infinity's advice. I remember finding it hard to accept that a view that was so different from mine could possibly be right, but if I ever mentioned to another Horse-Bonded that I was dragging my feet, they would always warn me against ignoring Infinity's counsel. They had already learnt what I quickly learnt and what Will is so helpfully trying to teach you; the horses are wise beyond your comprehension. If Mettle gives you advice then it is for a good reason and it will be your best option. Always.*

Jonus trudges on in silence, thinking. When his thoughts turn to his friends, I immediately know everything about them all. At various stages of their lives, they all realised that guaranteed safety can only exist by limiting self-worth. By stifling the soul. They found the incredible courage to leave the tightly controlled "safety" of the cities for a world of variety of colour, thought, texture, sensation, expression, food, company and choice. They found that their new world of uncertainty allowed freedom and creativity and for a while, their euphoria at surviving the early weeks and months carried them along. Now, they are exhausted by their constant struggle to survive and they have begun to doubt the intuition that brought them here in the first place. Doubt has allowed fear to take hold and their choices and behaviour are beginning to revert back to the ways of The Old that they were so desperate to escape.

It hits me again, the difference between reading about an event in the Histories, and experiencing it first-hand. When I used to read about The Ancients, I already knew that the outcome for them was positive. I didn't stop to think that at no point did they know that. They had nothing to keep them going other than an inner sense – that had been discouraged at best, criminalised at worst – that life could be something amazing and colourful, instead of dull and grey. I didn't appreciate their strength and determination in continuing to listen to this inner voice, even when they were hungry all of the time, even when their efforts to make tools and homes consistently failed, even when they were cold and wet or ill, with no sense of imminent relief. And I didn't appreciate their misery when they felt themselves doubting their decision to leave The Old, doubting whether their inner voices were real or just the voices of insanity. Without these souls living the incredibly difficult lives that they agreed to live, humanity would never have had a chance to break away from the worst of itself. And now their survival is teetering on a cliff edge.

I've been a bit hard on Jonus. My immediate affinity with him both as a person and as a catalyst for change, has caused me to forget the fact that he hasn't entered his situation as the first Horse-Bonded from a position of strength. Mettle is most of what he needs, and Am and Infinity step in with additional help when necessary, but he also needs a friend. He needs me.

And he will know then, how to be a support to the other Horse-Bonded when he founds The Gathering, Amarilla agrees. *Infinity and I will continue to provide a link that his mind can accept and we will help when necessary, but otherwise, Will, it's over to you.*

TWENTY-ONE

Amarilla

*T*he perfection of our roles in the dream strikes me, as it has so often before. Neither Jonus nor Will has been in a position to have a real friend of their own age before and as two upon whose shoulders so much rests, they are uniquely placed not only to understand but to help one another.

It isn't long before Will has Jonus laughing at his jokes. When we stop at the edge of a small woodland, Mettle drops his head to graze and Jonus sets off into the trees to search for the vines that Will assures him are there. He returns with an armful of them and is soon combining them into ropes, when he isn't doubled up laughing at Will's apparently endless stream of witticisms. I had no idea Will could be so funny and my heart warms as I realise that it's the first time he has allowed himself to be so.

When Jonus stops for lunch, he asks Will about his life and then listens in silence as Will tells of his family and his youth. Will avoids any mention of the horses achieving perfect balance, of the Kindred, of Awareness or of the Drifters, since knowledge of them will serve only to distract Jonus from the task ahead of him.

When Jonus has finished eating, he is on his feet and heading back into the trees for more vines as, unaware that Will already knows everything, he relates his own story of growing up. Will teases him at every opportunity and Jonus loves it and begins to make attempts at teasing Will back.

The vines with which he returns this time are the kind suitable for fishing nets and Jonus is soon plaiting, twisting and then knotting them at Will's direction. His fingers are raw by the time the light begins to fade, but he's thrilled at the fishing net and short length of rope that lie on the ground before him.

The discussion as Jonus eats his dinner is about the Horse-Bonded. Will restricts what he tells Jonus to what he learnt from the Histories and what he knows from his experiences with his father, me and Justin, and Jonus listens in rapt silence.

When Mettle wanders over, lowers himself to his knees and then allows the rest of his body to drop to the ground, it is time for Jonus to rest his tired fingers and mind and for Will to return to his dog and the horses.

We're off now. Rest easy, catch more fish, make more ropes and nets and when you next need us, we'll be back, Will tells his friend.

Is there a way I can call for you to come? Just in case I need you and you miss it? Jonus asks.

The catalysts will miss nothing. Rest now, Mettle tells him.

Why do you keep calling them that? Jonus's question almost seems to follow us back to the present as we both open our eyes and sit up, just as the sun is setting.

'About time too, you must be starving.' Vickery hands Will and me a bowl of stew each.

I take mine gratefully but Will pushes his aside. 'Thanks, Vic,

I'll eat it in a bit. I just need to take Maverick for a run and a play, and spend a bit of time with the horses.'

Vickery nods. 'No problem.' When Will and Maverick have disappeared into the twilight, she adds, 'He's doing brilliantly but he's affected in a way that you aren't.'

I nod while blowing on a spoonful of stew to cool it. 'He's doing a great job helping Jonus, but as far as his Awareness is concerned, he's having to sprint when he's only just discovered how to walk. Maverick and the horses are the crutches he needs, he knows it and he's looking after himself.'

'Which is more than can be said for you,' Rowena's voice precedes her arrival with a plate upon which are three cakes, all of which she clearly expects me to eat once I've finished my stew. 'Will may be able to go all day without sustenance, but at your age, you need to eat and drink regularly or your body will start to complain.'

'At least it would complain silently,' Marvel calls out from where I can see his silhouette by the camp fire. I can hear the grin that accompanies his words.

Justin appears with a mug of tea, which he puts down beside me. He sits down behind me and rubs my back. 'You didn't move, either of you, the whole time your attention was in the past. I think we're going to have to turn you over every now and then, or you're going to get sores.'

I shake my head with a grin. 'Does anyone have anything to say that isn't related to my supposed old age and frailty?'

'I do,' says Holly. 'I think it's amazing that it's even possible for two lads to be forming a friendship across time, but the fact that it's these two who are doing it, when they've both had so much difficulty making friends before, is just fabulous. I think we should raise our chipped, stained, ever-so-slightly-disgusting mugs to Will and Jonus.'

'I'll definitely drink to that,' says Vickery and there is a chink of mugs being raised together as we all agree.

Once I'm busy tucking back into my stew, Rowena says, 'It's not going to be a quick process, is it, you, Fin and Will helping Jonus and Mettle to bond and be taken seriously?'

I shrug. 'I don't know, exactly. To be honest, I thought it would take longer for Jonus to learn to keep his cool, but I'm learning not to underestimate Infinity's influence. When she told me what she would be able to do once she was free of her body, I understood, but I didn't appreciate quite how powerfully she would be able to affect things. You've all witnessed it, she doesn't force anything, she just makes sure that the most positive choice can't be ignored, and that speeds things up more than I thought would be possible.'

'Hmmm, you're right,' says Vickery. 'I mean, I never thought that Will would turn himself around as fast as he did. With Infinity's energy fuelling events in the past too, Jonus and Mettle could be accepted back into the fold in no time.'

'That's not the only objective, though, is it? Will knows now, so we can talk about it,' says Justin.

'Will needs experience being exposed to the emotions of others whilst in his super-Aware state, before he returns to help the Drifters,' says Vickery. 'Otherwise he'll be knocked off-centre by their fear and if he keeps having to rebalance himself, he'll be of less help to them.'

I nod. 'The past is an extreme environment. The Ancients may have stepped away from The Old, but they're still capable of being frightened, volatile and violent, and Will is Aware of everything about them, all at once – their histories, the abuse they've suffered, the depth of their feelings. It's a massive assault on his consciousness. Thankfully, he's protected by the strength of his character and that means he can use his exposure to the

Ancients to learn. Each time we return our attention to the present and Maverick and the horses become the focus of his Awareness again, he puts his experience of The Ancients into perspective. He'll be less thrown by them each time and quicker able to return completely to himself afterwards, until there'll be nothing that can unsettle him.'

'So, we might not need to move camp, then? The horses have moved around behind us to find fresh grazing, but we were thinking that it won't be long before they'll run out and we'll need to move to a new area for them,' Holly says. 'They've got no intention of leaving Will, so by staying here, he's kind of trapping them, but if he's not going to need to be here too much longer, they might be okay.'

'I think we leave that to Will to decide. He'll know the situation as well as we do and when he says it's time to go, that's when we go,' says Rowena.

'Well, strike me down with lightning,' Marvel's voice penetrates the falling darkness. 'I'll bow to Will as the better man. How long have I tried to help my darling beloved to see that decisions are for others as well as her to make? I mean seriously, Jus, how long?'

'About as long as you've forced the rest of us to listen to it, mate. Just be as grateful as we are that, at last, you can well and truly put a sock in it.'

'But what else will you have to talk about, Marvel?' Holly says.

Marvel grins. 'Ale.'

'Give me strength,' Rowena says, laughing.

Once I've finished eating, I realise how stiff I am and I'm glad it's dark as I find I have to turn onto my hands and knees in order to get to my feet.

Justin chortles. 'The dark is no use to you whatsoever when we know what you're thinking, Am.'

'It hides the visual indignity, though,' I groan as I slowly uncurl myself and stand tall, rubbing my lower back. 'I'm going for a walk before turning in, otherwise I'll be in an even worse state by morning.'

'I'd offer to come, but you want to be alone with the horses.' Justin kisses the top of my head. 'Don't worry if you wake me when you come to bed, I'm not expecting you to be able to crawl in with any degree of finesse.'

I laugh. 'Well thank you for your kind understanding. See you later.'

Once I'm clear of the almost total darkness awarded by the branches under which I've lain all day, I find I can easily see by the moonlight. I make my way to where my Awareness tells me I will find the horses, and as I get closer, I hear the munching of those who are grazing. Immediately, my mind flies back to all of the times I went to seek out Infinity in the dark, whether to check she had enough hay and water, to adjust her blanket or just to be with her. After following my sense of her, I would pinpoint her final location by that exact sound that has always been so soothing to me. A lump forms in my throat and a lone tear slides down my cheek. Then I smile and hold my hand out to the dark shape that smells and sounds so wonderfully of horse, as she approaches.

The mare sniffs my hand and explores Infinity's presence as part of my being, somehow bringing the two actions together into one and helping me to accept, all over again, that Infinity is part of my physical existence here. She breathes my scent in slowly and loudly in the still night, until she's satisfied that everything is as it should be, then wanders off into the night, my silent, unnecessary thanks following her in her wake.

I drift between the horses, breathing in their peace and unity. It

takes me a while to realise that one of the herd is Will. It's only
my familiarity with him that has allowed me to pick up the tiniest
of distinctions between him and the horses; he IS them in a way
that none of the rest of us can be. I am Infinity because she is me.
Will is the horses without necessity for them to help him, accept
him, even acknowledge him or be any different from how they, as
wild horses, just are.

I make my way over to where he is lying back, resting against
a young filly, with Maverick asleep in his lap. 'You need food,
Will,' I whisper.

He sighs. 'I know, I just can't bring myself to move.'

'Stay there, then. I'll bring it to you.'

'Thanks.'

I return to him with a bowl of reheated stew, a mug of water
and one extra cake on top of the amount that Rowena practically
force-fed me.

'You know where I'll be. When you're ready to return to
Jonus, I'll be waiting. Rest well,' I whisper to him and then leave
him where he needs to be.

I am first to the campfire the following morning and by the time
Will sits down next to me, I have a mug of tea poured and ready
for him. I spoon porridge into a bowl and hand him that too. We
don't speak. We know that we're both ready. Maverick is the only
one who makes any noise. I smile at his little yelps of excitement
as he nudges the remainder of his bone at my and Will's feet in
turn, wanting us to throw it for him. I marvel at the pup's senses
when he finds the bone straight away, even though the moon is
behind a wisp of cloud and the sun is nowhere near ready to make
an appearance.

When all three of us have eaten, Will and I carry our blankets back to our spots under the horse chestnut tree. I have brought an extra couple with me, hoping that they will cushion my body better and leave me a little less stiff when I return my attention to it.

Ready when you are, Will. Before I even finish the thought, we are back with Jonus and Mettle.

Jonus hurls his anxiety at us as soon as Mettle advises him of our presence. *Thank goodness you're here, I was beginning to panic.*

Beginning to? Sounds to me as if you're already there, mate. Will's response is accompanied by a sense of humour that dares Jonus not to find him funny.

Jonus relaxes and grins.

Will switches to being serious. *You know you never need to panic when your horse is with you, don't you? Mettle has you on your way back to your village because the time is right, and he'll tell you what to do when you get there, just like last time. He'll always know what to do. Amarilla, Infinity and I are just here to ease you into all this.*

I know that, I think, but it helps to be reminded, Jonus replies. *I've got so much going on in my head that I can't think straight and I'm worried about what's going to happen.*

Just know that whatever happens, you succeed. The three of us wouldn't be here with you if you hadn't. You can do this, Jonus. Whatever Mettle tells you to do, you can do it, Will assures him.

My attention may be away from my body at the moment, but I know there will be a proud smile on my face.

TWENTY-TWO

Will

The villagers gather in front of their shelters as they did the last time Jonus and Mettle approached. I know what they've prepared in case Jonus and his "beast" return. There are piles of stones, two catapults by each, at intervals along the boundary of the village, where the cleared earth meets the grassy tussocks of the scrubland. By the time Mettle is in range, there will be two villagers by each pile. When the command is given, the stallion will be assaulted by a barrage of stones which will hopefully fell him, providing the villagers with many days' worth of food rations, and giving Jonus the opportunity to return to his senses.

I am initially sickened both by their plan and their eagerness to carry it out, but then I put their behaviour into perspective with their situation and realise that at present, they don't have the capacity to do any better.

As Jonus and Mettle continue their approach, some of the villagers move into their agreed positions by the catapults. Then they notice the vine-woven baskets attached to a rope around

Mettle's girth. They point at him and murmur to one another and then to the group standing behind them.

Jonus holds up the bundle of branches he's carrying, each of which has a net dangling from one end. 'THESE ARE FOR YOU,' he shouts. 'THEY'RE FISHING NETS. I'VE LEARNT HOW TO MAKE THEM AND THEY WORK REALLY WELL. SEE THESE BASKETS METTLE IS CARRYING? I MADE THEM TOO AND THEY'RE FULL OF FISH I'VE CAUGHT FOR YOU. OH, AND WE'VE BROUGHT SOME ROPE I MADE, SO YOU CAN SEE HOW TO MAKE MORE.'

A tall, black-bearded man loads his catapult with a stone and takes aim. 'DON'T COME ANY CLOSER, OR THE HORSE DIES,' he shouts.

We will halt our approach, Mettle announces.

Jonus puts his hands on his hips. *We aren't afraid of him.*

No but he is afraid of us. His fear is all the more uncomfortable for him since we have given him cause to doubt the reason for it. For our efforts to be successful we must allow him to continue to doubt whilst provoking him no further.

I feel Jonus wrestling with himself. He feels Mettle's calm confidence that everything is alright, and its influence over him to feel the same way, but he still wants to confront the man who was his friend, to shout him down for daring to threaten Mettle, to beat him into dropping the catapult if he has to.

Trust Mettle, Jonus. Trust him and do as he says, I tell him.

Jonus breathes out loudly in frustration. *Okay, fine. So what do we do now then?*

You will relieve me of my burden and assure your friends that we will go no closer. I will graze while you cook the food we have brought, Mettle informs him.

'You want me to cook? Now?' Jonus says out loud.

He won't answer you, you have your instructions, I tell him.

Mettle stands, patiently waiting until Jonus removes the baskets from the rope around his girth and then unties the rope. Then the stallion wanders off.

Jonus looks after him and throws his hands up into the air. *I haven't brought any wood with me for a fire, and I'm not even hungry.*

Your friends are though, I remind him. *Your flint box is in your pocket, there are dry sprigs of heather everywhere and you can use some of the branches that you made into poles for the fishing nets, as firewood.*

But then I'll have to give them nets without poles, Jonus protests.

I think they'll forgive you when they have full stomachs. And they'll see how to make new poles from those that are left.

I suppose. We're definitely out of range of those catapults, aren't we?

You could be standing right in front of black beard, there, and you'd still be out of range. He's more likely to hurt himself than anyone else with that contraption. By the time you're back on proper speaking terms with your friends, I'll make sure you can teach them how to make catapults that work properly, but for now, get that fire going and start cooking.

The villagers watch in stunned disbelief as Jonus busies himself lighting a fire and then begins spearing fish onto a stick to cook over it while Mettle grazes nearby. Black beard frequently lowers his weapon, only to raise and prime it again at the slightest movement from Mettle as he ambles from one patch of grass to another with a total lack of concern.

'I THOUGHT YOU SAID THOSE FISH WERE FOR US, JONUS,' a woman shouts.

'THEY ARE, BUT I'M ASSUMING YOU'D PREFER NOT TO EAT THEM RAW,' he replies.

The villagers exchange glances and mutterings but then return to watching him avidly. As the smell of cooking fish permeates the air, several of them groan.

'ARE YOU GOING TO BRING THEM TO US?' the woman shouts again.

'SINCE METTLE AND I HAVE BEEN THREATENED AGAINST COMING ANY CLOSER, THAT WOULD BE A BIG, FAT NO.'

'LEOD'S AN IDIOT, YOU KNOW THAT, YOU CAN BRING THE FOOD TO US,' shouts the woman. Black beard turns to her, scowling, and sticks his middle finger up at her, which I gather is an insult. His gesture is returned.

'METTLE AND I ARE STAYING WHERE WE ARE. AND I'M NOT SHOUTING ANYMORE, SO IF THERE'S ANYTHING ELSE YOU WANT TO KNOW, YOU'LL HAVE TO COME CLOSER,' Jonus replies.

There's more muttering among the villagers, which quickly turns into angry shouting. Finally, the woman who has been conversing with Jonus tries to leave the others. A man and woman grab hold of her and pull her back. She is shorter than both of them, but turns and punches the man in the face, slaps the woman and then stands, hands on hips and shouts, 'ANYONE ELSE?' Rowena would love her.

When two men step towards her, she turns and runs towards Jonus, her red, matted hair lifting and falling in one disgusting lump.

Do not involve yourself in their argument, Mettle warns Jonus.

My friend nods and focuses intently on the fish he is cooking.

Mettle moves further away from both Jonus and the approaching woman, his long, white tail swinging gently from side to side. The woman stops when she is halfway between Jonus and the villagers, who are all shouting and jeering at her.

'Did you really catch all of those fish?' she calls out, rubbing her hands up and down her grimy trousers.

Jonus looks all around himself. 'I don't see anyone else who could have done it, do you? Mettle's clever but it takes hands to catch fish and last time I looked, he doesn't have any of those.'

Not very helpful, mate, she's scared and hungry just like you were, I remind him.

'Always the smart mouth, aren't you?' the woman sneers.

Jonus sighs. 'Come on, Priss, I'm trying to help you. These fish are nearly ready. Do you want to take a skewer of them back to the others and then come back for some for yourself?'

'No, I want mine first.'

'Okay, fine, but you'll have to come and get it. I'm not allowed any closer, remember?'

Priss shoots a nervous glance at Mettle, who instantly ambles further away. 'Do you promise it won't hurt me?'

'I'm not answering any more of your questions until you start calling Mettle by his name,' Jonus says without looking away from the fish.

'Okay then, you lunatic, do you promise that METTLE won't hurt me?' Priss says the stallion's name as a child would say the name of someone who has annoyed them. Jonus turns his back on her, his hands shaking with anger.

Insult to me is no more possible than it is to you. Do not make something real that if ignored will never have existed, Mettle tells him.

Jonus's mind spins as he tries to understand his horse's counsel. *You're telling me that an insult is only an insult if I take it as one?* he asks and allows himself a smile as he senses Mettle's approval.

Remain calm. You do well here, his horse tells him.

Jonus takes several deep breaths to persuade himself that he's calm, but remains with his back to Priss, afraid that if he looks at her, his temper will flare again. She shifts from one foot to the other, frequently looking back to where the other villagers are still taunting her, before returning her attention to Jonus as he continues to turn the skewer of fish over the fire. Her stomach grumbles loudly.

'J… Jonus, do you promise that Mettle won't hurt me?' she says.

Jonus moves around the fire so that he can see her. 'I promise.' He holds out the fish to her.

She walks quickly, her eyes darting between Mettle and the fish, and then stops in front of Jonus. She looks up at him as if expecting trickery.

He looks steadily into her narrowed blue eyes with his own brown ones. 'Take them, Priss, they're all yours. Be careful, though, they're hot.'

Priss grabs the skewer and takes a bite from one of the fish, then from another and another, as if she's terrified that they'll disappear if she doesn't mark them all as hers.

Jonus picks a large leaf from a clump on the ground and hands it to her. 'Here. Slide the fish off the skewer onto this. They'll be easier for you to eat and I need the skewer back to cook more for the others.'

Priss does as he says without pausing her frantic eating.

'Slow down, you need to watch for bones, or you'll choke. PRISS!'

Priss jumps and glares at Jonus. He points to where a white bone is sticking out of one of the fish. 'See? Pull the rest of the flesh off with your fingers, not your teeth, and make sure you don't eat any bones. If you swallow one, you could choke. Okay?'

Priss nods and does as she has been told.

'Do you want to sit down? You could put the leaf on your knee and eat with two hands, it will be much easier,' Jonus suggests.

Priss remembers why she is standing in the first place and looks in panic over to where Mettle was when she last saw him. He's still there, grazing. He lifts his head to glance briefly at Priss and then lowers himself to the ground. He sighs deeply and allows his eyelids to droop, his white eyelashes standing out starkly against the black skin around his eyes.

'Sit down,' Jonus tells Priss softly, and she obeys him.

Jonus has just finished preparing another skewer of fish when he notices another red-haired woman heading his way, dragging a heavily freckled teenage boy with reddish-brown hair. The woman turns and shouts, 'YOU MIGHT BE HAPPY TO WATCH YOUR CHILD STARVE, BETH, BUT I'M NOT. I'M SICK OF YOU THINKING YOU'RE BETTER THAN ME AND TELLING ME WHAT TO DO, NOW YOU CAN JUST SOD OFF AND LEAVE ME TO DO WHAT'S RIGHT FOR BEN.' Then she yells at her son, 'WALK PROPERLY, YOU'RE SEVENTEEN, NOT SEVEN.'

'WELL, STOP DRAGGING ME THEN. WE SHOULDN'T BE GOING TO JONUS FOR ANYTHING. HE'S A NUTTER. HE BROUGHT A DANGEROUS BEAST THAT HE THINKS TALKS TO HIM, TO OUR VILLAGE. HOW DO YOU KNOW THOSE FISH AREN'T POISONED? DAD THINKS THEY ARE,' Ben yells back.

The woman sighs. 'Priss doesn't think so, or do you think your aunt is a nutter too?'

'When it comes to food, she is. I saw her stealing greens from the store shed last week and when I told her to put them back, she said she'd brain me if I didn't leave her alone and keep my mouth shut. She would have too, you should have seen her face.'

'Well, she's been tucking into that fish for a while now and she looks fine to me, so I don't want to hear any more about poison, okay?'

'But what about the horse? He could kill any one of us just by looking at us, that's what Oona said,' Ben says, never taking his eyes from Mettle as he snoozes peacefully amongst tussocks of grass.

'Well, maybe that would be a better end than starving to death, but seeing as he's gone to sleep, I don't think we have to worry about it right now,' his mother tells him.

Ben sinks into a sullen silence as they reach Jonus, and refuses to look him in the eye. His mother watches the fish turning over the fire. 'How did you do it, Jonus? How did you catch the fish and the horse?' she asks.

'I caught some fish with my hands to begin with. It's easy when you know how, but it's time-consuming. So, I made a net to speed things up, and that was how I caught all of these. I've made a load of them for you all, although some of them are going to need new poles. I can show you all how to fish once you've eaten properly, and there's loads more I can show you all, Trix, if you'll let me. As for my horse, he has a name and I won't discuss him further until you use it.'

Trix manages to tear her eyes away from the fish and looks up at Jonus. 'What's happened to you? Did you eat or drink something that's turned your brain? Your intuition has always been so good when it comes to knowing what's safe to eat and what isn't, but you're not talking like yourself. It's like the Jonus we knew ran away one day and this... this...'

'Nutter,' mutters Ben.

Trix nudges him and continues, 'This person we don't know came back in his place who suddenly knows all this stuff and has all this food and talks about a horse as if he's his best friend and some sort of saviour to us all – I mean, a horse! We've only ever seen them in children's books and suddenly you have one following you around, carrying stuff for you and you won't even tell me how you caught it.'

'He has a name,' Jonus says quietly.

'Fine, what's its name?' Trix says.

'Mettle.' Priss licks the last of her meal from her fingers. 'The password is Mettle.'

'Okay, so Mettle, how did you catch it?' Trix asks Jonus.

'Him. I've already told you all, I didn't catch him. He reached out to my mind and pulled me to him,' Jonus tells her. 'These fish are almost ready. Get yourself some of those leaves, and you and Ben can share the fish between you while I cook more. That'll have to be it, then, you'll have to take the rest back and cook them yourselves, I'm running out of wood.'

Trix and Ben dash to fetch their leaves, all thoughts of Jonus's insanity momentarily forgotten. It isn't until they're scoffing fish that Trix says, 'I don't know how to help you, Jonus, if you won't help yourself and tell us the truth.'

'I don't remember asking for your help,' Jonus says. 'I only remember offering it and here you are, eating the first decent meal you've had since we got here.'

'I'll thank you tomorrow, if I'm not dead,' Ben says.

'And I'll hold you to that, if I'm here,' Jonus replies.

'What do you mean if you're here? Where will you go?' Priss demands.

'Wherever Mettle tells me to go.'

Trix sighs. 'Oh, for goodness' sake, Jonus.'

'How will he tell you where to go?' Priss asks, winking at Ben.

'I hear his thoughts in my head.'

'Off your head, more like,' Ben says and he and Priss both cackle.

Their laughter would make the hair stand up on the back of my neck if my body were here. I want to push it away from me but I know that if I do, I'll just give myself something to deal with another time. So, I welcome the energy of the Ancients as it permeates my Awareness, knowing that their feelings and behaviour have their place as they develop and learn. Immediately, they lose their effect on me. I feel Am and Fin's presence, watchful over me as ever and I accept their observation that I am learning quickly. As is Jonus.

'You think I'm mad, yet I've provided you with ropes and fishing nets, I've caught and cooked you fish, and it isn't me who is shouting, threatening, punching people and laughing when crying would be more honest.' Jonus is shocked that he isn't feeling the need to shout. He smiles as he feels Mettle's approval.

'That's it, laugh at us as well as patronise us,' hisses Priss.

'I wasn't laughing at you, I was smiling because of something I felt from Mettle. And he's just told me to assure you that he won't come any closer, but he's getting up because he wants to graze.'

Priss screams and jumps to her feet as Mettle heaves himself up from the ground. She grabs a basket of fish and runs back to the village as if a swarm of bees is after her. Ben yelps and runs after her, cradling the remainder of his fish in his hands. Trix is slower to react and by the time she is on her feet, Mettle is grazing peacefully. She looks from him to Jonus. 'How did you know he was getting up? Oh, don't bother answering me, you'll just spout more rubbish. Can I take the rest of the fish?'

Jonus nods and hands her his partly cooked skewer of fish. 'Take this and the other basket. Come back for the ropes and nets whenever you want. And Trix?'

'What?'

'When you have a moment, sit and listen like we used to in the beginning. When we still believed in ourselves. Think of me and Mettle and notice how you feel inside.'

'Because that's worked really well for us, hasn't it? Listening to how we feel inside? I mean look at us all.'

'But what if we were right to take the path we have? What if it's been leading up to this point? The point where it starts to get easier? What have you got to lose by just sitting and asking yourself the question? Do it, Trix, please?'

'I have fish to cook,' Trix says and hurries off, carrying the basket.

The villagers are already squabbling over Priss's basket of fish. She's screaming that since she was the only one brave enough to go and get them, the fish are all hers, but the others are arguing that they should be shared out equally, as they do with everything. Jonus shakes his head in despair.

You were awesome, Jonus, well done, I tell him.

Mettle wants us to leave now and come back tomorrow, he replies.

Okay, well we'll be back when you need us next. If we're not here, it's because you and Mettle have it covered, so no panicking, okay?

Do you really have to go now, Will?

Sorry, yes. I want to get Am back while she can still move this time, she's getting on a bit...

Thanks a lot, Amarilla chimes in.

...and she gets stiff if she lies in the same position for too long. We lie down while our attention is here with you, as we don't know how long we'll be.

Oh, I see. What about Infinity? Does she need to lie down too? Jonus asks.

Err, no she doesn't. Horses are pretty good at being everywhere at once, all the time, whatever they're doing.

I'm relieved when he nods and adds that information to all the rest that he doesn't quite understand. *Okay, well take Amarilla back to herself, then. I'd say I'm looking forward to when you'll next be back, but seeing as it'll be when I'm in trouble again…*

You're never in trouble, it just seems that way. See you, Jonus.

TWENTY-THREE

Amarilla

I reach for Will's hand and squeeze it in approval for his quick thinking when Jonus asked about Infinity; Jonus doesn't need the complication of knowing the full truth of our situation. Then I sit up. It's only been a few hours since I lay down and that fact, combined with the cushioning from the extra blankets, means that I'm able to sit and then stand up with no extra stiffness to add to that from the previous day. 'Three blankets at a time it is, then,' I say to Will and he grins as he sits up beside me.

'And everyone moaned at me for insisting we bring blankets, tents, and all of the other things that make camping a civilised affair,' Rowena says, her finger on her chin as she frowns up to the branches of the horse chestnut tree, as if they'll be more likely to congratulate her on her foresight than we will.

'Ro, as ever, thank you for having my back, this time literally,' I say. 'I do object, however, Will, to being described as "getting on a bit". I'm forty, not eighty.'

Will winks at me. He stands up and stretches, then holds out his arms. Maverick, just back from a walk with Vickery, leaps into them. The pup's legs have grown so much that they look too long for his body, and his ears are trying to stand up. Will laughs and splutters as his dog frantically licks every inch of his face, ears and neck. Then Maverick twists in Will's arms and leaps to the ground, bounds once and then springs up at me, fully expecting me to catch him the same way that Will did. I manage to wrap my arms around him in time to stop him bouncing off me and landing hard on the ground, but I have no time to adjust my balance. I'm thrown backward against Rowena and then feel her moving away from me. The next thing I know, Maverick and I are landing on top of her as she hits the ground with an, 'oooof!'

Maverick is overjoyed and stands on top of me, licking my face. I'm pinned down on top of Rowena, who is moaning about her back and the fact that my hair is in her mouth, and I can't speak for fear that Maverick's tongue will find its way into my own mouth. When Maverick finally launches himself off me so that my senses are clear, I can make out the laughter of Will, Justin and Marvel.

I roll off Rowena onto my knees, and wipe my face against my arms. She sits up, grimacing and rubbing her back.

'So, there's this thing that the Horse-Bonded have, called perfect balance,' Will says, still laughing.

Rowena rolls her eyes at me and tries to grin, which turns into another grimace. I crawl behind her and rub her back for her. Apparently, that only adds to the comedy of the situation, until Rowena begins to cry.

Marvel is by her side in an instant and Justin goes to her other side. Between them, they get her to her feet and Justin supports her as Marvel tunes into her back muscles.

'Good plan, you sing her muscles out of spasm, and I'll go and get my herbs to help with the bruising,' I say to Marvel and with an effort, get to my feet.

'I'll get them, Am,' Will says, 'you'll be needing them too. Wait until I tell Jonus about this, honestly, he'll wet himself.'

'You're never going to be able to convey the full visual impact of what just happened, by describing it. That was hil-ar-ious,' Marvel says.

'What, funnier than you riding wild horses in your underpants?' Rowena says. 'Will, feel free to peruse that particular episode from what you know of my experiences, whenever you like, then you decide.' She grimaces and bends over.

'I'll get the herbs,' Will says and dashes off.

I notice that while he's delighted to be with Maverick and will no doubt enjoy spending time with the horses once he's carried out his errand, it's more because he wants to than because he needs to. I think back to how long it's always taken me to learn and change, and I'm in awe of the speed at which Will does it.

Will is eager to return us to Jonus within a matter of hours. He knows I know, and he smiles sympathetically across the campfire as we eat our lunch. There's no need. Marvel is an excellent Tissue-Singer and with his ministrations and my herbs, I've not only recovered from Maverick's exuberance, but my stiffness has eased greatly as well.

When our attention settles on the next event in Jonus's life that needs our support, it's gratifying to realise that Will has been drawn to a time some weeks after we were last with him.

'HOW DARE YOU!' Jonus's outrage shatters the peace of the night. 'YOU'D BETTER HOPE I DON'T CATCH YOU, BECAUSE I'LL BEAT YOU SENSELESS IF I DO.'

He's holding a large stick and chasing two shapes that are just managing to stay ahead of him in the moonlight. Mettle is sending him calming energy and counsel, but Jonus's rage is blocking his horse out of his mind. It is no match for Infinity's discarnate energy, however. She gets behind Mettle's thoughts and energy with all that she is and propels them through Jonus's anger. Love for my horse flows through me as Jonus stops mid-stride in shock, leaving those he was pursuing to disappear into the night.

Your behaviour is inappropriate for one who would offer help, Mettle informs him.

'MY BEHAVIOUR? IT'S MY BEHAVIOUR THAT'S INAPPROPRIATE? WHAT ABOUT THEIRS? THEY WERE TRYING TO THROW A LOOP OF ROPE OVER YOUR HEAD,' Jonus shouts back to where Mettle is standing.

Did they succeed?

'THAT'S HARDLY THE POINT.'

It is exactly the point. They would never have accomplished their goal for they lack both the skill and the speed. Do not indulge yourself with anger at their intentions. Celebrate the fact that they dared to come that close to me.

'INDULGE MYSELF? I WAS PROTECTING YOU.'

Further progression will not be possible until you recognise your untruth.

'MY... MY WHAT?' Jonus stands with his mouth open.

Mettle begins to graze.

Jonus throws the stick to the ground and it breaks in two. 'AAAAAAAGH!' he shouts up to the night sky.

Jonus, can I give you some friendly advice? Will asks him.

Well, about time. Yes, Will, you can. You can tell me what you would have done. If you had spent the last three weeks lying on the bare ground even though your hut and bed were a stone's throw away, so that the people you are trying to help can slowly adjust to the fact that you have a horse with you who can help them; if you had spent the last three weeks going off to fish as soon as it's light, so that you and your horse could bring a steady supply of food back for these people who are supposed to be your friends, and they take it without thanks but with a constant demand that I make Mettle carry out all manner of tasks for them; if you had spent all that time, doing all of that, and then you woke up to the sound of your horse thundering around with those two gits trying to catch him with the very rope that I made for them to bundle firewood – tell me, what would you have done?

Will pauses to think and then arrives at the answer that not only Jonus, but he needs. *I would leave it to the horses. Sorry, I mean, I would have left it to Mettle. You've done all you can for these people for now, Jonus. By catching their food so that Mettle can bring it to them, you've taught them to see him as one who can help rather than one to be feared. Because of you, they're more open to his influence. Now leave it to him.*

Leave what to him? Jonus asks.

Everything. Find yourself another pole for your fishing net, now that you've just broken the one you had, get food for yourself, but stop bringing it for everyone else. You've brought them the tools to do that for themselves. Keep yourself to yourself and let Mettle show you what the horses can do. Oh, and I'd follow his advice and admit your untruth, if I were you, you won't get anything else out of him until you do.

I'm not a liar, Jonus protests. *How can Mettle say I was indulging myself by being angry? I stopped those two chasing him and made sure that they never try it again. I was protecting him.*

Just because you've convinced yourself that's true, doesn't mean it isn't a lie. The horses see things as they really are. You can tell yourself that Mettle's wrong, but it won't change anything.

Jonus sighs, miserably and begins to walk back to where Mettle is grazing. *I don't understand.*

Okay, you say you were protecting Mettle. Was he in danger?

Well, not danger as such, no.

So why did he need your protection? Will asks.

Well I suppose he didn't need it, as such, but I just wanted those morons to stop harassing him.

Did Mettle feel harassed?

Jonus is thoughtful. *Now that you mention it, no.*

So why did you interfere?

Because, Will, it was the last bloody straw. Okay, fine, I chased them off because losing my temper felt better than taking any more of their crap.

I get it, mate, I do. You've held yourself in check for weeks and you needed to let it all out, but can you see Mettle's point?

I guess. Jonus reaches his horse and rubs his neck. Mettle lifts his head from the grass and nuzzles Jonus's shoulder. *I'm sorry,* Jonus tells him. *That was exactly what you were waiting for, wasn't it? A chance to interact directly with them? And I lost my temper and ruined it.*

You have ruined nothing. You have learnt much. All is well. Mettle accompanies his thoughts with such love for his Bond-Partner that Jonus gulps.

I don't deserve that. I would have brained those two if you hadn't stopped me, Jonus tells him.

Love is not conditional on thoughts or actions.

Something stirs deep within Jonus. He doesn't fully understand Mettle's counsel, but he recognises it as the truth. He is the first to begin to learn what all of the horses who follow Mettle will teach their Bond-Partners over and over again, with unswerving patience, until we get it. It all started here.

'You do realise that being nostalgic is another sign of old age, don't you, Am?' Will informs me as I open my eyes. His grin is so cheeky that I can't help but chuckle.

'I suppose so, now that you mention it.'

'I told you we should have just left him to be angry and

frustrated, he had so much less to say for himself then,' Justin says, holding a hand out each to Will and me and then hauling us to our feet. He winks at Will. 'But then you couldn't have helped Jonus like you just did. On balance, I suppose we'll put up with you as you are. Well done. Honestly, I'm proud of you.'

Will and I are both taken aback. We both know how intensely Justin tends to feel about things, but it's rare for him to vocalise his feelings.

'Thanks, Uncle Jus.' Will throws his arms around Justin and there is much back-slapping as they part. 'You too, Auntie Am.' Will hugs me too and I feel him including Infinity, emotionally if not physically.

'Well done, Will, not just for helping Jonus, but for seeing what you needed to see,' I whisper into his ear.

Will takes a step back from me. 'It should have been obvious, really, shouldn't it? It's the horses the Drifters need. I just need to stay out of the way and leave it to them, then the Drifters will have no reason to be wary of their influence. I'll be nearby if I'm needed.'

I shake my head and smile at him as images of him from the wilful child he was, all the way up to the man he is now, flit through my mind. I can't help hugging him again.

'Can I join in, or is this just a Nixon family thing?' Will and I turn to see Rowena walking gingerly towards us.

Marvel jogs to catch up with her and offers her his arm. 'Make way for the bruised old lady, come along with me, Ro, we can't have you tripping on anything, oh and here comes Maverick the missile, hang on tight to me, now, dearest, I'll protect you.'

'You're insufferable,' Rowena moans but takes his arm and doesn't let go.

Maverick launches himself at Will just as Rowena and Marvel reach us. A group hug between five people and one very excited dog ensues, with Maverick managing to climb from one of us to the next, until somehow, he finds himself balancing between Marvel's and Justin's shoulders. It is only at that moment that we realise we're all soaking wet.

'Maverick, come here, boy,' Vickery calls him and we all part to watch her crouch down and rub him all over with a big handful of grass. 'Sorry, I managed to persuade him to come with me to play in the stream for a while as it's so hot. I thought he'd be dry by the time we got back, but…' she shrugs and grimaces on our behalf. 'Anyway, group hug? Looks like I got back just in time. What are we celebrating? Oh, I see, Will's learnt what he needed to as well as saving the day with Jonus, and Justin and Am are proud. Got it, a group hug is definitely warranted. Come on, don't stop on my account. You know we're going to have to do it all again when Holly gets back, don't you?'

Will and I find Holly in our Awareness. 'She's with the chestnut mare who is in foal,' Will murmurs. 'She won't be back any time soon. The foal will be born this evening and he's huge. Holly can help the mare by being there and we can help by keeping ourselves and Maverick away.' He nods to himself. 'We'll return to Jonus and Mettle tonight, once the foal has been born and we've seen Holly. Okay, Am?'

I smile at him. 'Sure.'

We're all Aware when the mare goes into labour. We feel the energy of the herd shifting in her direction in the same way that in the body, blood is directed towards muscles during exercise or towards the gut when digestion is in progress; she is the part of the herd that needs more energy so it will continue to be concentrated with her until she no longer needs it.

Holly's energy is also with the mare, albeit in a slightly different way. Where the horses merely allow their energy to flow to where in the herd it is needed, Holly directs hers in the gentlest possible way to the parts of the mare's body that are directly involved in the birth process. She allows her energy to resonate with each of the different tissues, all at once, so that she can respond immediately, providing strength or healing as necessary. One by one, we all retreat slightly in our Awareness, so that we don't disturb Holly as we marvel at the talent she has honed since she learnt to combine her Awareness with her Healing Skills.

As the mare's labour progresses, she accepts the energy of her herd without reservation and as a result, is able to continue well into the night without tiring. But as Will observed, the foal is enormous and she isn't strong enough to push him out. Holly adds her strength to the mare's. With each contraction, Holly fuels the mare's muscles with her own energy and then when the foal's feet finally appear, she takes hold and pulls physically while still providing strength to the mare to help her to push. As the foal begins to move, Holly puts everything of herself into helping both mare and foal. When at last he enters the world, Holly is busy opening his birthing sack even as she silently heals with her intention each and every little tear the mare has suffered, as well as priming the relevant tissues to pull the pelvis back into a healthy alignment in the days and weeks to come. She leaves mare and foal soon after that, knowing her work is done. The energy of the herd settles with the foal for a short while, before redistributing evenly once more.

I have witnessed Holly assisting mothers of all species as they've given birth, and she has always given as much of herself as is necessary, but no birth has ever taken as much out of her as has this one. I'm suddenly Aware that she wishes it had taken more. I get to my feet to run to her at the same time that everyone else does, but then we all pull up short as we feel Serene's presence.

It has been eleven years since Holly's Bond-Partner passed on and Holly has never regretted her decision to stay while Serene moved on without her. But tonight, in her exhaustion, she misses her horse with all of the small amount of energy she has left and she's forgotten what is keeping her here. She's beginning to fade. Serene steadies Holly while Will gathers the rest of us to him in our Awareness. We follow him in allowing as much of our group energy to settle with Holly as she needs, just as the horse herd did for the labouring mare. We don't try to console her, to reassure her that she will feel differently once she has rested, to tell her how important she is to us all, we just allow as much of our love to flow to her as she needs, for her to use in whichever way she wants.

Slowly, steadily, we feel Holly's conviction returning that she still has a part to play here. She remembers that Serene is an unwavering constant, always accessible while Holly is here in the dream, and always there in the oneness for when Holly's time finally comes. And that time isn't now, Holly suddenly knows that for certain. She sends her love to Serene, who stays with her as Holly gets to her feet and makes her way back to us. Our group energy begins to redistribute itself, and by the time she reaches us, the redistribution is complete. Will releases Maverick to welcome her as only he can, and when she enters the firelight, she's smiling.

TWENTY-FOUR

Will

I accept hugs and thanks from the others for showing them what to do to help Holly, but the truth is, I didn't actually do anything.

And that is why we are thanking you, Amarilla tells me. *We are grateful to be taken with you as you find new ways for us to be.*

You were already close, you were giving your light to those who needed it before I was even born.

I know what my aunt's response will be even as she gives it. *Yes. My light. We all know how to send our own light and even combine our flows when there is someone who needs the strength of more than one person, but you showed us how to allow the energy, the power, of the group to be used by one who needs it. We've felt the horses do it for one another many times, but it never occurred to us to do the same. We don't have the openness of mind to translate how the horses are to how we can be, even though as soon as you show us, it seems so obvious. Thank you, Will, for being you.*

Marvel and Vickery are either side of Holly with their arms

around her, and they beckon to the rest of us. 'Groooooup huuuuuuuug,' Marvel says.

As we all join in, chuckling, or in Rowena's case, groaning and warning Vickery and Amarilla not to hug her too tightly, I can feel the energy of our group swirling around us with increased momentum.

'I feel it too. We need to be back with Jonus,' Amarilla tells me.

'But you haven't rested enough,' Rowena says. 'You need to sleep so your minds can rest. Oh, okay, I get it, the momentum's building, you don't think you'll be with Jonus very long. Poor lad, I almost feel sorry for him.'

'We'll settle down in our tents, shall we? That way, we won't need watching over and everyone else can get some sleep,' Amarilla suggests.

'No way, we're not missing whatever it is that you two will be up to in the past. We'll all stay right here and keep the fire going so that none of us gets a chill, and you can both get your blankets and bed down where you are,' Rowena orders.

Everyone else nods, so I shrug and Am and I do as we're told.

Maverick snuggles up to me and I hear his sigh of contentment as I find Jonus and my attention is drawn to where Amarilla, Infinity and I are needed next.

But I can't, I'll fall off and hurt myself, Jonus is telling Mettle.

It is necessary, Mettle replies.

It has been many weeks since we were last here. Jonus has done as Mettle told him and not only kept himself to himself, but managed to resist every provocation that the villagers have thrown his way. When they have jeered at him for keeping company with Mettle instead of returning to his position in the community, insulted him with regard to his perceived insanity, and shouted at him for refusing to bring them any more food, he has kept his silence. When they have attempted, time after time, to sneak up on Mettle to try and catch him, Jonus has sat back and watched his horse evade them with ease. Mettle has stunned his pursuers and their onlookers with his speed and agility. He has shown neither fear nor aggression, and his calm demeanour, combined with the gentleness that radiates from his dark eyes, is beginning to affect everyone in a way that they feel but don't understand. It is indeed time for Jonus to ride his horse, to cement the idea in the villagers' minds that Jonus and Mettle are a partnership.

It's been a while since I rode a horse, but I can teach you, Jonus, I tell him.

Oh, thank goodness you're back, I've had a hell of a time, Jonus replies.

I know, but you've been amazing. Honestly, well done. You chose your horse's name well.

Huh?

You remember when you looked into Mettle's essence and chose his name because of what you saw in him? I ask.

Err, yes.

Well, what you saw wasn't just what he has in him, it was what you have the potential to be, and I'd say you're well on the way to being it.

Jonus frowns. *What?*

You have the potential to be what you saw in Mettle. You have spirit, courage and determination already. When they are the whole of you, the horses will call you "He Who Is Mettle", I tell him.

When they are the whole of me?

Yes, when you don't have to work at them, when you just are them, you will have reached the potential you saw for yourself. It's important that you remember what I'm telling you, so that you can explain it to the Horse-Bonded who come after you. We'll be in a right mess if there's no one to explain it to Amarilla when her time comes. I'm joking by the way.

About me having spirit and courage and... whatever else it was? Jonus asks.

Nope, about Amarilla. Sorry, I'm confusing things. Just know that the qualities you saw in Mettle when you chose his name are the ones that are ripe for development within you, Jonus. Some day that will make sense. When it does, pass it on to the other Horse-Bonded, okay?

Err, okay, I think. So, I called Mettle that because he and I both have it, and when I have more of it, I'll understand.

Yes. My point in telling you was that you've proved to yourself how much mettle you have by doing such a brilliant job following your Bond-Partner's advice. And the fact that you have it means that riding your horse will be no problem for you. You have the courage to try and the determination to keep working at it. You need to ride, Jonus, not just because of what you need to do now, but because you'll need to teach the future Horse-Bonded to do it too.

Jonus sighs. *Okay, you've persuaded me, but it'll be up to you to cheer me up when I make a total prat of myself. How do I even get on? I can't jump that high.*

I feel Amarilla nudging my mind, reminding me how she helped Fitt, the Kindred Horse-Bonded, to ride her Bond-Partner, Flame.

Jonus, how do you feel about me showing you how to ride by being in your body with you? I ask him. *Your mind has accepted a link with Infinity, which is how you can hear me in the first place, so I can send my mind down that link to ride Mettle through you. What do you think?*

Well, I don't know. I mean isn't that a bit... weird?

What, weirder than everything else that's happened to you recently?

Well, yeah, I mean, I'm a guy, you're a guy...

Seriously? That's what's weird to you, Jonus? That we're both male? You're fine taking instructions in your head from a horse – who is male by the way – you're fine with the fact that a horse from the future is helping two people, also from the future, to communicate with you, but the thing that's weird is allowing me to show your body in the fastest, easiest possible way, how to ride your horse so that you don't, in your own words, make a prat of yourself?

Jonus chuckles. *When you put it like that, I suppose it doesn't seem so weird. And I'm not sure I have the strength to argue, so fine, carry on. How will I know when you're in here with me?*

I'll be there as soon as I know you're ready. I'll be quiet in your mind, because I want you to concentrate completely on allowing your body to follow the suggestions I'll be giving it. If you need me to leave at any time, I'll know and I'll go, so just relax and concentrate on feeling how your body is riding your horse. When you're ready, go and climb on that boulder over there, so you can mount more easily.

Jonus takes his time thinking through everything I've told him and then I feel him gather himself together. He lifts his head, sets his chin and strides over towards the boulder. A villager points at him and shouts to the others as he climbs on top of the boulder and waits for his horse to come alongside it. Mettle canters over to him. His white, wavy mane is carried on the breeze, making him look even bigger than he is, and his thick, white tail streams magnificently out behind him. More villagers gather to watch as Mettle slows to a halt alongside the boulder, turns his head to his Bond-Partner and whickers his encouragement. Jonus takes extra heart from his horse. He is ready.

When his right leg follows my suggestion to bend and lift, it makes him jump. I allow him to put his leg back down and take a breath. Now he knows what to expect, he'll find it easier. I lift his leg again and swing it over Mettle's back. I take hold of a chunk of mane with Jonus's hand and then have his standing leg push against the boulder so that he leaps across and lands sitting on Mettle. I allow Jonus a moment to savour his unexpected delight and then set about rearranging him so that he's sitting in as balanced a position as his body is able.

After witnessing Amarilla's experience of inhabiting Fitt's body, I'm prepared for the fact that I need to work within the limitations of Jonus's body, but it still feels strange to be riding a horse whilst neither of us is in perfect balance. Achieving that is not what this is about, though.

Jonus's shoulders are still hunched in the defensive posture that he was forced to adopt during all of the beatings he endured. Having never felt secure in his family, his body or his situation, he can't sit down securely into his pelvis, but rather sits on the back of it with his spine curved all the way up to his rounded shoulders. There is so much hurt and fear buried within his curled, self-protective posture that releasing it all, clearing what blocks him from being able to achieve perfect balance, will be too difficult for him in this lifetime, even if he could find the time to try.

Mettle is entirely in agreement that this is merely about helping Jonus to ride as well as his body is able, so that he can do what he has agreed to do. The big stallion knows that Jonus is preparing the way for those of the future to be in a position to give the horses the help they need to achieve perfect balance, and he's content to play the part he's agreed to play to get the process underway. My heart goes out to this gentle, patient horse and all of those who will follow him in helping us to find our way until the day comes when finally, they'll get the help they need in order to be all that they were always destined to be.

Once Jonus has had a little time to process how I've arranged his body, I close his legs around Mettle's sides a little and give a very gentle nudge with his heels. Mettle moves forward and Jonus laughs with delight as I show his body how to follow his horse's movement while staying balanced. I show him how to turn his body so that Mettle turns with him, and I show him how to slow his movement and then stop it so that Mettle comes to a halt. I teach him to follow the smallest change in Mettle's movement so that if the horse speeds up, slows or turns of his own accord, Jonus can stay with him. Then I leave him to practise asking Mettle to move, turn and stop while I make sure his body remains in as good a balance as it can.

I feel Jonus's confidence in Mettle, in himself and in me, so I nudge Mettle gently from a walk into a trot. Jonus doesn't panic. He continues to allow his body to follow Mettle and do everything I want it to do, sitting easily to Mettle's trot and then his canter. He whoops with joy at the feel of Mettle's strength and speed beneath him, and at the increased feeling of partnership he's discovering with his horse as Mettle canters around between the bushes and boulders of the scrubland. When I bring them to a halt in front of where the villagers are standing, open-mouthed and speechless, Jonus is breathless but his eyes are sparkling and his smile is infectious. A few of the villagers find themselves smiling in response. I stay with him, holding his body in place so that he can concentrate on what he will need to say.

'How did you know he'd let you get on him like that?' Ben asks him.

'Because it was his idea,' Jonus replies.

'Oh, not this again,' says a tall man, standing with a hand on Ben's shoulder.

'Do you think he'll let me sit on him?' Ben says.

'No.'

'Why not?'

'Because he isn't here for your entertainment. He isn't here to be used in any of the ways that the horses you've read about in books allowed themselves to be used. As I've already told you all, he's here to teach us to live the life that we all dreamt of when we left the cities.'

'Oh, for heaven's sake, he's just a horse, Jonus. How can you possibly expect us to believe that he can teach us anything?' the man with Ben says.

'Because he already has, Tomlin. He's taught you all that you don't need to be afraid of things you don't understand. He's taught you that there are ways to respond to provocation other than by retaliation. And he's shown you that there are ways to communicate other than by the spoken word. You've just seen it for yourselves.'

Some of the villagers nod uncertainly, others shake their heads and look around to see who of their friends is doing the same. Most of them stand in thoughtful silence.

'It's true, he has shown us all of those things,' says Ben.

'Tomlin, can't you shut your boy up?' says the black-bearded man who was all for stoning Mettle.

'Oh, go and play with your catapult, Leod,' Ben says.

'Why, you...' Leod lunges towards Ben, his fist raised. Ben steps neatly to one side, leaving Leod to stumble awkwardly past him until he is caught and held firmly by Tomlin.

Ben runs to Mettle and stops awkwardly in front of him. 'I learnt to do that from you,' he tells the stallion. Mettle stretches out his neck and sniffs the boy's freckled face, then blows warm air into his ear. The villagers watch in uncomfortable silence but none of them intervene. Ben lifts a shaking hand and strokes

Mettle's long nose. 'Why won't you talk to me?' he asks the horse.

Jonus smiles down at Ben. 'He says he does, but you don't hear him.'

'But why not? If you can hear him talking to you in your head, why can't I?'

'I don't know, exactly. I can tell you what he says, though.'

'Oh, for goodness' sake, are we all really going to stand here and listen to this?' This time it is Priss who speaks up. 'Have any of you heard anything so ridiculous as a man hearing a horse talk to him in his head?'

'Is it more ridiculous than all of us leaving everything we knew, just because of a feeling inside that there was a better way to live? Any madder than following that feeling into the wilderness with no clue about how to survive, because we knew it was better to do that than to just wither away in the cities?' It is Trix who is speaking, and everyone turns to look at her. 'I believe Jonus. I've watched him with, er, Mettle and he knows exactly what the horse will do before he even does it. And he's different since Mettle's been with him. He talks sense, he acts like there's nothing to worry about and he's learnt skills he couldn't possibly have just discovered by accident. And it's like Mettle is one step ahead of us. Look how we've behaved towards him, yet he's tolerated everything in the same way we do with naughty children. He bears us no ill, it's like he's just waiting for us to learn whatever it is we need to learn.'

Trix holds a hand up as some of the others begin to shake their heads and protest. 'It's not just about believing Jonus though, it's more than that. I believe myself. When I watched you ride Mettle just now, Jonus, it was like something came over me and I felt calmer than I have in ages. I managed to find the part of myself, inside, that told me to come here in the first place and I listened to it as you asked me to when you first came back. That inner feeling tells me that everything you've said is true. I trust you and Mettle, because I've just remembered that I trust me.'

She holds both hands up this time and raises her voice as others begin to speak. 'I know you'll think I'm as mad as Jonus, but everything inside me is telling me to trust him and his horse. Don't waste time arguing with me, just ask yourselves like I did, and you'll come up with the same answer, I know you will.'

The villagers all begin to talk amongst themselves. Tomlin lets go of Leod and goes to his wife's side and then they both join their son, who is now stroking Mettle's neck. As Mettle greets Tomlin and Trix, someone shouts out, 'So, if the horse is here to teach us, then prove it. What does he think we should do?'

Jonus is silent while Mettle tells him exactly what to say. Then he relays the information in a loud, clear voice. 'Mettle says that we will find the answers to our building problems in memories buried deeply within us all. We all have memories of a race that lived long ago. They built enormous, four-sided structures on a square base and each of the four sides was a triangle.'

There is silence. Then someone laughs loudly and says, 'That's it?'

'What the hell is that supposed to mean? Does anyone know what he's talking about?'

'I told you Jonus was an idiot, we need to get back to work and stop wasting any more of our time.'

'You almost had me there, Jonus, you and the family stupid there. Take that horse, go back to wherever you found him and stay there.'

Ben says to the villagers, 'If they go, I'll go with them and so will my parents, and they're the best builders you've got.'

Trix and Tomlin are looking from Jonus to Mettle thoughtfully. 'No one is going anywhere, son,' Tomlin says.

'We're going to trust your mum, Mettle and Jonus, and see what happens next.'

The villagers disperse, muttering and shaking their heads. Jonus allows his body to follow my suggestion to lean forward, throw a leg over Mettle's back and dismount. I leave it immediately and tell him, *Good job, well done, you're going to feel...*

Sore. And stiff. Bloody hell, Will, what did you do to me? I can't stand up, Jonus complains.

Don't be such a baby, just put a hand against Mettle while you straighten your legs.

Jonus is crouching as if he is still astride his horse.

'Are you alright, Jonus?' Trix asks him while Ben and Tomlin try to hide their grins behind their hands.

'I'm fine, I just seem to have forgotten how to make my legs do what I want,' Jonus replies with a grimace.

Tomlin chuckles. 'I don't think that's going to help your credibility with the others. Here, lean on me while you move your feet closer together and then try to straighten your legs. Slowly now, does it really hurt that much? Why didn't you get off before, if you were in that much pain?'

'I wasn't in pain until I landed on the ground. It's as if my body's forgotten how to arrange itself on its own two feet. Remind me to stay on Mettle's back until I'm out of sight, next time, will you?'

Trix, Tomlin and Ben all laugh.

Mettle begins to graze. *There are plants here that will ease your discomfort,* he tells Jonus.

What, those small ones by your nose?

Mettle doesn't answer, so I do. *Yes, that's arnollia. It's the leaves you need, you can chew them as they are if you want, but we usually make them into a tea. Mettle's left you enough for now, but you could do with finding more, ready for the next time you ride.*

Why has Mettle eaten it? Mettle, are you in pain? Jonus asks his horse.

Being ridden is as unfamiliar to my body as it is to yours, his horse tells him. He doesn't tell Jonus that he expects to need to find the herbs that ease discomfort every time he is ridden. He knows that Jonus will never be capable of helping him to carry his rider in a way that doesn't compromise Mettle's body, and he accepts it as an inevitable side-effect of helping his Bond-Partner to achieve all that he needs to.

'Please could you pick me the rest of those little plants there, where Mettle's grazing? He says they will ease the pain in my legs, oh and my back, that hurts too, now.' Jonus rubs his back as he points the arnollia out to Ben. The boy immediately drops to his knees, picks the herbs and then hands them to Jonus. 'It's the leaves I need. Apparently, they can be made into a tea, but I can't wait that long.' Jonus rips the leaves from the stems and crams as many into his mouth as he can, and then grimaces as he chews them.

'Those leaves take away pain?' Trix says. 'Can Mettle tell us if there are plants that cure anything else?'

'He says he can but he won't.'

'What? Why?'

Jonus smiles. 'He says that you'll be better served learning for yourselves how to find herbs that heal.'

'Well, okay, I see that. So, will he teach us, then?' Trix says.

'He says that in due course, he'll give me the words that will awaken memories of all of the abilities we need, but his advice is to concentrate on one thing at a time for now.'

'Building,' says Tomlin.

'Yes, building. Wow, that arnollia's good, I feel better already, in fact I'm pretty sure I can walk now. Mettle and I'll leave you to the rest of your day.' Jonus turns to go.

'Don't you want to go and rest on your bed? I don't think Mettle's in any danger now,' says Tomlin.

Jonus chuckles. 'He never was. Thanks, but I'll go back to our little camp over there, it's beginning to feel like home. Just remember the words that Mettle told me to tell you. We all have memories of a race that lived long ago. They built enormous, four-sided structures on a square base and each of the four sides was a triangle. Got it?'

Trix and Tomlin both nod thoughtfully and say, 'Got it.'

Ben isn't listening. He stands looking crestfallen as Mettle turns and walks away from him.

'Mettle's hungry now, he needs time to himself to graze, but we'll come back over tomorrow, Ben, okay?' Jonus says.

Ben nods and his parents each put an arm around his shoulders. The three of them turn together to go back to their hut, Trix and Tomlin both looking back over their shoulders thoughtfully at Mettle.

We aren't needed here anymore, but I realise that I don't need a break. *Okay to carry on, Am?*

Absolutely.

Amarilla knows how keen I am to be back riding Mettle, even if it is by proxy and far from ideal in terms of balance. She knows that in showing Jonus's body how to ride, I'm reminding myself. When the time comes for me to do it, I'll be ready.

TWENTY-FIVE

Amarilla

*A*s always, Will is drawn to the next point in time that the energy of the second and third catalysts can bring balance to that of the first. Jonus is standing on the boulder from which he mounted Mettle last time. He is desperately trying to remember how Will arranged his body so that he landed on Mettle's back without sliding off the other side. Will and I are immediately Aware that this is not the only event occurring in the vicinity, however.

Less than a day has passed since we were last here, and the village is in uproar. A few of the villagers are hiding in their homes with the doors barred shut, while the rest are gathered around Trix and Tomlin, most cheering but some shouting angrily.

Trix is humming as she stares at one of the disused piles of stones that were to be used as missiles against Mettle. A stone from the pile begins to quiver and then slowly rises up into the air where it hovers for a while, before it is lowered back down again. Trix stops humming, smiles and looks to her husband. Tomlin then focuses on the pile of stones and begins his own humming.

Almost immediately, two stones of similar size begin to quiver and both rise up into the air. One quivers more violently and then plummets back down to the pile. The other rises smoothly until it is level with the roof of the nearest shelter. Tomlin holds it there with his intention, then lowers it very slowly to land in the very centre of the pile from which he took it.

The cheering increases in volume, drowning out those who are shouting their angry protests at the danger of Trix and Tomlin playing around with forces that they don't fully understand. The protesters point frequently to a large rock that has been deposited in the doorway of one of the shelters; when Tomlin lost control of it, scaring some of the villagers almost witless, he and his wife agreed to practise their rock-singing on smaller, easier stones until they are more proficient at their newfound talent. But the protesters still think they should stop doing it altogether. The most nervous of the villagers are hiding, trembling in their huts, muttering about witchcraft and evil.

Mettle has advised Jonus to leave events to develop without either of their involvement for the time being, and concentrate on improving his ability to ride.

Infinity touches Jonus's mind and he accepts her and therefore me, as he has every time Will has brought him to our attention. As Will once again uses our link to reach Jonus, I feel him acknowledge, very briefly, my observation that this is becoming a very familiar way for the four of us to be. Then he tells Jonus, *If you jump on the way you're just about to, you'll be talking in a much higher-pitched voice than you normally do. Want some help?*

Yes, obviously, Jonus replies. *I mean I've only done this once and it wasn't even really me doing it, was it? Are you in here with me yet?*

No, but once I am, I'll get you onto Mettle's back as I did the first time, then I'll get you off again and leave you to get back on by yourself while the movement is fresh in your memory. Then we'll do everything else the same way – I'll do a bit and then leave you to do it by yourself so you'll remember what you did, and then you can practise without me.

But why would I want to do that? I mean you'll always be there when I need you, won't you? When Will doesn't answer immediately, Jonus repeats, *Won't you? Will? And you, Amarilla, and Infinity?*

I know everything feels a bit overwhelming at the moment, but believe me when I tell you that there will be a time when you won't need us, I tell him.

Amarilla's right, Will agrees, *and that time isn't very far off. But when you get there, if you want me to, I can leave a small amount of my energy with you. That way, we can stay in touch without the link that Infinity has been providing for us.*

Jonus frowns. *But how can you do that? I mean how will it be possible for you to leave but not leave?*

Because I've learnt to be like the horses and it's normal for their energy to be in different places at once. At the moment, the only way your mind can accept communication from me is through the link we both have with Infinity. But if, after I've helped you to ride for the last time, I leave a tiny part of myself with you, I'll know whenever you want to tell me something or ask me a question, and because I'll already be with you, your mind won't block me out. And if you ever wanted me to take my energy back to myself, I'd know and I'd leave you in peace. Think about it, Jonus. But for now, we need to get you riding again.

After you've just told me all that? How am I meant to concentrate when you've just told me that you can leave a part of yourself with me?

The same way you've dealt with everything else that you

haven't understood to begin with, Will tells him. *Accept it and think about it when you have time to yourself. That time isn't now. Mettle's waiting for you to ride him. Come on, you're not under pressure like you were the last time, your friends have got more than enough to keep them distracted with everything that's going on over there – you could fly through the air making bird noises and they wouldn't notice. It's the perfect time for a riding lesson.*

As I witness Jonus practising what Will is showing him, I'm taken back to my own early efforts at riding Infinity. Since I tend to only remember the feeling of the two of us in perfect balance together, I had forgotten that I found riding her so difficult in the beginning. My heart goes out to Jonus every time his body tenses and doesn't quite follow Mettle's movement, so that he either bounces around, landing painfully on areas of himself he would rather protect, or loses his balance completely and falls off. He never stops trying though. By the end of the session, he's able to stay in a rough sort of balance by himself in walk, trot and canter, he can physically communicate his suggestions of speed and direction to Mettle, and can often follow Mettle's movement when the stallion decides for himself when to turn or change speed.

When Jonus attempts to dismount, it's more a case of slithering down from Mettle's back until he lands on the ground, at which point he sinks straight to his knees, sits back onto his bottom and then lies down flat on his back, his arms and legs straight out on either side of him. He's in agony, but is delighted with what he and his horse have achieved. Mettle, too, is sore, and has already wandered off to where he knows there is arnollia growing.

Do you have some arnollia picked, ready? Will asks Jonus.

Yes, it's just over there, but I'm too tired and sore to get it.

Mettle's had to go and find his, and he's no less tired and sore than you are, Will tells him.

Jonus sits up immediately and winces. He looks around for his horse and sees him grazing in the distance. *How do you know he's tired and sore? He didn't tell me.*

You can know how his body is if you want to, you just search his perception of himself, see how he is feeling. Really, you should do that before you take care of yourself, if you can.

Jonus does as Will tells him and immediately, he knows that Mettle's back is sore, his front legs ache and his hind legs feel a little stiff. He is mortified.

There is no cause for concern. Your balance and skill will increase alongside my strength and tolerance, Mettle tells him and accompanies his thoughts with a sense that everything is happening as expected.

But you need arnollia. Hold on, I'm coming, I have some. Jonus gets slowly and painfully to his feet and begins to hobble over to where Mettle is grazing.

I have what I need. Take care of yourself. Rest and recover and then we will try again.

But then I'll just make you sore all over again, Jonus protests.

We will both be sore. We will both recover. Then we will continue. Mettle very obviously transfers all of his attention to selecting the particular herbs he wants to eat, so that Jonus is in no doubt that the conversation is over. He staggers back to his campfire and lowers himself painfully to the ground just as a loud cheer goes up from the village.

Tomlin and Trix have figured out how to work together, Will tells Jonus. *They've combined their strength and have just moved the rock that Tomlin dropped in someone's doorway, right out beyond the village boundary. Hello, they're lifting it again... and putting it down again. Jonus, stand up, this is worth watching.*

Jonus groans, but reaches for the pole of his fishing net and puts one hand above the other in turn as he pulls himself to his feet. He then leans on the pole and watches what his friends are up to.

Ben takes a stone from one of the missile piles and runs to a spot on the village perimeter, far enough away from the shelters that the protesters are shouted down, but close enough that the onlookers can see what is happening. Ben moves away from the stone and watches as Trix and Tomlin start humming together. They focus intently on their rock and it lifts to around the same height as their son. It then moves slowly and smoothly to hover exactly over where Ben has placed the stone. The couple lower the rock so that it lands on top of the stone.

The protesters are silent this time as their friends cheer. Even those who have been hiding in their huts begin to poke their heads out to see what is happening. When they see Trix and Tomlin being hugged and patted on their backs, heads, wherever anyone can reach, they venture out to gather explanations. Soon, everyone has a smile on their face as they begin to believe what Trix and Tomlin have been trying to show them – that they will be able to build houses of stone. Finally, the villagers will have houses that will shelter them from the weather, and houses that have a chance of staying up, so that the villagers won't keep having to rebuild them at precious cost of time and energy that is needed elsewhere.

People begin pointing to various small rocks and boulders lying around, and then to huge rocks further away, of similar sizes to the villagers' shelters. Trix and Tomlin walk closer to one of the largest rocks, holding their hands up to the villagers behind them, warning them to stay where they are. They hold hands and focus intently on the rock, their humming much lower than before. All of a sudden, there is a loud bang and some of the villagers scream and run away. A crack has appeared in a straight line from the bottom to the top of the rock, separating a neat slice of it away from the main bulk. The slice is lifted into the air and deposited to one side. Trix and Tomlin continue to focus on it and another loud crack accompanies the slice separating into six smaller rocks. There is much cheering and even some dancing by the villagers, as they watch Trix and Tomlin move the six rocks, one by one, to sit in a line at the edge of the village clearing. Then there is another loud crack as the couple separate off another slice of rock. When the huge mother rock has been reduced to an even larger pile of smaller rocks, Trix and Tomlin, the first ever Rock-Singers, are exhausted and delighted in equal measures. Tomorrow, they will get to work building the first house of The New.

'Mettle said it wouldn't take long for them to remember what they can do, but I can't believe it, they've done it already,' Jonus whispers to himself. Then his eyes widen as he sees Ben running in his direction, followed by his parents and then the rest of the villagers.

Jonus groans as Ben flings his arms around him, hugs him tightly and then runs off to where Mettle is grazing with a complete lack of concern for the hoards heading in his direction. Trix and Tomlin copy their son's actions and once they are on their way to see Mettle, Jonus is besieged by the rest of the villagers hugging him, thanking him, apologising to him, begging him to move back to the village – a cacophony of voices shouting, laughing, even singing their words to him. Two of the men hoist him, groaning and protesting, onto their shoulders and carry him, with the rest of the villagers leaping and dancing along behind, over to where Mettle continues to graze even as he is being hugged at various parts of his body by Ben, Trix and Tomlin.

When they reach Mettle, Jonus holds his hands up and there is much shushing and scolding until everyone is finally quiet. 'I'd just like to say that it should be Ben, Trix and Tomlin who are being hugged and carried around, not just because they're awesome but because I'm in so much bloody pain. Now sodding well put me down, will you?'

There is laughter all around as Jonus's friends do as he says, and he can't stop himself smiling at the sound of it. Then he grimaces again. He leans on one of the men who carried him and says, 'Ignore me being grumpy, I've been riding Mettle in between falling off him, and there's nowhere in my body that doesn't hurt.'

'Haven't you got any of those leaves that eased your pain yesterday?' Ben asks.

'Yes, they're in my basket over there in my camp, I didn't get a chance to eat any before Trix and Tomlin started breaking rocks, and then you lot assaulted me,' Jonus grins and Ben runs off to fetch it for him.

'There are leaves that help pain? Mettle told you which ones?' Jonus turns to see that it is Priss who is asking.

He manages to smile at her. 'Yes, he showed me them after I rode him yesterday and they really do work. At some point, he'll tell us the words that will help us remember how to find lots of other plants that heal, just like he told us the words to help Trix and Tomlin remember how to affect rocks.'

'When will he do that? I'd love to be able to use plants to make people feel better.' Priss blushes and glares at everyone around her, daring them to laugh.

'I think his answer to that was "in due course". Oh, wait a minute, he's telling me something now.' Jonus pauses while he concentrates on memorising the exact words Mettle has placed in his head. Then he says, 'Mettle says that we all have memories of being able to feel the energy of plants and ailments as easily as we feel the heat from the sun.'

Priss frowns as she looks from Jonus to Mettle and then back again. 'We all have memories of being able to feel energy?'

Jonus says, 'Yes, of being able to feel the energy of plants and ailments as easily as we feel the heat from the sun. It doesn't matter whether the words make sense to you, just remember them, think about them and see what happens. Okay?'

Priss nods thoughtfully.

'Right, so can I get back to being in pain in peace, please?'

'You're not sleeping out here anymore, Jonus, we'll take you back to your hut,' Trix says.

Jonus shakes his head. 'Honestly, I like sleeping out here with Mettle. And anyway, once you know everything he can teach you, we'll be off to receive abuse at other villages, so there's no point me getting comfortable.'

'You're going to leave us?' Ben says and looks frantically at his parents for them to tell Jonus that he and Mettle can't leave.

'Not for a while, there's still lots that Mettle needs to teach you, and I need to get a whooooooole lot better at riding him before we can go anywhere. I mean, look at me, an hour on and off his back and I'm crippled.'

Ben shoves the arnollia into Jonus's hand and says, 'Well then, that's lots of time for a horse to find me. When I have a horse of my own, I can come with you both.'

I see the thread that links Ben to his future Bond-Partner. She hasn't been born yet but when the time is right, she will tug him, he will find her and then he will, indeed, join the ranks of the Horse-Bonded. But for now, he'll do as his soul agreed and continue to fuel the change occurring in his community, with his open-mindedness and enthusiasm.

Will and I aren't needed here until Jonus is ready to ride again, but we're both finding it hard to tear ourselves away. It's heart-warming to be witnessing the point where the Ancients' lives turned around and became easier, the point where their courage was finally rewarded and their dreams of creating a new way of life became possible.

When we finally open our eyes, dawn has broken. I hear water bubbling in the pot and smell the smoke of our campfire.

Vickery hands me a mug of tea. 'It's all been very humbling, hasn't it, actually witnessing for ourselves what the Ancients went through. If they had been even a fraction less than the people they were, humanity would never have made it out of The Old. And before you say it, Am, I know everything happens as it should. But it doesn't take anything away from the fact that those souls chose to live very difficult lives so that things could change. And don't even get me started on the horses. I mean, seeing how sore Mettle is from being ridden and knowing that he's prepared to compromise himself every time Jonus rides him so that at some time in his future, the horses will help us to reach the point where we can finally help the horses in return... I mean, it just brings it all home, doesn't it?'

Justin puts an arm around Vickery and says, 'It's not like you to be morose, Vic.'

She shakes her head and blinks. 'No, sorry. I guess it just shows, I'm never too old to be knocked off-centre.'

'It was guilt that did it.' Will rubs Maverick's chest as he looks up at Vickery. 'Witnessing what Mettle is prepared to do reminded you that Verve did the same for you until you finally helped him to achieve perfect balance. It's a funny thing, guilt. We all know it's unnecessary because making mistakes is just part of learning, but it does have a place in the balance of everything. There was a time when admitting a mistake was tantamount to signing your own death warrant, so denying mistakes became ingrained and the ability to learn from them was lost. Guilt was the soul's way of nudging the personality to acknowledge its mistakes. In that way, it played a valuable part in re-establishing the learning process and therefore the path to balance. It's bound to come up now and again when a lesson is remembered. Interesting, isn't it?' Will gets up. 'See you in a bit, this one needs a run and a game.'

The rest of us watch Will as he turns and runs off with Maverick, who barks with excitement in anticipation of the game he knows is coming.

Finally, Rowena says, 'I'm going to go ahead and say it. That was like being counselled by our Bond-Partners, wasn't it?'

We all nod in amused silence.

TWENTY-SIX

Will

Maverick makes me laugh as he splashes around in the stream, trying to catch droplets of water and barking at them when they disappear back into the current. I love his sense of fun, his ability to be continually delighted by life and, as he is growing up, his increasing sense of loyalty to his pack. I don't need him to be loyal to me, but I love the fact that it gives him the sense of belonging that he needs. As long as he can express his limitless, unconditional love as often as he wants and however he chooses, he is the happiest, most joyful pup alive. He carries me along with him in his delight, a continual reminder to enjoy life at the same time as accomplishing it.

Some of the horses come to the stream to drink and, used to Maverick as they are now, they pay no attention to his antics downstream from them. I notice that the chestnut mare who gave birth last night is with them, accompanied by her foal. He is jet-black and his legs look much too long for his body. He hasn't got full control over them yet, but even so, I'm Aware that his body is primed to grow easily into perfect balance. I'm pleased to see him drinking hungrily from his mother as she draws in water from the stream and then waits patiently until he's taken as much milk from her as he needs.

All of the other horses are well on their way back to the area they have been grazing by the time the foal finally releases his mother's teat, steps back from her and catches sight of me. My breath catches in my throat; his eyes are the most beautiful amber colour. Against the black of his face, they're like pale orange embers glowing from the charred ashes of a bonfire.

The foal holds my stare with a confidence that contradicts his age and experience in this lifetime. I am seeing an old soul who has entered this incarnation relatively soon after departing his previous one. He has been drawn into this body, at this time, because of the contribution his experience and energy can make to improving the balance of the human situation. I nod to myself and breathe out my love and respect. Even now, with how far we've come, the horses are still there for us when we need them – the bringers of balance within the dream.

My focus on the foal so soon after his birth, my recognition of who he was, who he is now and why he is here, gives him an awareness of himself as an individual that is greater than either the lead mare, who I always recognise as such whenever I visit the herd, or the grey mare, who I can't help but single out, as she still selects me as her grooming partner from time to time.

The foal remembers himself and who he was to me in his previous incarnation. He whickers his greeting – such a cute little noise and so far-removed from the loud, shrill whinny he used to generate. His mother immediately moves between me and her baby and ushers him back to the herd. I smile. She's a strong mother. Now that I've inadvertently assured that her foal has a strong sense of himself, she'll need to be.

My stomach is cramping with hunger by the time Maverick

and I get back to camp. I don't resist Rowena as she manhandles me over to the shade of the horse chestnut tree and sits me down with the bowl of porridge that I should have eaten with the rest of them at breakfast, followed immediately by the bowl of stew that she has just finished preparing for lunch. Maverick lies at my feet, happily ripping the meat from a bone that Rowena has given him and oblivious of her order to make sure that I don't move. When she returns carrying my bedding, I groan.

'Everyone else has gone to sleep in their tents, against my advice – it'll be way too hot in there before long. You can do as you're told and sleep under here in the shade. You aren't going back to help Jonus until you've caught up on sleep,' she tells me.

'You need to sleep, too, Ro, you were up all night with the rest of us.'

'Yes, I was, but if I'd gone to bed as I, er, told everyone I would once I'd done a few jobs, then you wouldn't be sitting here eating a proper meal, would you?'

I nod. 'You remind me of Maverick, only without all of the joy.'

'And how, exactly, am I meant to take being told that I remind you of a dog? And a joyless one, at that?'

'You know it was a compliment. You and Maverick are both devoted to others, he just doesn't hide it as you still seem to think you can.'

Rowena's voice softens. 'And do you know who you remind me of, Will? My Bond-Partner, Oak. He had the same disregard for my feelings whilst telling me the truth. That was a compliment too.' She grins at me.

'I SMELL STEW!' Marvel's shout from within his tent is followed seconds later by his head appearing between the door flaps, his brown and grey hair sticking up at all angles and his eyes squinting in the sunlight.

'Remarkable. Even deep sleep and a layer of canvas can't keep him from knowing there's food ready.' Rowena gets to her feet to go and ladle him some from the cookpot.

Marvel's shouting has woken everyone else and they all emerge from their tents looking sleepy and hot. Rowena hands each of them a mug of water and bowl of stew and nods at their thanks.

Amarilla puts her mug and bowl on the ground and goes into Rowena and Marvel's tent. She reappears with an armful of blankets, takes Rowena's hand and leads her over to where Maverick and I are resting under the tree. 'There are times when you have to take what you give out, now settle down against the tree trunk on these blankets and eat some of this delicious stew you've made for us all, and then sleep,' Amarilla tells her friend. 'If you try to get up, I'll sit on you. That goes for you too, Will.'

As Amarilla glances at me, she instantly knows where I've been this morning and who I've seen; having spent so much time with our minds linked as closely as they have been, she can pick up disturbances in my equilibrium much quicker than anyone else, however small the disruption, however quickly it was rectified and however deeply I bury the fact that it happened. Her eyes widen slightly but, sensing that I'm enjoying relishing the situation by myself for now, she buries what she knows, as she is so practised at doing. She gives the faintest of winks and shouts, 'MARVEL, BRING RO'S MUG AND BOWL OVER, WOULD YOU? AND MINE, WHILE YOU'RE THERE.' She turns to Rowena. 'I'm staying right here until you've eaten and are asleep, so don't think I won't carry out my threat if I have to.'

Everyone joins us sitting under the tree and there is excitement as the events of the night are discussed in detail by everyone except Rowena and me, who are both fading rapidly. As soon as I've finished eating, I lie down and drift off to the sound of my family and friends laughing at Rowena, who has fallen asleep with her spoon in her hand while Maverick finishes off the half-eaten bowl of stew that she's dropped into her lap.

When I wake, the sun is setting and I'm alone except for Rowena, who is still propped up against the tree trunk, snoring softly with her mouth half open. I find Maverick in my Awareness, and smile. He's been enticed away from his place at my side by Vickery, and is thoroughly enjoying scenting out the small pieces of meat that she's hidden all over for him to find.

As I sit up, Amarilla kneels down beside me and hands me a plate of sandwiches. 'Here you go. When you've eaten, we'll visit Jonus and Mettle for the last time, shall we? The others want to stay up again and witness everything, so they've already eaten and Vic is wearing Maverick out, so when you're ready, we'll be good to go.'

'Thanks, Am.'

She knows I'm not talking about the food. 'No need. The others will all respect the mare's need for space in these early days, so you have a little time to enjoy the new development by yourself, but it won't be too long after that before they realise who her foal is, especially if Holly gives more attention to the mare and foal than a cursory health inspection. I'll keep it deeply buried in my mind, though. No one, including your parents, will pick it up from me.'

I nod. 'There'll be a time for them to know, but it isn't yet.'

'Talking of whom, if your mother were here, she'd be asking you not to inhale your food,' Am grins.

'Bu' I'd be doin' i' anyway,' I manage to say through my mouthful, and we both laugh. I swallow and add, 'They won't recognise me when we finally get home, will they?'

'They've followed you closely enough in their Awareness to know what to expect, but it'll definitely be strange for them to begin with. I mean, it's strange for us and we see you every day. You don't question anything, you don't even think about anything. Whatever happens, you go with it, just like the horses, and that means you're always ready for more change. I saw who you would become and I knew the part Infinity and I would need to play in it all, but I didn't see all of the process of how you would get there. I'm glad I'm here with you, Will. It all felt so difficult to begin with, losing Infinity and dealing with…'

'Me being a pain in the arse.' I grin.

'Well, yes. But I'm glad I trusted her. She told me that seeing this through with you would be the culmination of her and my contribution here and that there would be a point where all of the pain I would feel at her physical loss would be worth it. She was right, as always.'

'You were both right,' I say. 'You talk about her as a being separate from you out of habit but I know you feel her as part of you just as she knows you as part of herself. The only difference between you is that she accepted the situation straight away, and your grief prevented you from doing the same, at least for any length of time. But you're past that now, Am. You don't need to keep dreading that sorrow will come over you and block her out. You don't need to keep feeling for her to make sure she's there. You don't need the mirror that Marvel dug for you to see that Infinity's eyes shine out of yours, because you feel them. You don't need to talk about her as if she isn't physically here, because you know that she expresses herself through you. We all talk about Infinity creating the link to Jonus for us and Infinity using her energy to drive events, because it's convenient for us to think of it that way, but the truth is, she doesn't do anything and she isn't anywhere without you. The small amount of grief you still feel is for an idea of Infinity and nothing else. Let it go, Am, you don't need it anymore.'

Amarilla and Infinity nod and smile warmly out of their blue eyes at me. I feel the last of Amarilla's hurt and doubt dissipate into the ether, leaving the two souls fully able to share their existence here in the dream. Never before have two souls achieved the same relationship within the dream as they have in the oneness. And it is unlikely it will ever happen again.

'Let's get back to Jonus,' I say and they nod.

'JONUS, JONUS, JONUS, JONUS,' the villagers are shouting encouragingly as Jonus manages to mount Mettle from the one boulder in the vicinity that Trix and Tomlin haven't shattered into smaller rocks for their building. He settles himself into place and cheering erupts as Mettle obliges him by walking forward onto a circle. Jonus concentrates on each and every part of his body in turn, trying hard to make sure that everything is doing what he thinks it should be.

I'm here, Jonus, I tell him. *Carry on as you are, you're doing great. I'll only intervene to correct you if I can feel you struggling, otherwise I'll keep still and leave you to practise. Okay?*

I thought you were going to leave me to struggle on my own. Yes, that's fine, thanks.

He's already doing well. He's remembered to sit up as straight as he can and he's trying to open at the hips enough for his legs to hang down beneath him, instead of sticking out in front of him. He's following Mettle's movement with his pelvis so that he doesn't impede him and he's just remembered to look up, so that he doesn't put more weight on Mettle's forequarters than he can help.

He practises asking Mettle to turn to the left and right, and when Mettle offers his own changes of direction, he notices immediately and allows his body to follow without loss of balance. It is once Mettle is trotting that I'm needed to step in and loosen Jonus's lower back muscles as they begin to tense, so that he continues absorbing Mettle's movement without bouncing. I leave him be when he asks Mettle to trot circles to the left and then to the right, but step in once it's Mettle who is deciding when to change direction, as Jonus doesn't adjust his body to match Mettle's quickly enough, and needs my help to regain his balance before he falls off.

Once in canter, I remind Jonus's legs to remain hanging down beneath him, against their inclination to lift and grip his sides. He's remembering to do everything else I've shown him, so I leave him be. As Mettle carries on cantering beneath him, Jonus gets more and more confident in his balance. He even allows himself to smile at the continuing cheers of encouragement from his friends. He remembers how to slow his movement until Mettle slows to match him during the downward transitions to trot and then to walk, and he manages to keep his weight back so that he doesn't lurch forward onto Mettle's withers as his horse slows down. The only help he needs from me is to keep his lateral balance for him, so that he can concentrate on following Mettle's movement as it changes between the three paces, without sliding off either side.

Well done, Jonus, I'm proud of you, I tell him. *You just need more practice, now, so that your strength and balance improve, and then you'll wonder what you ever found difficult. You've spent enough time in the right position for your muscles to be able to remember what to do and Mettle now knows how it should feel to him, so he can give you feedback to stop you getting into bad habits.*

Does this mean you won't be coming back again? Jonus asks.

Amarilla, Infinity and I have done what we came here to do. But as I told you before, I don't have to leave completely if you don't want me to. You don't need to decide right now, it looks like someone wants your attention.

Jonus looks over to the villagers to see Priss pushing her way between them, calling Jonus's name and waving some plants around. Mettle halts beneath him and he swings a leg over his horse's back and jumps to the ground, landing with a grimace.

'I have some… arnollia, you said it's called, for you both, and I have this,' Priss holds out some herbs with white flowers, 'for the bruising on Mettle's back and on your thighs and backside.'

That's starflower, it will help with bringing out bruising more quickly, I advise Jonus. *Ask her if she knows which part of the plant will help.*

'Err, that's starflower, apparently. Do you know which part of the plant will be of help?' Jonus asks Priss.

'Of course I know, it's the petals. What I don't know yet, is whether you eat them, make tea with them, or grind them with water into a paste and smear them onto the bruising.'

'And how is it that you know exactly where Mettle and I are bruised?' Jonus says.

'As soon as I knew how to tune into plants, I knew how to tune into bodies, it's the same. You know, you could stop causing Mettle's back to bruise in the first place if you put some sort of padding between it and your seat bones. You've got no flesh on you, so they're pretty sharp and when you bounce around on him like that, it hurts him as well as you.'

Jonus flushes red. 'I hardly bounced around at all that time. Well, not as much as the time before, anyway, but okay, point taken, er, thanks, Priss.'

He notices that she looks different. She and her ragged clothes are now clean and she has cut off the matted bulk of her red hair, leaving the short length that remains to stick up in all directions. She has wrapped a clean piece of flowered fabric around her head and tied it at her forehead.

'Umm, why did you cut off your hair?' Jonus asks her.

Priss glares at him. 'Because it was a mess. I was a mess.' She looks around at the other villagers. 'We arrived here so happy and so optimistic for the future, and then we got lost in all the hunger, tiredness and frustration and we forgot who we were, me more than most. When I dreamt last night that I could tune into plants and find out what they cure, and then woke up to find it was true, I remembered who I used to be. I know I've been a right bloody nightmare and I'm sorry, okay?'

Trix bursts out of the crowd and hugs her sister. 'I'm so glad to have you back, Priss. And you can really do it? You can feel the energy of plants, the way I can with rocks?'

Priss nods, smiling. 'It'll take time to find which plants cure what, but I know how to go about it. It feels like I've always known and just needed reminding, and that's all thanks to Mettle.'

She pulls back from her sister and turns to where the tall, dappled stallion stands with Jonus. She lifts a trembling hand up slowly towards his face and then flinches and steps back when he clears his nostrils.

Jonus chuckles. 'You're fine. Hold your hand out to him again and let him sniff you.'

Priss follows Jonus's suggestion and a faint smile curls her lips as Mettle touches her hand with his muzzle and breathes in her scent, his dark eyes soft and reassuring. Priss's smile widens as Mettle takes a step closer and sniffs her face and then her hairband. She reaches a hand up and strokes his neck. I feel how much emotion she keeps in check so as not to embarrass herself in front of her friends as she says, 'Thank you, Mettle.'

Jonus grins. 'Mettle says that gratitude is not necessary. The herbs you carry are, however, and he would like a preparation of them for his back when you have honed your new skill sufficiently that you understand their use. I think he'd like them sooner rather than later, if you can manage it.'

Priss steps back from Mettle. 'Well, of course. His bruising isn't going to go away while I stand here chatting, is it? My instinct is to grind the petals into a paste, so I'll try that first. I'll be back very soon to apply the paste and see if it helps. That is, err, I'll apply Mettle's, not yours, Jonus, you can put yours on your thighs and, er, backside yourself.' She blushes furiously and hastens off towards her shelter.

A man with grey hair tied back in a tail steps forward from the crowd and takes great care to look at Jonus and Mettle in equal proportion as he says, 'I'm sorry I ever doubted you both. Thanks to you, we have the means to build proper homes, we have a healer and we have a plentiful supply of fish. We need other foods too, though. Do you have words that can remind any of us how to hunt and grow food better than we've managed to so far?'

Jonus looks to the ground and frowns slightly as he memorises Mettle's response. Then he turns his attention back to the villagers. 'First of all, Mettle says that the words he has given you so far, and those he will give you now, can remind ALL of you of the skills you have forgotten, not just some of you. Second of all, he says that the skills are all the same. If you can tune into plants to see what they will heal, you can know which of them will be appropriate for food and clothing, and you can influence them to grow. If you can tune into and influence rocks then you can also influence soil, sand and metal. You can move what you need, make what you need and grow what you need. Those are the words you need. You will remember.'

The villagers are silent for a few moments after Jonus finishes speaking and then they begin to chatter excitedly.

'So, we'll be able to identify more plants that we can eat without fear of being poisoned, and we'll be able to influence them to grow?'

'If we can influence sand, we can make glass. We could have windows, and proper food containers and...'

'If we can move soil, we wouldn't have to dig anymore, think how much quicker we could plant and harvest the crops we already know about, and Mettle's saying we'll remember more of them.'

'If we can influence metal, we can make knives out of those old gates we found, and axe heads and spear heads and arrow heads...'

'We'll be able to make clothing from plants?'

As I listen to the voices, I know their futures. I know that each will remember the particular skill on which they are choosing to focus, and Mettle's counsel that the skills are the same and can be remembered by everyone, will be forgotten. It doesn't matter. The first catalyst introduced the message. The second catalyst will drive it home.

Jonus and Mettle leave the villagers to chatter about what it will mean when they can do as Mettle has said they will be able to.

By the time they're well and truly making use of Mettle's words, you'll be riding as if you were born to it, I tell Jonus. *Then it'll just be influencing the weather and hunting they'll need your help with, and your work here will be done. You and Mettle can be off to work your way around the other communities. Some of them are in an even worse state than this one was, some are doing better, but they all need you.*

And you, he replies.

They don't need me. You and Mettle are a force to be reckoned with on your own. Don't forget, I know that because you've already succeeded.

Mettle is more to me than I ever dreamt anyone could be and I don't doubt that with him teaching me, I can live up to being who you say I'll be. That doesn't mean I don't need you too, though, Will. This is too big for me to take on without your help. I want you to leave part of yourself with me, as you offered to. I need you to teach me more about caring for Mettle and when the time comes, you can help me to help the other Horse-Bonded. But aside from any of that, I want you to be my friend. I need you to be there for me as I'll be for you, although I know you don't need me, with you being superhuman and all.

I'm very normal, believe me. I breathe, eat, drink, feel, all the same as you and believe me, Jonus, I value your friendship every bit as much as you value mine. I'll leave the tiniest part of myself with you but it'll be enough that you can just think your thoughts to me and I'll reply. And if you feel a little nudge to your mind that doesn't feel like Mettle, it'll be me asking to talk to you. If we're not communicating, then my attention will be elsewhere so you'll have as much privacy as you've always had.

Thanks, Will. Amarilla and Infinity, this will be the last time you're here with me?

Yes, this is the last time. We're glad to have shared this time with you, Jonus. Without you and Mettle and everything you have done and will do, we would never have been who we are. Thank you.

Jonus sighs. *I'm still struggling with all that, I mean, I know Mettle told me that time isn't linear, but...*

Jonus, are you sure about this? I interrupt, *I'm warning you, there'll be tears.*

...but it still feels very like a circle to me, he continues. *I pave the way for what you will do, Amarilla, and then you pave the way for what I will do in order to pave the way for you.*

If it were a circle then you and Mettle would be positioned at a different location around it from us. And yet here we all are, together. All events occur simultaneously. All time is now, Amarilla tells him.

I don't understand.

Yes, you do. There is a glimmer of understanding within you that will expand if you so allow. But you will not.

I won't? Why not?

Because if you allow yourself to accept that time is not as you thought it was, then you will be forced to question whether everything else is as you think it is and that is not something for which you are ready. Do not concern yourself, your reaction is part of the human condition and perfectly normal.

The human condition? You make it sound like an illness.

Not an illness so much as an imbalance.

Oh. Jonus frowns to himself.

Frowning is how it starts. When you're several hours in and no closer to being able either to grasp or let go of the conversation you've just had, the tears will come, I tell him. *I know, I've been there. It does help one not to miss them when they're gone.*

Jonus chuckles. *I'll miss them anyway. Amarilla, Infinity, thank you for all your help, whether I understand what you did, how you did it, even when you did it, or not.*

Goodbye, Jonus. Amarilla and Infinity withdraw from the past, leaving me behind.

I'd better take the greater part of myself off too, I have a lot to be getting on with, I tell him.

Did you learn everything you needed to from being here?

I did. And more than I was originally led to believe I would learn, actually.

Amarilla deceived you? Jonus asks.

She put me in a position to realise for myself what I needed to learn. Enjoy this time with your friends, Jonus, you all deserve it.

Bye, Will.

I'm glad to have a continuing link with Jonus, giving me constant Awareness of his experiences. I'm glad of his friendship and I'm glad it was from him that I learnt the best way for people to accept help from horses is to be exposed to the horses' energy until they realise it for themselves.

It's time to take the horses to Goldenglade.

TWENTY-SEVEN

Amarilla

I return my attention to the present to hear Vickery and Marvel clapping, Justin, Rowena and Holly cheering, and Maverick barking enthusiastically. Will sits up only moments after I do and then is flattened back down by a thoroughly over-excited Maverick.

'Maverick, come here,' Justin calls, laughing. He doesn't repeat his request when the dog ignores him.

When Vickery finally tempts Maverick away with a piece of meat so that Will can sit back up, he says, 'Job done.'

'Job done?' Vickery says. 'The three catalysts connect through time and confirm the course of history, and all you can say is, "job done"? By the wind of autumn, Will, that has to be the understatement of the century, it was flaming well miracle accomplished.'

We all laugh and then Will says, 'So, are you all ready to ride again?'

'Err, ride?' Rowena says and reflexively rubs her back.

'Yep, we have a herd of horses waiting to travel with us to

Goldenglade. We saw signs of wild cats on the way here, and a herd of horses is going to attract their attention far more readily than we did, not to mention the fact that we know there are packs of wild dogs roaming nearer to Goldenglade itself. There are times when the horses are going to need to move at speed, and it'll be far easier if we can go with them. They know we all have perfect balance and won't compromise them, it's the obvious way to go and they're expecting it. They're ready when we are.'

The rest of us sit in silence, considering. I surprise myself as I realise that the thought of riding a horse other than Infinity doesn't present me with a problem. Then I remember Will's counsel before our last experience of the past. Putting the reality of my situation into words in the way he did, with the timing he chose, has resulted in my complete acceptance now that I suffered no loss when Infinity departed her body. I knew that would be the case before her departure, but the human part of me, the anchor that holds me in the dream, has needed time, support and strength from my human partner and friends, and, finally, the help of one who is integrating what it is to be horse into what it is to be human, before I have finally been able to fully accept the truth.

I don't try to hide my thoughts and feelings from those who have helped me to get here. They are all watching me and smiling with heartfelt happiness that, at last, I have the same relationship with Infinity here in the dream as that when she and I fly the oneness together whilst my body sleeps. As Will told me, I don't need a mirror to see in my eyes what I know they see.

'Thank you, all of you, for being there for me. Again.' I grin at them and hug Justin back as he draws me to him.

Rowena comes over from her place across the fire and kisses me on the cheek. 'It's just what we do, Am.' She winks at me and then returns to her place by Marvel's side.

'So, Will, when do we ride?' I ask him.

'We'll move on from here on foot in the morning. Not too far, we'll stop when we reach fresh pasture for the horses. We'll set up camp and catch up on sleep and rest while the horses graze as much as they need to and then, when they're ready, probably after a few days, we'll pack what we can carry on our backs and ride for Goldenglade.'

We all nod, and even Rowena accepts Will's instructions without question or complaint. Will notices the same peculiarity and raises his eyebrows before continuing, 'We'll be limited by how far the horses can travel in one go now that they have a young foal with them, but he's stronger than most and he's drawn to the imbalance at Goldenglade, so he'll be wanting to be on the move as much as his body will let him.' He pauses and then says, 'He's as eager to help as he ever was.'

Holly is the first to understand. She gasps and then Marvel lets out a low whistle.

'Flaming lanterns, Candour? It's really him?' Rowena says. 'But why has he come back? Oh, I see how his experience with you will help. Does your Dad know, Will? No, he doesn't and it would be hard for him if he did. Thunder and lightning, not hard, excruciating. What does this mean? Are they all coming back? No, they don't...'

'Ro, much as your conversations with your Awareness are amusing when they're about normal stuff, this isn't really the time,' Marvel says.

I'm Aware that everyone except for Will and me yearns for their Bond-Partner to reincarnate as Candour has done. At the same time, though, everyone understands, whether they want to or not, why it is Candour's energy alone of the bonded horses that is needed here. It was his energy that grounded the young wild-child that was Will. Able to remain completely unaffected by the little boy's screams and tantrums, he allowed his calm sense of balance to reassure the sensitive soul within Will, to allow it to express itself through the raging strength of his personality. Once he is close enough to the youngsters of Goldenglade, in his foal's body – the most endearing and least imposing he could possibly be – his energy and experience will allow him to cope with drawing them within the range of influence of the rest of the herd. The perfection of the dream as it strives towards balance strikes me, as it so often has before.

'This won't be easy for your Dad, Will,' Vickery observes. 'Not only is Candour back, but he's here with us and...'

'Dad will understand. Candour is as available to him as ever. Nothing has changed except that now he is also incarnate and helping me. He won't go back to being a bonded horse again, he has no need and neither does Dad.'

'I think Jack might disagree with that,' Vickery murmurs.

'He might to begin with, but any disagreement on his part would be based on emotional want rather than actual need,' Will says. 'As would disagreement from any of you,' he adds quietly, respectfully, but firmly.

No one can argue with him and not only because they all know he is right. He's giving the exact advice that their Bond-Partners would give them if they were here, in exactly the same way that they would give it; he speaks the truth with absolute confidence, lots of love and a total lack of concern for the outcome. I feel the emotion that had risen in the group begin to dissipate and they all manage to smile.

'One day, we'll look back on this and feel honoured that we were counselled by you as you were in the process of becoming a phenomenon, but at the moment, it feels a bit like swallowing a worming preparation,' Marvel grins ruefully. 'I'm out of practice at being counselled by someone so much wiser than me – Rowena's contribution to the appropriate living of my life not withstanding – and while it's welcome as an echo of being pulled up constantly by Broad, it's strange being told how to feel by a fresh-faced young lad, even knowing that I'll be taking your advice, Will.'

'And so say all of us,' says Vickery. 'It was galling when it was Amarilla who was always so far ahead of us, and she was only ten years odd younger than most of us, but these flipping catalysts are getting younger.'

'Will's older than I was when we went off to find the Kindred, Vic,' I remind her. 'He just seems younger from the grand age that you're all looking down from. Not you, Ro,' I say and blow her a kiss.

Rowena laughs and says, 'My back would argue with you. And in a few days, I'm going to be riding a wild horse, I can't believe I'm going to be so stupid.'

'And you can't wait,' says Holly. 'Let's be honest, none of us can. It'll be weird not to be riding Serene, but lovely at the same time, I mean they're all one, Serene is part of them as much as she's part of me.'

'Trust you to see it that way, Holly,' Rowena says, a rare fondness in her voice. 'Okay, fine, I can't wait. We'd better all go to bed and get some sleep so that we've got the energy to pack up and go off hiking in the morning, hadn't we?'

By the time we exit our tents at dawn, the horses have gone. They know our intention for the day and their eagerness to find fresh grazing has taken them on ahead of us.

'That's good, they'll stop to graze as they go, so the foal will have lots of time to rest and feed from his mother. We'll catch up with them when they've chosen where they want to spend the next few days,' says Justin as we all gather around the campfire for our last breakfast at the camp that has been our home for the past weeks. 'Are we going to keep calling him "the foal", or do we call him "Candour"? Will?'

'Unlike the rest of the herd, his sense of individuality is strong enough that I don't think it will disturb him if we give him a name, but Candour isn't who he is now. That was the name my Dad chose for his Bond-Partner, and the only meaning it has is as the potential that Dad saw for himself at the time. When I saw those amber-coloured eyes glowing out of his black face, I knew how I would always think of him.'

'Ember,' I say. 'The spark who will guide the Drifters home.'

Will grins and nods. 'Ember.'

Marvel raises his mug of tea. 'To Ember. May he drink his fill from his mother's teat and grow strong.'

'I think I'd rather drink to the spark who will guide the Drifters home, but whatever, Marvel.' Justin gulps a mouthful of tea.

'I'm not sure I want to drink anything to anyone from these mugs, they really are disgusting now.' Holly wrinkles her nose as she inspects her battered, wooden mug.

'I packed them because they're light. You can drink from the teapot if you'd prefer,' Rowena says.

Holly holds up her hands. 'Sorry, Ro, I'm grateful to you for organising everything so that our stay here has been so easy, really I am. I guess I'm just looking forward to the comfort and, er, cleanliness of being back in civilisation.'

'Don't look forward to it too much, we're a way off it yet,' Will warns.

'Right, well we'd better get going then, hadn't we?' Justin says. 'The sooner we get to Goldenglade, the sooner the horses can help the Drifters and the sooner Holly will be able to drink out of a clean mug.'

There is a hasty scraping of spoons in bowls as we finish our porridge and then set about breaking camp.

It's mid-morning before we're ready to leave, and the heat of the day is building again. We reach out to the horses in our Awareness and are relieved to learn that, as Justin foresaw, they have moved slowly and aren't too far in front of us.

We have considerably less to drag on our litters than on our outward journey, since our food supplies have dwindled and we've whittled down our clothes, cooking and hunting equipment to that which we'll be able to carry once we are on horseback. Maverick no longer has need of space on Will's litter to rest, which is fortunate for Will, as the pup is almost twice the size and weight that he was.

I look around at our group as we set off. All of us are brown-skinned from the sun, and Will's, Holly's and Vickery's hair, blond before we started out, is now bleached almost white. The rest of us have golden streaks in our hair and, apart from Will, all look leaner and younger. Justin and Vickery have come out in freckles, which amuses the rest of us no end.

Will has converted the portable shelter that Justin made for him to use when he was trailing the horses, into a smaller one which he can hold above Maverick, providing him with shade as he trots happily at Will's side. We stop frequently for water breaks and Maverick is always delighted, convinced that we're stopping solely for him to refresh himself and then greet us in turn with licks while bouncing around on his hind legs. No matter how hot, tired and sweaty we are, he never fails to make us smile. He's grown into his long legs, but still has a gangly appearance. His ears now stand up into points but are still a bit big for his head, and his tongue lolls out of the side of his mouth as if he has no control of it. When he pants, he looks like he's laughing. We all love him dearly.

It's a relief when we finally see the horses in the distance. They've found a wide, flat valley that clearly holds water in its soil, since there are clumps of reeds everywhere. Where there is grass, it's unusually green and lush for the time of year.

'Fantastic, that grass will give Ember's mother loads of milk,' says Holly.

'And there's a stand of trees over there.' Marvel squints into the distance. 'They'll give us shade and firewood. Everyone okay to keep going until we reach them?'

Rowena lets out a long sigh but we all nod and carry on dragging our litters until we reach the shade of the trees. Maverick is overjoyed to find a very shallow but wide pool of water nearby, fed by an underground spring judging by the way the water is bubbling at the centre of it. He lands in it with a splash and a bark and then lies down and begins to lap the water.

'Nice one, Maverick, you go ahead and have a nice, cooling bath in what looks like our only source of clean water,' grumbles Vickery and then rolls her eyes and grins as he answers her with a cheerful bark.

'Personally, I think we should all follow his example.' Will leaps into the pool with his dog, lies down on his back and says, 'Ahhhhhhh!'

'WILL, SERIOUSLY?' Rowena shouts.

'We can clear this water out and it'll soon be replaced by fresh, I think Maverick and Will have the right of it,' says Marvel, and joins them.

Very soon, we're all lying on our backs in the water, enjoying its coolness while the sun continues to beat down on us all.

'We've sunk to an all-time low,' moans Rowena. 'Holly, I'm with you, I can't wait to get back to civilisation.'

'You'd honestly rather have a bath on your own in clean, scented water, than swill around in the mud with all of us? I mean, are you crazy?' Will laughs. 'And now the horses are planning on joining in. Moan all you like, Ro, but as far as I'm concerned, life just doesn't get any better than this.'

We all lift our heads up to see that some of the horses are indeed heading our way. We jump up and hastily splash the water out and away from the pool. It is quickly replaced by the fresh water bubbling up from the ground.

Ember's mother appears as the horses fan out to drink, and then the little foal himself emerges from just behind her. His foal coat is jet-black and as Will said, his eyes do appear to glow like embers. His ears, like his mother's, are fluted delicately at the tips and I can see two indentations in his neck, likely where his back feet rested when he was in the womb. He stands as if the whole world is his. As a foal, he's gorgeous and cute. As a stallion, he will be breathtaking.

He lowers his head down to the pool beside his mother's and watches her drink. He dips his little black nose into the water and then lifts his head and curls his upper lip, baring his toothless gums. We all chuckle quietly with delight. He eyes us all and we feel his recognition of who we were to him before, as well as who we are to him now. Then he decides that we are less interesting than his reawakening hunger and turns his attention back to his mother, who has turned to wander back to the rest of the herd. He gambols alongside her and as soon as she drops her head to graze, he begins to suckle.

'Am I the only one finding this a touch surreal?' Vickery says.

Her question is rhetorical, so none of us speak. Seeing the situation with Infinity as I do means that I have no trouble accepting it, and Will, despite having been the closest to Candour, has been able to understand and accept who Ember is from the moment he first saw him. Everyone else becomes consumed with reconciling the fact that the adorable baby Ember is the same soul who incarnated as Candour, the powerful grey stallion whom we all knew so well – and yet the two horses, whose bodies have different heritages and whose lives have different intentions, are not the same at all.

When Rowena gets there, she says, 'When I first realised that Candour was back, I wished with all of my heart that it was my Bond-Partner who had returned. Now, I'm glad that it isn't. I'm not sure I could cope with him being here yet not as I knew him, even though I know we've incarnated together before and we were both different then. There's just something inside me that I can't let go of, but that I would need to, to make that okay.'

'It's your humanity,' I tell her. 'Don't be letting go of it, else you'll fade away and then where would we all be?'

'Allowed to drink ale in peace?' Marvel says.

'Able to travel without the paraphernalia of the elderly?' Will grins cheekily.

'That's just earned you two the job of putting the tents up and making the beds, unless you'd prefer to sleep outside with these… horrid… little… biters eating you alive?' Rowena swipes at several of the flies that are beginning to swarm, and then continues, 'No? I thought not. Set to it, then, and the rest of us can focus our efforts on getting a particularly smoky fire going. That should repel the little monsters.'

It isn't only because more of the biters are descending on us that we leap to follow her instructions, but out of ingrained habit, I realise with a smile to myself.

By the time the sun is setting, we're sitting as close as we can bear to a campfire that is every bit as smoky as Rowena planned. It's hard to decide which is easier to tolerate – coughing from smoke inhalation, or stinging and itching as a result of the biters.

Maverick isn't affected by them at all and amuses himself by watching a selected biter and then snapping at it when it's close enough. He has us laughing every time his eyes cross as he tries to watch the biters that approach the end of his nose.

'We're going to need to keep the fire going so that the biters don't swarm here, and that means tending it in shifts through the night,' Vickery says. 'Tomorrow, I'll see if I can find any nightreed to make a repellent against the little pests, there should be some about.'

I nod. 'Good idea, I'll help you. As long as we dilute the sap enough, it'll repel the biters without making us blister.'

Everyone nods their agreement except Will, who has a momentary faraway look in his eyes. Then he's back with us. 'Sorry, I was listening, Jonus just wanted to ask me something.'

'And you ended up spending the day with him in, what, a few of our seconds?' Justin says.

'Yep, pretty much.'

There's silence as we witness Will's most recent experience in the past, and then Vickery says, 'Wow, Trix and Tomlin have finished the first house of The New!'

'And the community voted that Priss should have it, so she has somewhere decent to store all of her herb samples and to work. She's really pushing on with it,' Will says with a smile. 'And the Glass-Singers have got a move on too, they've nailed not just making glass from sand, but singing it into window panes for the house.'

'And now that the Earth-Singers and Tree-Singers have gone to work, they'll have fresh crops planted and growing in no time,' observes Holly. 'And the Metal-Singers have made new cutlery, tool heads and hunting gear from all the old farming gear they found lying around. Wow, it's all coming together for them, isn't it?'

Will nods. 'It is, thanks to Mettle.'

We all look over to where the horses are either grooming one another, grazing, or resting nose to tail, flicking biters away from each other.

'And here they are again. The bonded horses did everything they agreed, and yet there are still horses ready to step in and help us when we need them to,' says Rowena.

'There always will be, it's who they are and what they do,' Will says. 'How lucky are we that the situation this time calls for us to ride them, though?'

We all smile.

'I know which one is willing to carry me,' says Rowena.

'The stallion of the herd,' agrees Justin. 'They'll follow the pattern in their collective consciousness from when you guys rode the wild horses before. I wondered if Infinity's presence with Am would change anything, but apparently not. The lead mare will take her, the mare with the six-month-old foal at foot will choose Holly and one of the colts will choose Marvel. The other two colts are likely to take Vic and me, and it'll be the grey mare for Will.'

Will nods. 'She chose me as a grooming partner from the beginning and she knows that Maverick and I'll help them to take care of the little guy; she's full sister to his mother, and she's always with them.'

I pick up the vaguest sense in my Awareness that there is more to Will's "taking care of the little guy" than his casual mention of it suggests; there's a pattern present in his energy that I recognise from my own experience of burying what I've seen in the future. He's seen something and buried it so deeply that none of us have a hope of finding it. He learnt how to do that from me. I smile at the turning of the tables and then I stifle a gasp as I too catch a glimpse of what has to be the incident that he has already seen. Immediately, I bury what I saw.

Will gives the slightest of nods in my direction and then turns his attention to Vickery, who is saying, 'I can't help it, I'm still finding it weird. I mean, Ember's so little and helpless, and he was so strong and sure of himself when we knew him before... I know, I know, I'm well Aware of how it is, it's just that my brain is still arguing that it can't possibly be.'

'Sleep on it,' advises Marvel, yawning, 'that's what I'm going to do, starting right now. I'll take the last shift and then I'll be off hunting straight afterwards at dawn. Whoever takes the shift before me has my permission to slap my face if that's what it takes to wake me up, because it probably will. Goodnight, all.' He stands and then dashes to his tent, hastily tying the flaps tightly shut against the biters that try to follow him in.

'I'll take the first shift tending the fire,' I say, looking around at my tired friends. When Rowena and Justin go to object, I interrupt them with, 'No arguing.'

Justin kisses me on the forehead and then sprints to our tent, and Rowena hugs me and then hurries to hers, cursing and slapping at her arms and legs as she struggles to unknot the ties on the door flaps that Marvel tied in such a hurry.

'Goodnight, Am,' Holly says as she hugs me. Then she whispers, 'I'm so happy for you, now that you're finally at peace with everything.'

'I love that Holly whispers louder than she speaks,' Vickery whispers loudly as she hugs me in turn. She stands up and says, 'Seriously though, Am, good on you. It was hard enough for the rest of us when our horses moved on, and we could still communicate with them in the same way we always had. What you and Infinity have done, merging your essences so that you could do everything you've done – that was so much harder. I mean, we all know how happy Adam and Peace are existing that way, but they're both in the oneness. Infinity is mostly there and you're mostly here, with all the grief you've had to wade through as a result of being human interrupting your acceptance that everything has changed for you. It was excruciating to watch, let alone to experience, but you've done it. I'm in awe of the two of you and I love you.' She turns and runs after Holly for their tent.

'We love you too, Vic,' I call softly after her. 'We love you all.'

TWENTY-EIGHT

Will

We have spent two long days in the swamp, as we've taken to calling it. Thankfully, the biter repellent that Amarilla and Vickery prepared has been effective, but it only lasts for a few hours at a time and we're immediately very miserably aware the second it needs reapplying. Thank goodness the horses are ready to move on.

Rowena divides our stuff between us and we pack our back-sacks, strap them onto our backs, and wait. One by one, the horses who will carry us leave the herd and make their way over to us.

The black lead mare walks purposefully towards Amarilla and then stands patiently while Justin gives Amarilla a leg up onto her back. Even with a back-sack on, Amarilla is instantly in perfect balance with the mare. I feel her delight at the mare's immediate acceptance of her as a rider and of Infinity's presence, as if being ridden by a human who shares her being with a horse is as normal to the mare as is being ridden in the first place.

The big, rangy black stallion of the herd approaches Rowena, sniffs her briefly and then also stands patiently while Rowena is given a leg up onto his back by Marvel. We all smile at the broad grin that spreads across Rowena's face. She draws Oak to her, wanting to include him even though she knows that for him at least, it isn't necessary. He brushes her mind and then fades away again.

As predicted, it is the three eldest colts of the herd who approach Justin, Marvel and Vickery. I watch Marvel help Vickery onto her mount and then I heave him and Justin onto theirs.

It's a long time since I've seen anyone except Amarilla ride, and as I stand back for a moment, I remember why the Horse-Bonded are so revered. Their achievements alone are impressive, but the sight of them on horseback is even more so. They change so effortlessly from being humans standing on their own two feet, to being at one with the horses they ride, a fact that strikes me even more as I compare it with my recent witnessing of Jonus riding Mettle. I appreciate all over again how much the horses have been willing to tolerate and how far they have brought us.

I feel a nudge at my back but am prevented from turning around to see what's happening. I manage to turn my head and see that Ember is there; he's grabbed my back-sack in his mouth and is pulling on it. His mother lunges towards it, showing the whites of her eyes, her ears flat back. I turn quickly away from both her and her foal, slip out of the straps of the back-sack, lower it to the ground and walk away, calling for a frantically barking Maverick to come with me. I feel the mare's maternal panic subside and she sniffs the back-sack at which her mischievous foal is still trying to pull, although he's losing grip as his gums begin to slide on the material made wet by his own saliva.

Everyone roars with laughter and I can't help joining in, despite the fact that my back-sack is now sitting in a patch of mud and Ember is beginning to paw at it. Happily for me, his mother chooses that moment to nudge him away from the offending item.

When I can feel that she's moved her foal to what she considers a safe distance away, I hoist it onto my back, reassure Maverick with a quick stroke of his head and then wait for the grey mare to approach me, which she does immediately. I vault onto her back, my present height making it so much easier than when I used to mount Candour as a boy, despite the weight on my back. As soon as I am astride the mare, I feel the same elation as my friends. Being one with the horses in my Awareness is one thing. Being physically at one with a horse is another entirely, and an experience I have missed.

The grey mare sidesteps as Maverick barks up at me anxiously. I wrap him in a net of energy to soothe him and he whines, sits down and puts his head to one side.

'Are you ready to run?' I ask him, knowing he'll recognise the words I always use before he and I run together.

He barks excitedly and gets to his feet just as the horses begin to move.

We all realise immediately that this is nothing like our previous experience of riding horses. All of those any of us have ridden before were either bonded horses or wild horses needing help – either way, they were receptive to our suggestions. These horses carry us out of necessity. They are drawn, through me, to the imbalance of Goldenglade, so they know where they are going. We are riding them purely in order to be able to travel at their pace and they have no need for any contribution from us; we are merely passengers. And it feels right. I look around at my friends and see that they're all smiling.

The lead mare sets off in the direction of Goldenglade at a canter and as the other horses follow, I find myself at the edge of the herd, about halfway back, with Maverick racing along on my outside. The colts carrying Marvel, Vickery and Justin are just ahead of me, and to my right there is a grey filly. On her other side is Ember's mother, who glances over at my back-sack every now and then with suspicion and makes sure to keep Ember on her other side. Rowena brings up the rear on the stallion.

The horses canter up the gentle slope that takes us away from the swamp, across some grassland and into a forest. Here, they slow to a walk as they negotiate the trees, nibbling at the leaves of low branches as they pass underneath.

When we reach the grassland on the other side, the horses pick up a canter again. I glance across to see that Ember is keeping pace with us. His long legs don't have much weight to carry, but he is so young and I feel him tiring. Then I feel the energy of the herd shifting in his direction. They know how much they can support him so that he keeps going and strengthens his muscles, they know when they need to slow the pace for him or for the older mares, and they know when they need to stop so that he can rest. I am glad not only for Ember, but for Maverick, who, much as he loves to run, is vulnerable to the heat and lacks the strength and endurance of a mature dog.

We spend the day closely attuned to the herd, so that we're ready to dismount when they need us to leave them to graze and rest in peace, ready to remount when they're ready to move on, and prepared for changes in gait and direction. They rest when they need to, graze and drink when the conditions present themselves, and then move on if the circumstances are favourable. As we become used to the rhythms of the herd, we realise that the horses are likely to continue throughout the night.

'Good job we didn't bother bringing the tents,' Marvel says as we stagger away from the horses. 'By the time we'd put them up, we'd be needing to take them down again to move on.'

'I like travelling this way, the rhythm of it feels comfortable,' says Vickery and we all nod our agreement.

'Unlike my back, which is anything but,' moans Rowena. 'It's one thing being able to slot straight back into riding in perfect balance, but another entirely to have the strength and suppleness for it not to hurt, especially carrying a back-sack.'

'Well, at least travelling during the night means we won't have time to stiffen up as much as if we slept straight through. We're going to have to get into the habit of sleeping and eating when the horses do, though, otherwise we'll never have time for either,' says Holly.

'Vic and I are going to need to hunt too,' says Marvel. 'Although judging by the amount of wild cat spoor I've spotted today, we have a fair amount of competition.'

'They've kept their distance from us though, so there must be plenty of easier prey about,' says Vickery. 'Will? Am? You two are quiet.'

Amarilla blinks and says, 'Sorry, just tired. Are you sure you need to hunt? I mean we have food with us and with the speed we're travelling, we'll be back at Goldenglade in no time. The horses are carrying us in case we have to move quickly, and if you go off hunting, you might not have time to get back here if they want to leave in a hurry. Do you think you should leave the hunting for now and see how we go?'

'Good point,' says Rowena. 'Let's see how we get on, then.'

I've been on the receiving end of Amarilla's dissembling enough times that I would have recognised she's doing it now, even if I hadn't expected it and known the reason why. She's skilled enough at it that she gives the others no reason not to take her at face value though, except for Justin. He doesn't know why she's doing it, but he trusts her, so barely a second passes before he changes the subject. 'Right then, let's eat now, and then grab some sleep, although at least one of us will need to be awake at all times to pick up on when the horses are preparing to move on, so we don't hold them up. Am, we'll take first watch, shall we?'

'Sure.'

I grin to myself. Justin will ask my aunt what she's up to, but she won't tell him. She's seen a glimpse of the future because she and Infinity have a part to play, but she knows that if the information were given more attention than the two briefest of flickers she and I both gave it when we saw what's coming, it would disturb the horses. Events just need to be left to play out without the distraction of prior warning.

We move on twice during the night, both times only at a walk, but for several hours each time. When dawn breaks, Holly wakes the rest of us from our exhausted sleep to warn us that a female wild cat and her two cubs are nearby and they have sensed the horses. Amarilla shoots a quick glance in my direction but says nothing as everyone reaches out in their Awareness for details of the threat to the herd.

The two cubs are mature and approaching the point where they will leave their mother. She wants to show them how to hunt larger prey than they've brought down before. They are nearby and slowly getting closer.

The horses begin to whinny nervously. They stretch their necks up high, breathing in the early morning scents, their ears flickering wildly and their eyes wide. Some of them begin to shift around in readiness for flight.

'Get your back-sacks on and hurry, we need to mount before they bolt,' says Amarilla.

I upend my back-sack, shake it until it's empty, and then join everyone else in racing over to the herd, with Maverick running uncertainly by my side.

Amarilla's and my confidence that our friends will do what is needed without prior warning is proven justified as together, we all send light to the herd. A bright, white haze settles over the horses, warning them of our approach and keeping them just calm enough that they don't react to us in the way that they are preparing to react to the approaching wild cats.

When we are close to the herd, I hold my back-sack open and signal for Maverick to jump in, as I used to when carrying him in his sling. He jumps in without hesitation and I enclose him in a net of reassuring energy as I pull the draw string closed so that only his head is sticking out. I hoist him onto my back and he licks the back of my neck. I feel the trust and confidence he has in me. I can do this.

The grey mare is wild-eyed when I get to her, and only just short of bolting. I don't want to risk disabling her flight response by calming her down much more than the light of our group already has, but I need her to allow me to mount. I increase my light flow towards her just long enough for her to acknowledge my presence and stand still. I rub her neck and then vault onto her back, releasing my light flow completely the second I am in place, so that she's free to react according to her instincts.

I increase the strength of my energy net around Maverick so that he's heavily cocooned in a feeling of safety, even as the grey mare spins beneath us both. He licks the back of my neck again, but is otherwise still and calm.

I look around to see that all in our group are mounted. Amarilla is effortlessly absorbing the lead mare's rapid changes in speed and direction while the mare tries to decide where and when to flee. My aunt feels my attention.

You can do what is needed. To be human is to have a sense of self, she and Infinity advise me and then, all of a sudden, the lead mare leaps into a gallop. Ember and his mother spin and go after her as she tears past them and the rest of our horses follow suit. I find myself near the back of the herd, with Rowena and the stallion.

I feel the cats approaching stealthily from off to one side. The lead mare also knows exactly where they are now, and has chosen a path at right angles to that of the predators. Travelling at our current speed, we should pass the point where the two pathways meet before the cats get there, and then there is grassland for as far as the eye can see, giving the horses, who are able to move at top speed with far greater endurance than the cats, the best chance of escape. The lead mare knows what to do for the benefit of her herd as a whole, even if it leaves the weakest member vulnerable.

Ember is falling back rapidly through the herd. His mother shrieks for him to keep up but her own terror prevents her from slowing to his pace. Soon, he is alongside my grey mare and tiring at an ever-increasing rate. The herd energy is of necessity spread evenly between its members, with none available to boost him. He tries to call for his mother but his cry is cut short by his lack of breath. His eyes are wide with terror and his fluffy foal coat is streaked with sweat. My heart goes out to him but he'll be okay, Maverick and I are here. Just as Ember looked after me when he was Candour and I was a small child, so I will look after him now that he is Ember and I am who I am. But I can't help yet. The rest of the herd cannot witness what I will do.

I look behind me to see that there is only the stallion behind Ember now and he is screaming at him every bit as loudly as Rowena is, and weaving from side to side behind the foal, trying to keep him from falling out of the herd. Then the three wild cats burst from their low, slow advance through the cover of the grass to the side of us, into an all-out sprint. I feel the grey mare's pace pick up even more, but the wild cats aren't focused on her. They fan out behind Ember as the stallion finally overtakes him. Rowena looks back at him and then across at me in panic from the stallion's back.

'DON'T WORRY, I'VE GOT THIS. JUST KEEP GOING,' I shout to her.

She senses my confidence and frowns uncertainly. Then she nods.

As the grey mare feels the wild cats' attention shift from the herd to its weakest member, she experiences a brief moment of relief. I seize it and resist her forward movement ever so slightly. She slows enough for me to vault from her back and land, with a yelp from Maverick, on my feet and hands, before she continues her flight.

The rest of the horses are safe and Amarilla will make sure they stay that way. She won't influence the lead mare unnecessarily, but she'll encourage her to keep going until I've done what I need to do.

Ember is exhausted and trotting on wobbly legs to the left and then the right as the wild cats harry him. Now that he is their sole target, I can step in. Infinity and I act in concert. Ember recognises her essence as she infuses him, and in his exhaustion, he welcomes her influence. She moves him behind me and then keeps him still, confusing the cats' chase instinct. I wave my arms around until the cats shift their focus to me. I make sure that Maverick is still safely cocooned within the energy net I wove around him and then I allow my sense of him to be all of me. Instantly, I am the collective consciousness of the dogs.

We have an innate willingness to accept those unlike ourselves and to love them unconditionally. We were confused and afraid when so many of us were thrown out of human cities, deprived of our families and left to fend for ourselves. We have a strong pattern of loyalty to humans, a desire to provide them with calm and comfort, and now that it has been reignited by Maverick and his siblings, more of us will gravitate back towards human civilisation. We have a deeply ingrained pattern for protecting those we love.

I feel a momentary hesitation as I wonder whether I will forget who I am. Then I feel Ember's panic, only just held in check by Infinity. I will protect him. I remember the words Am and Fin placed in my mind. *To be human is to have a sense of self.* I can do this. I can be the dogs while being me. I am Will.

The cats have lowered themselves to the ground and are stalking me, confused by my lack of motion. Now, they stop dead in their tracks and flatten their ears, hissing with terror as I allow the full force of what it is to be dog, to erupt out of me.

TWENTY-NINE

Amarilla

I see out of Ember's eyes as Infinity and I continue to hold him still. We infuse him with reassurance that he is safe and his little heart gradually calms its beating. He'll be fine. Will is with him and about to become all that he can be.

Just as sharing my physical existence with Infinity has meant that her eyes look out of mine, so Will sharing his physical existence with the collective consciousness of the dogs, allows them all to look out of his eyes. A multitude of brown, blue and yellow eyes glower out of Will's blue ones with a blazing fury at those who would threaten a member of their pack. And it isn't just the eyes. Will's mouth appears to contort into countless fanged muzzles that snarl the lengths to which they will all go to protect one of their own.

It's like having double vision. I can still see Will standing there, calm and expressionless, but I also see the dogs as their collective consciousness explodes visibly out of him.

The cats turn tail and run back the way they came. They won't stop running until exhaustion forces them to and they won't visit that location, ever again. They will have to rest and recover from their experience before hunting elsewhere – but everything happens as it should.

As soon as the threat to Ember is over, Will focuses on his sense of self to the exclusion of all else, and his physical appearance returns to normal. Infinity and I cease our influence over Ember but continue to reassure him with our presence.

I'll suggest to the lead mare that we pull up now, I tell Will and feel his assent.

I hold the idea in my mind that the danger to the herd is over and I resist the lead mare's movement by pulling back slightly with my thighs. Her adrenaline would have kept her running longer but there is no need for her or the rest of the herd to tire themselves further, or to increase the distance between Ember and his mother. My friends feel the change in situation as soon as I do, and reinforce my suggestion to the lead mare by asking the same of their mounts. We all direct strong flows of light to the herd, to help them to calm as they slow and then come to a halt as one. We all dismount immediately and move away, so that they can come back completely to themselves in their own time.

'By the wind of autumn, what just happened?' Vickery says breathlessly.

I turn around and grin. 'Will was being awesome again.'

My friends, all having been too busy reacting to the situation to follow in their Awareness exactly what was happening, now witness what Infinity and I saw through Ember.

'Flaming lanterns, Will was one with the dogs physically as well as in his Awareness,' says Justin.

Holly nods thoughtfully. 'It was like all the dogs who have ever been just radiated right out of him. Poor Ember, he must have been terrified... oh I see, Infinity had him, well you and Infinity had him, Am, oh it's so confusing. You and Infinity are where she is as well as where you are, and now Will can do whatever it is that he just did, what does it all mean?'

It means that We Who Are Infinity and He Who Is no longer need the boundaries that human minds have needed up until now to feel secure. We Who Are Infinity share our being with one another and express such in our eyes. He Who Is can share his being with any other and express them physically in whichever way he chooses.

'That's insane,' moans Marvel out loud.

It is a concept that is new to you. That does not render it insane. You believe that there are physical and mental boundaries. While dispensing with the boundaries will not necessarily improve the human experience, it will be helpful if they are more widely recognised for what they are. They are merely ideas in which you need to believe so that you can feel secure in your identity whilst you are here. Yet to be human is to have a sense of self. He Who Is has proven that relaxing belief in the physical and mental boundaries has no effect upon his sense of who he has chosen to be in this lifetime. As such he has laid the template in the human collective consciousness for Awareness of the fact that there is nothing that can diminish the human sense of self within the dream.

Everyone stares at me thoughtfully. Then Holly's eyes widen. 'The barriers that the Drifters have erected in their minds to make sure they don't lose their sense of individuality are just a magnification of the boundaries we all believe in to keep us safe in our knowledge of who we are, aren't they?'

Justin nods excitedly. 'If the Drifters calm down enough for Will to show them that his sense of identity stays intact even when he lowers his physical boundaries and visibly becomes someone else, then they might just trust that they won't lose their individuality by lowering the mental barriers to merely being Aware,' he says.

'Or they could freak out and cross the final stretch of the bridge to insanity,' says Vickery. 'But then, I'm guessing the plan is for the horses to get them to a place where that won't happen?'

'Not the plan. The inevitability,' I say.

'Flaming lanterns, Am, I get that you're settling into the whole sharing-your-being-with-Infinity thing now, but just so you know, it's easier when we only hear her in your thoughts; when she comes out of your mouth, it's unsettling,' says Rowena.

I shrug my shoulders and smile, and Rowena can't stop herself smiling back at the happiness she feels bursting out of me.

Marvel is still deep in thought. 'It had to be Will, didn't it? He's the only one open enough to be someone else completely, and strong enough to know he wouldn't lose his sense of himself in the process.'

I still needed help. It turns out that even my will has a limit – I know, who'd have thought it? Will's amusement accompanies his thoughts. Then he is more serious. *If it hadn't been for Maverick's confidence in me, advice from Am and Fin, and then having Ember to protect, there's a chance I might have bottled it.*

'Advice from Am and Fin,' Rowena repeats and then turns to me. 'You knew it was going to happen. That explains a lot.'

'You didn't tell us because the horses would have picked up on it,' says Vickery, nodding. 'But would that have been such a bad thing? I mean, they would have bolted there and then, but it would have saved Ember from having to go through all that.'

'Will needed to be in a situation intense enough for him to risk pushing the boundaries. The horses are bringers of balance and Ember ensured that Will can accept or ignore his physical boundaries at will, which, as you've seen, will help the Drifters closer to balance when the time is right. If we'd prevented today's episode from happening, something similar would only have happened another time instead. Everything finds the balance it's looking for. Everything happens as it should,' I say.

Everything happens as it should, echoes Will.

I'm Aware that he is stroking Ember with long, gentle strokes as the foal lies exhausted in the grass beside him. Maverick snuggles up to Will's other side and I feel my nephew's love infusing the two souls who have provided him with so much love and support. I'm glad for him that he has this time alone with them both, but I know it won't last for very long; Ember's mother has calmed down enough to know of her foal's survival and his hunger. She sets off in his direction at a slow, tired canter with Will's grey mare following in her wake.

The other horses watch them go but make no move to follow. It is not their company that will be of most help to the mares, but their energy. As a herd, they either lie down or stand with their heads drooping, resting, so that as much of the herd energy as possible is available to the mares.

The chestnut mare whinnies loudly as she approaches her foal. Will and Maverick move quickly to one side, giving Ember's mother plenty of space to inspect her foal all over. She nudges him to his feet and then towards her teats. Once he's suckling, she drops her head to the grass to eat. Her sister does the same and many of the horses in the main herd do likewise. The emergency is in the past and they leave it there – unlike us. We move into the meagre shade awarded by some sparsely-leaved ash saplings, lie on our backs in the grass and discuss it, dissect it and celebrate Will's latest achievement, until Rowena remembers that since Will carried Maverick in his back-sack, that must mean that he emptied it of its contents first. The contents that she so carefully selected and gave over to his care.

We all chuckle as she assaults Will's mind with her objections until he agrees to jog back to where we camped, to collect his things.

'You really are a tyrant,' says Marvel.

'He was planning to take Maverick for a little run to loosen him up after being squashed into his back-sack like that, I just told him where to run to. It's not far,' Rowena says, but we all catch her thoughts to Will to make sure he and Maverick have a drink and a rest before jogging back to Ember and the mares, and to make sure he remembers to use Maverick's sun shade so that the dog doesn't get too warm as the heat builds.

Justin chuckles and then feels Rowena's annoyance. 'Sorry, Ro, it's just that today we saw Will stretch the limits of what we thought was possible as if it were nothing, and then you boss him around as if he weren't capable of tying his own shoelaces. You wouldn't be you if you hadn't, it's just that it was funny when Am was way ahead of us and you used to do it to her, but when you do it to Will…'

'It seems ridiculous, I get it,' Rowena says. 'But as Will told Jonus, he's human, the same as the rest of us. He breathes, he sleeps, he eats and he drinks. He excretes his waste…'

'Delicate,' says Marvel.

'… and he does silly things, just like the rest of us. At the end of the day, he's a twenty-two-year-old lad who may be capable of the extraordinary, but still has a bit to learn about living with the mundane. He had food in that back-sack that he's going to need, so he had to be told to go back and get it, it's as simple as that.'

'I think Will knows it won't be as simple as that. He'll never hear the last of this,' chuckles Justin.

'So, anyway, the mares will let Ember rest but they'll make sure they have him back with the herd before nightfall, so we can rest too, until then. I mean we'll need to take turns keeping watch, but at least we know the herd is likely to stay put for a while,' says Holly.

'Yep, and then we push on for Goldenglade,' I say, feeling suddenly sleepy.

'I'll take first watch,' Justin says, shifting sideways on his back until he's next to me. He whispers, 'Sleep, Am.'

I snuggle up to him and the next thing I know, I'm flying the oneness with Infinity. It no longer feels like the escape from the dream that it once was, but merely a different medium in which to express ourselves, one where we can immediately be anything we choose, but one where there is nothing external to observe, to experience or to push against – one where there is no reason to learn. When Justin gently shakes me awake, I am still smiling at my realisation of why the dream exists.

As Holly predicted, it's dusk by the time Will and Maverick join us; the mares gave Ember plenty of time to rest before wandering back slowly in the heat, and Maverick and Will stayed behind them, guarding their rear.

There are whickers and whinnies as the mares and foal are welcomed back into the herd, around which Maverick races to where we are sitting, eating. He leaps from one lap to the next, convinced that our shouts, groans and laughter are encouragement. Then he races back to Will, who, hot and tired as he is, still manages to laugh at the chaos his dog has left behind him. Maverick leaps into Will's arms ecstatically, as if it has been weeks since he last saw him, rather than minutes.

Justin and Marvel both get to their feet and wander over to welcome Will back and there is much back-slapping as they congratulate him on his latest achievement. Vickery, Holly and I line up to take our turns and by the time Will gets to Rowena, she's waiting with a sandwich for him.

'That's the last of the bread. We don't have the time to keep digging and lining ovens, even if we still had flour left, which we don't, so enjoy this. That's how low our supplies are now, and they'd have been even lower without your share, Will.'

'It's a good job we'll be back at Goldenglade soon then, isn't it,' Will says cheerfully. He takes a bite of his sandwich, bits of which he then spits out as he continues, 'Mum's so excited. She's going to meet us there with food and, knowing her, fresh small clothes for me. I've persuaded her to leave Dad at home to keep everything running smoothly at the Rockwood Centre, so that Ember and I can concentrate on what we need to do.'

'For goodness' sake, Will, either stop talking or stop eating, that's disgusting,' Rowena tells him.

Will just grins at her.

By the time the horses are ready to move on, the sun has long gone down and the grassy plains are lit grey by the moonlight. When the lead mare comes for me, Justin gives me a leg up onto her back and then wanders over to where his own mount waits nearby. I rub the mare's neck with affection. For now, she's conscious of her individuality due to the attention that both Will and I have paid to her, but that will change. I know that, in the same way that a splash of water is reabsorbed by the puddle from which it originated, her sense of individuality will fade and disappear once her interaction with us is over.

As the days go by, we humans gradually forget what it is to be awake by day and asleep by night. We succumb completely to the rhythms of the horses' daily existence and we revel in doing so. When we are on the move, our group energy joins that of the energy of the herd in being distributed among us all in the most beneficial way for the single being that we are. Maverick is included as he runs by the side of Will's grey mare; if he tires or stumbles, more energy shifts in his direction, giving him both the reassurance and speed to catch back up and retake his place. By the time we reach the woods where Will found Maverick, we find ourselves feeling rested, relaxed and... blissful, despite having followed a way of life that has been both strenuous and unfamiliar.

We decide on a camping spot by a stream at the edge of the woodland, so that we have shade whilst being close to the grassland where the horses have settled down to graze. Marvel and Vickery immediately go off hunting while the rest of us set about collecting firewood. Maverick darts between us, grabbing hold of sticks in our bundles and pulling them out, then tossing them away before darting in to grab another.

'Maverick, seriously, you're not helping,' Will groans. He laughs as his dog tries to run away with the stick he has just stolen but comes to an abrupt halt when it lodges between two trees. Maverick growls and tries to push the stick between the trees, but it is sturdy and holds fast. Then all of a sudden, Maverick lets go of the stick and looks past it, into the woodland.

I reach out in my Awareness to see what has caught his attention and my heart leaps. I shout, 'KAT!' at the same time Will shouts, 'MUM!'

I drop my sticks and run past Maverick to where I sense my sister approaching. Will gets there first and almost bowls her over with the force of his hug. Maverick is soon with him, his tail now wagging furiously.

When Katonia and her son finally disentangle themselves, she holds him back from her and says, 'Oh, Will, I've missed you so much.' Then she crouches down beside Maverick and offers her hands for him to sniff, saying, 'And what would we all have done without you, gorgeous boy? Look how much you've grown, aren't you handsome?'

Maverick thrusts his head into her hands to be stroked and then, before Katonia can divert her attention elsewhere, throws himself to the ground and rolls onto his back, his tail sweeping the forest floor into two piles either side of him. My sister laughs delightedly and rubs his chest, telling him, 'I could just fuss you forever, yes I could.'

Will looks at me with a grin and rolls his eyes.

When Katonia finally tries to stand up, she overbalances backward with the weight of her back-sack. Will catches her and pulls her upright before she can fall. She holds on to both of his hands in hers and shakes her head. 'Just look at you, my handsome boy. Even if I couldn't feel the difference in you, I can see it. You're so...' she continues to look up at him.

He raises his eyebrows. 'So...?'

'I'm not sure that there's a word for it,' I say with a wink.

My sister looks past Will to me, and smiles. She comes over to me and takes hold of my hands as she's just done with her son. 'Or for you,' she says. 'For either of the two of you who share those blue eyes of yours.' Katonia looks from me to Will and adds, 'Neither of you are the people you were when you left. I'm so proud of you both.' She looks deeply into my eyes. 'Thank you, Am and Fin, for everything you've done for my son, I'm just sorry I wasn't able to do more myself.'

'If you were able to fix all of the imbalances in the world by yourself, Kat, nobody else would have a chance to learn anything or to change,' I tell her gently. 'You know what's happened to me, and you know that without Will and Maverick, I wouldn't have quite got there. I helped Will, and in the process, he helped me. I couldn't be more grateful to you for your ineptitude.'

She laughs and hugs me. 'Only you could get away with

speaking to me like that about my children, do you know that, Am?'

'She knows everything, Mum, just like you do. It's a Nixon family trait,' Will grins and hugs us both.

'Is anyone going to take that back-sack from Katonia, or are you both just going to wait for her to collapse under the weight of it?' Rowena says from behind me.

Will duly jumps to relieve his mother of her load and then winces. 'You carried this all the way from Rockwood? Are you nuts, Mum? You could have done yourself an injury.'

'I could and I did. I just healed myself each time and carried on. I know you lot can hunt and scavenge but I've brought tea, oats, flour, dried fruit, spices and...' Katonia is cut short by another hug from Will.

'Thanks, Mum,' he says.

'You, Kat, are a wonderful human being.' Rowena heaves the back-sack up onto her back from where Will dropped it. 'Come on, let's get this lot unpacked. Holly's just got the fire going, so we can make tea. How long has it been since we ran out? I'm gasping.'

'Two days,' says Will, 'but with all the moaning, it seems like longer.'

'Will!' Katonia gasps, but Rowena and I just laugh. He does have a point.

'You'll be looking forward to spending time with people closer to your own age, I should think, Will? Less prone to moaning and more prone to being pretty? Like Lia?' Rowena says as we make our way back to camp.

'You asked for it,' I tell Will as he rolls his eyes.

'I'm looking forward to seeing the Drifters again once the horses have done what they can, yes,' he says. 'On that note, Mum, there's someone I think you'll want to meet. You can't let

Dad know he's here just yet though, it'll be too difficult for him to stay away and he needs to until we've done what we need to do.'

I feel Kat reach out in her Awareness for an impression of who Will is talking about but he puts the suggestion of a block in her way. He takes her by the hand and says, 'It's a surprise. Come with me. Rowena, we'll be back by the time you've brewed tea. And if you can see your way to digging another oven, some of your amazing cake would be welcome later on, now we have flour.' He gives her a cheeky wink and ignores his mother's raised eyebrows.

'You've been spending far too much time with Marvel,' Rowena tells him, but she doesn't argue and I see the corners of her mouth turn up into a smile.

Tea is indeed just brewed when Will and Katonia reappear. Justin and Holly jump up to greet my sister and Justin tells her, 'Don't worry, you'll get your head around the whole Ember situation, it just takes a bit of time.'

She nods. 'I just feel bad for Jack, with him not knowing, but I understand, now isn't the time; Ember and Will have work to do first. When are you planning on starting, Will?'

Will grins. 'I'm not planning anything. The horses have got this. Feel that?'

We all feel a shift occurring within the herd. Ember and the older mares have fed and rested sufficiently for the pull of the Drifters' imbalance to now be the horses' greatest priority. They are preparing to move.

THIRTY

Will

$\mathcal{I}$ follow the herd in my Awareness as it makes its way unhurriedly towards Goldenglade. Various horses stop to graze when they come across herbs they need, or particularly attractive varieties of grass, and then catch up as others do the same. When they get close to the village, they gather closely behind the lead mare and, as one, move up to a trot. The herd flows gracefully over the brow of the last hill and when the villagers catch sight of them and begin to shout and point, the horses move into a mesmerisingly slow, powerful canter. They breathe as one, feel as one, move as one, all of their hooves leaving and touching the ground in the same steady, hypnotic rhythm.

The horses canter alongside the back gardens of the houses on one side of the main street, turn as one around the end of the village and then continue along the row of back gardens of the houses on the other side. By the time the horses have circled the village, there are people shouting and tearing about everywhere. Some adults are collecting small children and rushing inside with them, others are shouting after the older children who are running around the village, trying to see what's happening.

Ember has been keeping up easily with the slow canter and is beginning to gain attention. People who were running away stop to look at the cute foal, and some even smile as he does little leaps and bucks before rejoining the rhythm of the herd.

By the time the horses are halfway around their second circuit of the village, its inhabitants are rushing to get a better view of the vision of oneness before them. Heads poke out of upstairs windows, villagers appear in back gardens and children run from one end of the street to the other in order to glimpse the horses from both vantage points. Then the lead mare heads away from the village and back towards us.

I feel the despair of many of the villagers as the source of the sudden feeling that has come over them that everything is alright, canters slowly away. Lia is among them and she isn't going to take the horses' departure lying down. She tears up the hillside after them with Maverick's brother, Breeze, racing along beside her, barking excitedly. When, gasping for breath, she reaches the brow of the hill and the horses are nowhere in sight, she drops to her knees, looks up towards the sky and screams. Her father catches up with her and tries to pull her to her feet, but she snatches her arm away from him and puts her face in her hands. Breeze licks them, trying to get to her tears to wash them away, and she puts an arm around him and buries her face in his fur. When she finally gets to her feet, she allows her father to lead her back down to the village. As they get back to where many of the other villagers are standing, waiting for them, they both turn and look up to the brow of the hill despondently.

Once the horses are a distance from Goldenglade, they slow down, separate out from one another and then meander back to us.

I look around at Mum, Am, Rowena, Justin and Holly. We're all smiling.

'It's begun,' Amarilla says.

I am with the horses in my Awareness as they visit the village at dawn the following day. They're already leaving by the time the villagers have realised that it is the rhythmic touch of the horses' hooves on the ground that has woken them, but when the horses return in the afternoon, the villagers gather quickly in the pasture by the village to watch them in silence and awe.

The horses canter a large circle around them, their perfectly balanced, rhythmic movement so beautiful and so moving that the villagers are captivated. They begin to open to the oneness that is being displayed so powerfully in front of them, unwittingly becoming more and more receptive to the very thing that terrifies them the most.

I am Aware of the Drifters as I wasn't able to be when I visited them before. Then, my more limited Awareness was filled with their emotions and their ways of coping with them. Now, I am Aware of them as a whole. I see the trait shared by all of the founding members and imposed on their children, that is at the root of their situation. They can't believe that they'll keep their sense of themselves if they succumb to Awareness of their oneness with All That Is, because they suffer the agony of believing that there is very little of worth to them in the first place. Having witnessed Jonus's upbringing, I know exactly when and how that belief entered the human collective consciousness. It is time for the last traces of The Old to be released from the human experience.

I feel the draw of the horses on the Drifters' minds, enticing them to flow along with the horses' peace and magnificence, to allow themselves to experience their oneness with the horses and with All That Is; to know their worth as being equal to any other.

The young, open minds of the children are the first to succumb to the horses' influence. They are pulled along the path to oneness that calls to them, but when they come up against the barriers to Awareness that their parents have insisted they put up in their minds to keep them safe, they panic and begin to cry. Ember immediately appears from within the herd and trots a smaller circle inside that of the other horses. The children pull away from their parents so that they can see the foal more clearly. He may not have the strength of the older horses, but he echoes their balance. He leaps into the air in a playful fly-buck, then lands and immediately continues his cute yet powerful demonstration of what it is to be young, balanced and free of fear. As the children relax and giggle at his antics, he takes them with him to Awareness, just as he did with me so many times when I was small. When they feel him in their minds as well as see him with their eyes, they laugh with pure, unadulterated delight. He slows to stand in front of them and is totally unfazed when they crowd around him. The children are as gentle with Ember as he is with them, their immediate sense of one another's youth and vulnerability ensuring mutual sensitivity and respect.

Some of the parents move towards their children, smiling. From nowhere, Ember's mother appears, her ears flat against her head as she snakes it towards them. The adults' presence will not be tolerated near her foal until they are free of the fear behind which they still hide. The rest of the horses continue their mesmerising dance of peace and power.

Lia is next to be affected. She's been battering against the barriers her parents have made her put up in her mind for so long that when she feels the horses' energy pulling at her, and then sees the children with Ember, she knows what she will do.

She sobs as she passes the first of her remaining barriers – the dread of disappointing her parents – and leaves it behind her. She cries out as she passes the next one – the fear of having to live apart from her family and friends if she rejects the Drifters' way of life. There is one final barrier left – Lia's fear that if she feels her oneness with everything, she will lose her sense of who she is and be nothing at all. The barrier has been steadily strengthened her whole life, all of the threats and horror stories she has been told having been funnelled into it, slowly making it bigger and stronger until, whenever she tried to get past it by herself, it felt insurmountable. Now, she hammers at the barrier, desperate to get past it, to be part of the oneness she sees in front of her.

The horses' dance draws her on, never allowing her to consider retreating or giving up. Their magnetic pull creates a crack in Lia's barrier and her mind immediately senses where to flee. The barrier screams out of Lia's mouth, desperate to frighten away everything that threatens its existence. None of the horses are afraid. Breeze whines and jumps up, trying to lick Lia's face and her parents rush to her side, but she has no need to be comforted. A smile lights up her face as she becomes Aware. She throws her arms around her stunned parents and then crouches down to take her dog into her arms, disbelieving for a moment the sense she has that he lives his life looking for ways to love and comfort her.

Lia moves closer to the horses with absolute confidence that they will welcome her. That is all it takes for the rest of the teenagers to follow the path she has opened up for them. Their minds blast past their barriers and they leave the group to join Lia where she stands just inside the circling horses.

The teenagers hold out their hands and are rewarded by

frequent touches of passing velvety noses. They feel their way around the peaceful, powerful energy of the herd, experiencing in the best way possible, what it means to be Aware. But their dogs are uncomfortable with the developments. Their whines soon become barks and snarls at the horses whose size and movement scare them from staying close to their humans. They are beginning to consider rushing at the horses in order to protect their loved ones from the potential threat. I immediately enclose all four dogs in reassuring, calming energy nets, as I've done for Maverick so many times. They lie down at the perimeter of the main group of villagers, and watch the teenagers calmly. The teenagers sense what I've done, and they all smile gratefully as they try to identify who I am.

I am the one who brought your dogs to you. They will be calm and safe while you enjoy your time with the horses, I tell them.

I sense them fumbling around in their newly-acquired Awareness and it is Lia who manages to reach out to me. *Will? You came back! And you brought the horses with you!*

It's more the case that they brought me with them, but yes, I'm not far away and there are others with me who will help you all to cope with being Aware. Please, Lia, make sure you and your friends do as they say, otherwise you'll all get distracted by everything you can feel and your parents will think you've lost sense of yourselves, just as they've always been so frightened would happen. I make sure that my thoughts reach all of the teenagers and I feel their relief and total, utter happiness as their new reality sinks in.

Thank you, Will. Lia is ecstatic to finally be herself with nothing restraining her, nothing trapping her, nothing holding her back from her Awareness of her place in existence.

Happiness and excitement are such new, unexplored emotions for Lia that they burst out of her with a childlike intensity and

Ember is drawn to her, wanting to investigate one who is on the brink of adulthood and yet has an energy that resonates so closely with his own. He gently pushes through the small knot of children and then trots over to Lia. Where he is cheeky and playful with me, there is a gentle innocence about him as he greets her, reflecting back to her the personality traits that make her the individual she has always been so terrified she wouldn't be without her barriers. He sniffs and nuzzles her hands and then moves closer, resting his head in the crook of her arm as she rubs his forehead. His mother moves closer to her foal, but doesn't intervene as he then greets each of the teenagers in turn.

I feel the increasing anguish of the adult Drifters. Their barriers have been added to and strengthened enough over the years by their fears, that they can resist the increasing pull of the human collective consciousness for them to be Aware. But the powerful, magnetic pull of the horses is something they have no practice at resisting, and the sight of their children behaving as they could only behave if they were Aware, makes them realise what it is the horses are drawing them towards. They try to slow their minds, to reverse the process and retreat back behind all of the barriers that make them feel safe. But their souls sense the opportunity the horses are creating and cause an intense restlessness within each and every Drifter, pushing them from the inside as the horses pull them from what they perceive to be outside. The pressure on them is fast becoming intolerable, yet still they resist. Their terror of losing their senses of self, their identities, if they allow themselves to feel at one with everything – a situation believed by them to be inevitable due to their lack of self-worth – is still greater than the combined encouragement of horses, children, soul and collective consciousness. They need a break from the pressure before the pressure breaks them.

Just as horses will always advance, retreat and then advance a little closer when approaching something that is new to them or scares them, so they recognise the Drifters' need for the same. Ember rejoins the herd and the horses canter back towards us as the single living, breathing, powerful entity that they are.

The children and teenagers calmly watch them go, knowing that they will return. The adults, as one, drop to the ground, exhausted.

Immediately, my mother introduces herself to the teenagers in their Awareness and begins to give them instructions so that they will be able cope with feeling their parents' distress. They stand still, listening, some of them muttering or moving their mouths as they answer her. Then, they run to the younger children, who are clinging to their parents and crying, overwhelmed by their parents' emotions. Each teenager takes the hand of a child and speaks quietly and calmly as Amarilla, Rowena, Holly, Vickery, Marvel, Justin and I each put suggestions of blocks between the children and their Awareness of their parents, shielding them from the pain that will cause their young minds to buckle. We add the suggestion of a temporary muting of their Awareness, until they have access to the coaching all young children have in order to cope with everything they can feel.

My mother continues her gentle coaching of the teenagers, determined that none of them will be overwhelmed by their Awareness, which would only give further confirmation to the Drifters that to be Aware is to lose sense of self. Her long experience of coaching people of all ages in how to use their Awareness comes to the fore and very soon, she has the situation stabilised. The younger children are calm and chatter happily amongst themselves about their time with Ember. The teenagers help exhausted adults back to their homes, while excitedly using mindspeak to discuss between themselves everything that has happened, at the same time as counting flowers, bees, houses, children – anything they can see – as my mother has instructed them.

I reach for my mother's hand and squeeze it. 'Mum, you're flaming well fantastic.'

She smiles and gently pushes me away, still concentrating hard on the children she has allocated to herself to coach.

'Shhh,' Rowena frowns. 'Just because you can monitor the children you've been given, communicate with them all at once and still have a conversation with your mother, doesn't mean the rest of us don't need peace and quiet.'

'And yet, you're talking, Ro,' says Marvel.

'You neglected to mention the additional distraction Will has, of one of his charges being the lovely Lia. Adept as he is at guarding his mind, he's not doing very well on that front.' Vickery winks at me.

'I'm not trying, Vic. What would be the point? You're all as Aware of the thread that links the two of us as I am. The outcome's inevitable.'

'And they say that romance is dead,' says Vickery.

'No, just an indulgence of human insecurity,' Amarilla says.

I chuckle and wink at the two pairs of blue eyes that smile at me in solidarity.

'Give me strength,' says Rowena.

'Don't you have children to monitor, Ro?' Justin glares at her. Then he turns to me. 'You did ought to hide your feelings from Lia, at least for now, she's got enough on her plate.'

'What, like you hid yours from Amarilla?' Marvel chuckles.

'I hid them until she couldn't help finding out for herself.' Justin throws a pine cone at his friend.

'Shhhh!' Holly and Katonia say together as they counsel several children each at once.

'We're just remembering back to our own youth, so that we can give Will the wealth of our experience,' explains Marvel.

'So then, you've obviously forgotten that he's Will and is already Aware of it in far better detail than you can remember it,' says Rowena.

'Hmmm, good point,' says Justin. 'Poor Lia has no idea what she's in for with him, does she?'

'The mistake all men make, no matter how Aware they are, is in choosing to believe that women don't already have the measure of them,' says Rowena.

Justin and Marvel groan, sensing one of Rowena's tirades coming on. The rest of us laugh as Rowena launches into her expected lecture and Justin and Marvel bury their heads under everything they can find.

I feel a slight shift and my attention is drawn to Amarilla. She smiles as I sense the peaceful finality that is settling about her and Infinity. They know that the way forward centres around me, and the rest of them can begin to wind down, their mission here almost complete. Almost.

I'm awake well before dawn. I shiver. Even under the cover of the trees, the nights now have a chill to them, warning that summer will soon give way to autumn. I sit up and Maverick stands up next to me, shakes the forest floor from his coat and licks my face. When he trots off to relieve himself, I look around at my sleeping friends and family, just visible in the glow of the campfire.

My mother sleeps next to me, her arm still outstretched. She fell asleep holding on to my shirt in the hope that I wouldn't be able to leave without waking her. On my other side, Amarilla is turned away from me, her head on Justin's chest. They're flying the oneness with Gas and Infinity, as they so often do. Marvel has both arms around Rowena, who, somehow, is asleep even though he's snoring in her ear. Holly and Vickery lie back to back. Vickery's arm is stretched behind her so that she can hold Holly's hand as they sleep.

I creep over to where our food hangs from the lower branches of a tree. I feed Maverick and eat a few slices of bread, then attempt to steal away from camp.

'Will.' I look behind me to see that my mother is sitting up, rubbing her eyes. She gets to her feet and tiptoes over, bending down to stroke Maverick on the way. 'You haven't had enough to eat,' she whispers.

'It's too early to be hungry. I need to go, Mum, the horses are preparing to leave for Goldenglade.'

She nods. 'I love you, Will. I know you don't need me to tell you that, but I need to say it.' She hugs me and then gives me a little shove. 'Go on then, don't make the horses wait.'

I roll my eyes and grin. 'No, Mum.'

I feel her watching me until I'm swallowed by the darkness. I follow my sense of the horses, until I hear a couple of them whicker a welcome to me. The sky is just beginning to lighten and I feel their intention to move at speed. The grey mare appears next to me and I vault onto her back. Maverick takes his place at her side as she wheels around and the herd departs at a canter.

The horses don't slow down until we're almost at Goldenglade. Ember has kept up easily; I'm amazed how quickly he's growing and strengthening. The grey mare stops to allow me to slide from her back and I rub her coat down to erase any sign that I was astride her; it won't help the Drifters to be confronted by anything that might suggest the involvement of the Horse-Bonded. Not just yet.

The horses trot over the last hill before Goldenglade, just as dawn breaks. When I reach its brow, I see that all of the Drifters are gathered in the pasture, waiting. I sense adoration for the herd from all of those who are Aware and I feel the teenagers' hope that today will be the day that their parents give in to the horses' influence.

I'm Aware of the adults' relief as the horses' display of oneness draws them in once again, easing them past the first of their barriers and relieving some of the restlessness that has intensified within each and every one of them since the horses left the previous day. They don't try to retreat back behind the barriers they have already passed, but when they come up against the final barrier of terror within their minds, they still manage to hold firm behind it. They stand on a knife edge, with intolerable restlessness waiting to torment them if they go back and the terror of losing themselves if they go forward. It is the horses' energy that will bring them to balance, but it needs an additional means of reaching them. Me.

THIRTY-ONE

Amarilla

---

*W*hen we wake at dawn, Will has already gone and Katonia is keeping vigil over him in her Awareness. All of us join her as we go about preparing and eating breakfast.

We witness Will walking through pasture with Maverick at his side, towards where the horses are trotting their beautiful dance around the Drifters. I can't see the herd with my eyes, yet I am every bit as captivated as those who can. The horses are different ages, different sizes, different strengths, and yet their bodies are arranged in an identical, perfect balance. Their hindquarters are underneath them, taking their weight. Their powerful hindlegs create the lift that travels all the way up to their withers and then to the tips of their ears. They leave the ground as one and land as one, although landing is too heavy a word for what they are achieving. They touch the ground with the lightness of snowflakes coming to rest, using it purely as a guide for when to lift up and away once more. Their energy swirls around the Drifters, entrancing those already Aware and enticing those who aren't to join them in their magnificence.

When man and dog reach the horses, Maverick jumps into Will's arms and puts his forelegs over the shoulders of the man whom he now trusts so deeply that he barely needs the energy net that Will weaves to keep him and the other dogs feeling safe and calm.

There is no break in the horses' rhythm, yet Will is able to move easily between them as those closest to him effortlessly shorten their strides to allow him to pass in front of them, and then lengthen their strides in order to regain their places in their display of oneness.

Ember is once again to the inside of the circle, delighting everyone with his paradox of cuteness and power. He stops to greet Will, nuzzling his shirt and then taking a mouthful and pulling at it. Will flicks his nose until he lets go, then rubs his head and neck. I feel the children's delight as they once more leave their parents' sides to go to Ember. A few of the adults tentatively try to follow their children, and I feel the parents' despondency as Ember's mother immediately appears and comes to a graceful halt between them and her foal. They watch the teenagers welcome Will and Maverick with a hug and then hold their hands out to be greeted by the passing horses, and they move to join them, only to find that the horses, as one, move their circle so as to keep the adult Drifters at the centre of it, unable to get any closer.

It is time for Will to be everything he is. He learnt from his time with Jonus and Mettle, not to get in the horses' way. But just as it was necessary for Jonus to be Mettle's voice, to speak the exact words that would reach the Ancients and propel them forward, so it is necessary for Will to be the voice of the wild horses. He is not Horse-Bonded and he must not be mistaken as such, so deep is the Drifter's fear of us. Any hint that we are trying to influence them will reignite their fear that we will make them Aware, and will only strengthen the very barriers that their minds are so desperate to breach.

Will puts Maverick down and walks towards the adult Drifters, softening his physical boundaries with each step. He knows himself. He is Will, and visibly so. But he is also the horses – each and every member of the herd. Ember's golden eyes look out of his own and then are replaced by the brown ones of the grey mare. He is the lead mare, then he is the stallion, then one of the fillies... but on closer inspection, he is always Will.

Lia, Brionie, Jake and the other teenagers follow Katonia's request to move close to the younger children and reassure them that all is well.

The herd moves as one into canter. Its serenity, grace and power lulls the Drifters ever more into the horses' influence, dispelling the confusion that wants to arise in the villagers as they see both Will and horses in Will's physical space. They have neither the time nor the mental space to do anything other than accept the approach of the man who appears to be bringing to them those whom they are so desperate to be near.

'Are you Horse-Bonded?' Lia's father says.

Will shakes his head. 'No. But I am of the horses.'

'They won't let us near them, but they're somehow with you? In you?' Lia's father says to Will and then shakes his head suddenly, trying to clear his head and think rationally.

'Don't take it personally, they're allowing you a lot closer than they allowed me to begin with,' Will says.

The Drifters see his grin amongst the shifting features of the horses and while some of them stare, most of them blink, as if that will help them to see him more clearly. I smile to myself, remembering that I used to do the same thing when I couldn't see

Justin separately from Gas. It won't help them any more than it helped me.

'What did you do to get closer to the horses?' A woman whispers. 'What are the children doing? They won't say. Any of them.'

'I stopped pushing them away.'

The Drifters all bristle and look more closely at Will, trying to find something human upon which they can fix, but the horses continue to observe them out of his being – peacefully, knowingly, lovingly. The Drifters all relax again.

Another woman says, 'How are we pushing the horses away?'

Will appears more himself as he says, 'They aren't capable of being anything other than honest. They show how they feel and they react to how those around them feel. You have a need to hold the world at arm's length. So, they stay at arm's length.'

Will softens his boundaries further so that the horses become more of him. As he does so, I feel his lack of need for boundaries of any kind. He is so firm in his sense of himself that he is everywhere and everything, all at once, yet he knows, always, who he is, strengthening further the pattern in the human collective consciousness for the knowledge that to be human is to have a sense of self. The more the pattern strengthens, the less the Drifters – here or in any of the other Drifter communities – will be able to doubt it.

The past and the present collide as Will senses Jonus speaking to the Ancients the precise wording given to him by Mettle, while he speaks the precise wording that the wild herd would give him if he had any notion of separation from them, that would give them the need.

'To be human is to have a sense of self. To have a sense of self is to doubt its worth until such time as the truth becomes obvious.

We are the truth. You see us. You feel us. Come with us. Know yourselves as we know you.'

The discarnate energy of We Who Are Infinity gathers the words within each of the Drifters and hurls them at the barriers of fear that remain. The barriers shatter with barely a whimper and are swept away as if they never existed. The horses disperse and drop their heads down to graze the lush pasture, as if nothing has happened.

A profound peace washes over the Drifters as they come to know themselves and their place in All That Is. They watch in amazement and wonder as their children run to them, smiling, laughing and talking to them using mindspeak. Then they look around themselves at the grazing horses. I feel their disbelief that what just happened could possibly have done, and then their renewed astonishment and joy as they realise that it did.

Will re-establishes his physical boundaries just in time for Lia to throw herself at him. As he catches her in his arms and swings her around, the thread that has linked them since before they were born flares to life with recognition. These two old souls will do as they agreed. They will continue challenging boundaries, taking along with them those who are ready for a different experience of this dream that we all dream.

It is several hours before the rest of us arrive at Goldenglade, yet the villagers are all still out in the pasture. They mingle between the horses, respectful of those who show no interest in them and delighted by those who do. Ember's mother is never far away from him, yet she allows his interaction with any of the humans he chooses – which is all of them.

Will is sitting with Lia, watching Maverick, Breeze and their sisters play. They both turn and wave at us. I am Aware of Katonia experiencing a whole host of emotions at once; pride in her son, excitement at meeting Lia, wonder at the life the two have ahead of them, grief that another now has the primary place in her son's heart, sadness that Jack isn't here to experience it all first-hand with her...

'Blimey, Kat, I think you need a hug,' says Rowena.

'I'm okay, it's just hard being a mother sometimes,' Kat says.

Rowena sighs. 'Tell me about it.'

When we both look at her, she nods her head towards Marvel, and we laugh.

As we make our way down to the villagers, many of them stop to watch us. When we reach them, it is Lia's father who approaches us first.

'Katonia, Holly, Justin and Amarilla. I never thought I'd say this, but you're very welcome here at Goldenglade,' he says. He looks to Vickery, Marvel and Rowena and adds, 'We've never met, but you walk with the balance and composure of the Horse-Bonded and... oh my goodness, I'm sorry for your losses, all of you, except... you, Amarilla. Infinity has gone, yet she hasn't. I can even see her in your eyes. How is that possible?'

'You met her,' I tell him with a grin.

A smile steals over his face and he begins to nod. 'I remember her snorting all over me once. I stopped in her path to tie my shoelace – well it was either that or stand on it and land face first in front of her – and then I had to go to lunch with my then future wife's parents, with the contents of Infinity's nose down the back of my shirt. She had very set ideas, didn't she?' His eyes widen. 'But now I feel all of who she was... is. By the breeze of summer, I had no idea, absolutely no idea, who any of the horses were... are. I had no idea about any of this.' He rubs his face with his hands. 'This has all been my fault. I've inflicted misery on my wife and daughter, and not just on them; many of the others would have accepted your help twenty years ago if I hadn't talked them out of it, if I hadn't scared them almost to death with what I thought could happen. And their children have suffered too, all because of me.'

Had Will not felt the depth of your distress he would never have sought his balance in order to bring to Goldenglade those who could bring balance to you. In time you will realise who you have helped him to become and what that means for the future. You have been who you needed to be and you have done what you needed to do. Everything happens as it should. Always.

Lia's father searches Infinity's and my eyes with his own. Finally, he nods his head.

'Oh, come here,' Rowena says, and pulls him into a hug.

The horses remain near Goldenglade for over a week, slowly grazing down the pasture that was resting ready to winter the sheep of Goldenglade. None of the villagers care; it's a tiny price to pay for what the horses have given them and they know that once the horses leave for the other Drifter communities with Will, they are unlikely to see them again. They also know that they will be more than welcome to move their sheep to the vast pastures surrounding Rockwood, should the need arise.

Jack arrives just as the horses are gathering themselves to move on. Candour has prepared him well. He has reminded him that horses can be in many places at once, since they know better than most of us that in reality, there are no places. Jack understands who Ember is and who Candour still is to him, and is more than excited to meet his Bond-Partner's current incarnation. We all feel Jack's emotion as Ember runs to him with a cute, shrill whinny and then nuzzles his ear, just as Candour used to. It is some time before Jack manages to dry his eyes and tear himself away from the foal, to greet his wife and son.

Katonia cries as he hugs her, even though she knows he understands why she kept Ember's existence from him until the Drifters were no longer such. When he reaches Will, he holds his blond-haired, blue-eyed son – his image – away from him so that he can drink in the sight of the man Will has become. There are few dry eyes as we all feel his love and pride for the son about whom he has spent more than two decades worrying.

The horses' increasing restlessness cuts short the opportunity for any prolonged expressions of emotion, or indeed the opportunity for Jack to properly greet the rest of us.

Will turns to Lia and kisses her forehead, then he hugs his mother. 'We have to go.'

'I know.' Katonia looks from her son to her husband. 'Look after one another, okay? And, Jack, could you at least try to disguise the fact that you're so eager to be off, when you've only just got here?'

The grey mare who carries Will appears and he vaults onto her back. Maverick, squealing with excitement for the run he's anticipating, bounces up and down at the mare's side. The chestnut colt who carried Marvel to Goldenglade appears by Jack's side, and Jack's grin splits his face in two as he accepts a leg up from Justin onto the colt's back. 'Kat, I'm sorry, but riding again, and with my son... and EMBER! I mean seriously, does it get any better?'

Katonia laughs as the colt spins and leaps into a trot to join the rest of the herd. The villagers all gasp at the sight of Will and his father merging into the oneness of the herd as it canters away from them.

Justin puts one arm around me and the other around my sister, and hugs us both to him. Rowena appears on my other side and her arm appears around my waist as Marvel puts his around hers.

Holly and Vickery join our human chain on Katonia's other side and we all stand, staring after the herd.

Jack will be the advance assistance to the Drifters of the other communities, as his wife has been in Goldenglade, helping them to cope with the Awareness to which they will be drawn by the horses and Will, and by the strengthening pattern in the collective consciousness that Will has laid down. Others from the Rockwood Centre are already on their way to the various Drifter communities on foot, ready to relieve Jack when necessary, so that he and Will can move on to the next community. When relief arrives here in Goldenglade, we will all go home and Katonia will reclaim her children from our parents. It will be a year or so before she will see her husband and son again.

There is a disturbance further down the line as Katonia welcomes Lia between herself and Holly. Lia will go to Rockwood to train with Katonia, until Will returns. My sister has the greatest Awareness of all who are non-bonded and I know she sees, as we all do, that Lia's will exceed hers. Lia has few blocks to experiencing greater Awareness than she already can, and she will not allow them to stand in her way for long.

'I think ale is called for,' Marvel says.

'You think that every minute of every day,' says Rowena, 'but on this occasion, I happen to agree with you.'

'Did everyone hear that? Ro agrees with me,' Marvel says. 'Of everything that has happened, I think that's the most amazing yet.'

'More amazing than Will being a physical expression of the horses?' says Vickery.

'More amazing than a herd of wild horses drawing a whole community out of fear and into Awareness?' says Holly.

'More amazing than seeing Ember with all the children?' says Katonia.

'More amazing than seeing Jack with the most recent incarnation of his Bond-Partner?' says Justin.

'More amazing than being in the company of the phenomenon that is Infinity and Amarilla?' says Rowena and squeezes my waist.

'Um, well maybe not the most amazing thing, but definitely the sixth most amazing thing,' Marvel says. We all smile.

Epilogue

*E*verything is always moving towards balance. Sometimes, the movement is slow, sometimes it is accelerated by the appearance of a catalyst, but its direction is constant.

Prey populations remain in balance with their environment by losing their weakest members to disease, starvation or predators, by increasing their fertility when food is abundant and decreasing it when food is scarce. Predator numbers remain in balance with their environment in turn, by losing their own weakest members to disease, starvation or injuries sustained in battles for mates, territory and food.

Historically, humans have maintained their population levels in balance with their environment by acting as predators, culminating in the obliteration of so many during the implosion of The Old. The advent of The New saw humans ready to live in a gentler way – by achieving internal balance. It has been a rocky road. First, there was the struggle to know the truth of existence, to know that we are one with All That Is. Then there was the effort to balance that Awareness with the sense of self, the personality, the mode of transport for souls incarnating as humans within this dream of ours. There have been those – and I was the first – who were so distracted by their Awareness that they needed reminding of self. There have been those so terrified of losing their sense of self that they have resisted being Aware. And there is one so strong in both that he has been able to forge the way forward for everyone, pulling us all along with him as he experiences and expresses ultimate balance. Through it all, the horses have been there to guide us, to wait for us while we learnt from experience, to reflect us back to ourselves when we couldn't see where we were making mistakes.

To be human is to have a sense of self. To be dog is to be a constant expression of unconditional love. To be horse is to bring balance. Humans are the least stable of all species, the most likely to be knocked off balance and lose their way, but as long as there are dogs to reassure us when we experience the discomfort of straying from the path, and horses to guide us back onto it, we will be okay.

Infinity and I are done here. There is nothing holding us here any longer, no reason to maintain my physical body. We can spend eternity flying the oneness together, ecstatic in our knowledge that we have no more need to incarnate in the dream, no more need to be anything other than infinity, while appreciating that the reason we have that knowledge is because we dreamt the dream in the first place.

Knowing that we would arrive at this point is all that kept me going when my grief separated me from Infinity, and up until very recently, I thought that once my job here was done, I'd be happy to relinquish my body. But what would be the point of that? Flying the oneness, living in the dream, it's all the same now. Infinity and I will do both until such time as my body is ready to expire.

While we are here in the dream, we will see it for what it is, and know our place within it. We are human and we are horse. We are past, we are present, we are future. We are Infinity.

Books by Lynn Mann

<u>The Horses Know Trilogy</u>
The Horses Know
The Horses Rejoice (The Horses Know Book 2)
The Horses Return (The Horses Know Book 3)

Horses Forever
The Forgotten Horses
The Way Of The Horse
In Search of Peace
The Strength Of Oak
A Reason To Be Noble
Tales Of The Horse-Bonded

I'd be very grateful if you could spare a few minutes to leave a review for The Horses Return where you purchased your copy. Reviews help my books to reach a wider audience, which means that I can keep on writing! Many thanks.

I love to hear from you!
Get in touch, receive news and sign up to my newsletter to receive free stories, exclusive content, new release announcements and more at: www.lynnmann.co.uk
I can also be contacted via the Facebook page:
www.Facebook.com/lynnmann.author

Acknowledgments

The Horses Know Trilogy has been a real labour of love for me. Without readers, I wouldn't have been able to write the books, so I would like to thank you all, from the bottom of my heart, for accompanying me on this journey and for all your support in the form of reviews, emails, and facebook comments and shares.

I would also like to thank my editorial team: Fern Sherry, Leonard Palmer, Rebecca Walters and Caroline Macintosh, I know how very fortunate I am to have you all keeping me on track.

Massive thanks to Jon Morris of MoPhoto for once again supplying the shot of Pie for inclusion in the cover. I am constantly in awe of Jon for his talent in transforming a sight that most wouldn't look at twice, into something magical.

Thank you to Liz Atkinson for sharing her memories with me of the late Smokey Joe. He was the inspiration for Ember, a character I found all the more enjoyable to write about for having a real horse on whom to base him.

Lastly, big love and thanks to my family (human, equine, canine and feline) for all being who you are.

Manufactured by Amazon.ca
Bolton, ON

30020934R00168